This Would Be I

By N. L.

Copyright © 2016 by N. D. Iverson

Chapter 1

Roy was a dead man. Or he would be if he didn't stop badgering me. He was chomping at the bit to canvas the Gretna area for the mercenary's hideout. I was very much regretting my offer to help, and I'm sure John was just as annoyed since he promised to aid Roy as well.

Life in Hargrove was *just* starting to settle down after the gruesome murder of my friend Darren, the exile of Byron due to him *killing* Darren and a bunch of other people, and Wyatt's *demotion* two weeks ago. Our secret meeting ended with every attendee agreeing that Wyatt needed to be usurped. The next day a petition was circulated to gather signatures calling for his resignation. He was voted out in a landslide.

To his credit, Wyatt handled it with more grace than I thought possible. He didn't pitch a fit, storm out, or scream bloody murder—I probably would have. He was allowed to stay, but his word would no longer be the last. A council had formed, each member from a different "household." No two members could be related by blood or law, dating, or living in the same condo. This way it was a fairer representation of the population. All major decisions, however, would be decided by a democratic vote of the populace. Our "family" voted John to be our voice on the council, even though he didn't particularly want the honor.

"Bailey, it's been weeks," Roy tried again. "I think one scouting mission couldn't hurt." Roy was my friend, but he was being seriously annoying right now so that might be amended.

I gritted my teeth. "Fine, Roy. By all means, grab a vehicle and go." I motioned for the gate.

We were standing in the middle of the cul-de-sac with people bustling around us. At least the impact on everyday life hadn't been too drastic. Most people knew their job and knew it had to be completed regardless of who was in charge.

"You and John said you'd help."

"And at this moment, I'm not too happy with my past self for offering."

Roy glared at me and opened his mouth to say something. But he must have thought better of it because he suddenly clamped his mouth shut. "I'll go find John," he muttered.

Roy stormed off and I breathed a sigh of relief. He would be John's problem for the next hour. I turned to head back to the armory for inventory. I had unofficially taken over Darren's duties – inventory and supply runs. Not that anyone had been outside the gates since Byron was thrown out. We would have to organize a run soon. Oscar, our resident doctor, came out of the medic center waving like a lunatic for me, so I stopped and let him catch up.

"Bailey." He flashed a smile that was ruined by him taking a big gulp of air. "Do you have a moment?"

"I think so." Truth be told, I was kind of dreading being hunched over for who knows how long trying to count guns and bullets.

"It's about Colin."

I narrowed my eyes. "What did he do now?"

Colin had been pranking people around Hargrove like he was in elementary school again, small but annoying pranks that ranged from ringing random doorbells to letting the chickens out of the coop. As if life wasn't exciting enough. Every time I gave him shit, he responded with,

"I'm sorry, Mom," which I hated more than finding a fake press-on nail in my breakfast. Hargrove didn't have the best quality control.

"No, nothing like that. Did he ever mention anything to you about him being sick?"

"What kind of sick? You were the one who examined him back when he got here."

Oscar scratched his head as Sheri passed by, pushing a wheelbarrow full of dirt.

"Hey, guys," she said with a friendly smile.

"Should you be pushing something that heavy?" I asked.

"Her kidney and wound are both healing very well, but I did say no heavy lifting." Oscar shook a finger at Sheri.

"No way am I sitting out after being confined to that chair." She made it sound like she was being tortured by the wheelchair. "Besides, I'm just playing delivery woman, not shoveling the dirt in and out."

"If I catch you..." Oscar warned.

"Yes, yes." Sheri brushed him off and continued on her way.

"Perhaps we should have this conversation in the medical center, where it's private," Oscar said.

"Sure."

I followed him to the other side of the road and into the medic building. I was concerned with all the secrecy. Colin never mentioned anything to me, or anyone else, that I was aware of. He did tire easily for a fifteen-year-old and often, would be asleep even before Chloe. At least we got a reprieve from his pranks at night.

The inside of the center was silent. Not surprising since there had been no accidents since Darren's untimely death, but it was still eerie. I was still struggling with the fact that Darren was gone. A week ago, when we had all been relaxing in our condo one evening, I absently said, "We should save some popcorn for Darren." Zoe had burst into tears and ran back to her condo, leaving me horrified and hollowed. I felt like an asshole after that, not just because of the slip, but because I realized that I wasn't dealing with Darren's death properly.

It was like I was in denial. Instead of tears pouring, I got angry. So that night I went to his grave and allowed myself to grieve. I told him about how I angry I was with Hargrove, with Byron, with Wyatt, and with myself; I told him how helpless I felt; how I didn't know how to help Zoe—I'd been almost avoiding her. The tears finally came when I finished my venting to the dirty patch that was Darren's final resting place. Death never got any easier.

"Bailey?" Oscar asked.

I guess I had zoned out.

"Sorry, you were saying about Colin?"

"Let me show you some of the blood test results. We don't have advanced equipment here, but we do have some simple tests that can be run."

After he had closed the front door to the frame, but not completely, he motioned for me to follow him into the operating room where all the equipment was located. I looked back at the front door that Oscar hadn't closed all the way; it was almost like he'd left it open because he was expecting someone else. Goosebumps broke out on my skin. Something felt *off*. I swallowed and put aside the weird vibe I was getting. I needed to know what he knew about Colin.

Oscar used a key to unlock the tall filing cabinet in the corner of the room. He shuffled through the files while I swayed awkwardly in the doorway. The metallic glint of the tools and machines were putting me even further on edge. The odor of bleach overpowered my sense of smell, making me breathe through my mouth.

"Here we go." Oscar pulled out some sheets, walking over to me. "His white blood cell count is way below average."

I took the sheet he passed to me. His eyes kept darting behind me and I barely resisted the urge to turn around. There was no one behind me, so I don't know what he kept looking at. Oscar pointed to one of the sets of numbers on the sheet.

"See, the range our lab usually went with back at the hospital I worked at before all this was four thousand five hundred to ten thousand WBCs per microliter. As you can see, Colin's is over one thousand lower than even the bottom of the healthy range, and I suspected that when he told me what he had."

"What do you mean, *what he had*?" My heart rate elevated as I began to panic. What was wrong with Colin?

Oscar looked away, then back at me. "Colin told me not to say anything, but eventually he'll be sick enough he can't hide it. He was diagnosed with Non-Hodgkin lymphoma before the breakout and began receiving chemotherapy treatments at the Ochsner Cancer Institute."

I stilled. Everything started to click into place. This was why he was so tired and sickly all the time. Why he acted like he had nothing to lose—after all, we had found him running down a street like an escaped mental patient, shooting off rounds *and* his mouth at the infected. He lied about being down here for boarding school, although with the way he acted, I thought boarding school sounded pretty realistic.

My lungs deflated. "Can you treat him? How long does he have? Will he get even worse?"

Oscar held up his hands. "I'm not an oncologist, so I don't know what would be the best treatment for him. Usually radiation and chemotherapy are the first step, but there are different types and doses that correspond to each type of cancer being treated. Maybe if he could remember what type of chemo drug he was on before, we could try to find some at nearby hospitals, but patients don't generally know that stuff."

I wanted to sit, but there was nothing to plunk down on besides the sterile operating table and I had no desire to touch that thing. So I settled for leaning against the wall as my eyes glazed over the report in my hand. *That poor kid.* Why did he not tell us?

The front door opened and closed, footsteps heading our way. Oscar stood straight as a pole, his pupils dilating. The goosebumps broke out on my skin again when I heard the deadbolt being flipped. I looked into Oscar's eyes.

"I'm *so* sorry," he pleaded.

I slowly turned around to see Wyatt heading toward me through the waiting area, while Grant remained at the front door like a guard dog. My breathing shallowed as Wyatt loomed closer. This was an ambush. My foot went to step back into the operating room, but Oscar blocked my way—not that I had anywhere to go.

"I just want to talk," Wyatt said, flashing his empty hands at me.

"Yeah?" I said, my voice surprisingly steady. "I really don't feel like talking to you, so..."

"That's rude."

Don't let him see you're afraid. I took a step toward him into the waiting area, his eyes widening. Even Grant shuffled on his feet by the front door.

"Byron killing Darren was as much your fault as it was Byron's. If you hadn't covered up for that monster, Darren would still be here," I practically spat at Wyatt. If he wanted to talk, then we were going to *talk*.

"I made ... a mistake in regards to Bryon. One I've paid dearly for." He must have been referring to being voted out as leader of Hargrove. Like he gave a shit about all the innocent people Byron had killed.

"Not as dearly as Byron's victims."

My eyes darted around the main area of the medic center to try and find an escape. I'd throw myself out a window if I had to.

"Well if you want to play point the finger, I know it was you, Roy, and John who broke into my condo."

I swallowed. *Shit.*

"Grant, here"—Wyatt pointed a thumb at Grant—"saw you guys running out of my backyard the night of the wake. We know you got to the radio equipment, but I don't know how much you poked around. It's probably safe to assume you know about who we've been contacting."

There was no point in denying I had seen anything at this point. "You mean the mercenaries? The ones you're in bed with?"

"Sweetheart, everyone is." His endearment grated at me like a fork scraped across a plate. "And you're going to help me get my town back, since you're immune and all."

"How the hell did you know that?" I couldn't stifle the look of shock that crept onto my face.

"We have eyes everywhere, but perhaps you should ask your boyfriend, Ethan," Wyatt deadpanned.

What? Ethan would never ... would he? I felt the urge to scream and cry at his betrayal.

"Enough stalling, they've already been contacted to come get you. Oscar, grab her!"

Oscar didn't listen. He just stood glued to the floor. Wyatt let out an angry breath and started toward me. Without thinking, I swung a fist as hard as I could, hitting Wyatt on the left side of his face. He went flying back and stumbled to the ground.

Then, I snapped.

I dove to Wyatt's fallen carcass on the floor and attacked with everything I had. If I'd had my gun on me, I would have shot him. Wyatt was too shocked at the beginning of my assault to protect himself. I went for the throat first, his eyes bulging from their sockets. He wheezed, gasping for air. I punched and kneed wherever I could land a hit, wanting nothing but to inflict pain. After a couple of hits to the face, blood began to coat my fists.

As I was readying for another haymaker, I was tackled from the front. Grant and I flew to the ground beside the bleeding Wyatt, knocking the breath from me. I was beyond caring at this point. Despite my lack of oxygen, I lashed out viciously at Grant.

"You're not doin' yourself any favors," Grant grunted as he put me in a vise grip.

My arms were now pinned to my sides, Grant using his weight to immobilize me. I kicked and flailed trying to get free, but he was astoundingly strong. Wyatt scrambled up, cradling his bleeding face. He leaned on a wall, glaring at me with hate in his eyes.

"My people will get you for this," I sneered. "Even if I can't!"

"We're not going to kill you, if that's what you think," Wyatt said.

No, I was being traded off to the highest bidder again.

"Oscar! The anesthesia!" Wyatt ordered.

Oscar finally came back to reality, and handed Wyatt a syringe filled with a murky liquid. My pulse spiked at the sight—I didn't stand a chance drugged. He loomed over me as Grant's hold tightened even more.

My arm stung as the needle jabbed into the upper muscle.

"What the hell did you just give me?" I screamed, my face half pushed into the worn linoleum.

"Best you don't fight it," Wyatt said in lieu of answering.

I renewed my struggles as he removed the syringe. A trickle of blood ran down my arm, dripping onto the floor. I panicked as I realized that fighting against Grant would make my blood pump faster, delivering the drug that much quicker through my blood stream. I began to feel like I was falling asleep. A wave of nausea hit me and I started to retch.

Wyatt leaned down so his face was right in front of me. My sight wavered, making him seem more like a mirage. "Don't fight it," was the last thing I heard before my body lost the fight.

I slowly came to. Disoriented and confused, I tried to look around, but my head was just so heavy. This wasn't like the last time I had been knocked out. The drugs that Wyatt had stabbed me with were keeping me on the cusp of consciousness, like I had woken up in the middle of a dream. It was so bright that I had to squint. My stomach convulsed and churned, but I managed to stamp down the urge to vomit.

"He—" My mouth was too dry to form words. I swallowed a few times before I had enough saliva to speak. I tried again and managed to croak out, "Help."

There was no movement or sound in the bright room besides the noise I was making. Slowly, I tried to sit up. My body was too weak, and I collapsed back onto the padded surface I was on. I twisted my head, looking around. The room looked like a post-op recovery room. There were curtains in between the beds that were pushed against the wall. Tubing and equipment lined the rest of the walls. It reminded me of the recovery room I'd been in after I had my wisdom teeth removed—except this room wasn't crowded with people trying to get as many patients through as possible.

I'm not in Hargrove anymore.

I went to raise my arm, only to have it yanked back down, the sound of metal clanging against the bed. Craning my neck, I peered down to see my right hand attached to the bed with handcuffs. The door to the room opened. A woman in a lab coat walked over to me in a hurried stride. Her black hair was held back in a tight ponytail and a pair of those overly large hipster glasses were held up by a sturdy looking nose.

"You're awake." *Obviously.*

My mouth was still too dry to speak back.

"My name is Amelia. I run this research facility."

My spine tingled when she said research facility. Unwanted images of experiments being done on my body flashed behind my eyes.

"Don't worry, it's not want you're thinking," she said, having registered the blood draining from my face. "When the effects of the drug wears off, I'll send someone in to take you to the others."

Others?

"In the meantime, have some water."

Amelia reached for the bedside table and brought a cup with a bent straw in it to my face. When I didn't take it, she said, "Don't worry, it's just water."

I smacked my lips, but ultimately my thirst won. I put my lips around the straw and drank. It was stale, like it had been sitting out for a while. *How long was I out for?*

After I downed the entire glass, Amelia set it back down on the table and I immediately bombarded her with questions. "Where am I? Who are you people? Are you the mercenaries? Why am I handcuffed to the bed?"

Amelia sighed. "I should prepare a script. Everyone seems to have the same questions when they wake up."

"Or you could stop kidnapping people."

She shot me a tired look and cupped her face with her hand. "I'm not up for this today. We had a major setback earlier with one of the tests. I'll send Josh in for you." She pivoted and walked away from me, her heels clacking on the floor with every step.

"Hey! Get back here!" I screamed as I fought against the handcuff latched around my wrist.

She ignored my protests and walked out the door. A male dressed in scrubs came into the room next. He was tall and muscled like a UFC fighter. Both arms were entirely tattooed with color and black ink, looking like the pages of comic book.

"I always have to deal with the mouthy ones," he muttered. His accent was lightly Irish.

"Ever think that, hey, maybe you shouldn't be taking people against their will? Maybe we wouldn't be mouthy then." I was too pissed to filter my words.

"Yeah, yeah, yeah. They all talk big until their first test. Then they usually stop." His eyes bore into mine as the side of his lips curled up in a taunting manner.

Like hell I was going to be intimidated by this tattooed *murse*. That's probably why they sent him in here for the "mouthy" ones. Normally a person would take one look at him and decide better of their words. I leaned closer to him. "I killed the last mercenary who tried to kidnap me because I was immune."

"Never cared for those mercenaries. Bunch of savages and degenerates."

That threw me off. "You're not part of their group?"

"Nope. We just hire them to bring us people like you—outsourcing. This is our research facility. It used to be the East Louisiana State Hospital which was known for treating mental patients. Amelia, who you met just before me, used to run the place. Lots of handy equipment left lying around, and lots of special cells meant to keep people in. This is her brain-child."

His words were meant to instill fear, but I never listened anyways. "So if you aren't bad guys like the mercenaries, then why am I being held prisoner?"

"Well at first we tried the volunteer method. Oddly, no one ever came back." He snickered at his joke.

"Why am I even here?" I had an inkling: test subject.

"Within you, and the others who can be bitten and scratched without turning into dead-heads is the answer to all this," he said, motioning around him.

"So we're your cure?" I asked.

"We're not looking for a cure. You can't help what's already dead, but you can make everyone who's still alive, immune. Once we find out what it is inside you that makes you safe from the dead-heads, we can eliminate the threat and re-start society. No longer will a bite or a scratch be a death sentence. Think of us as this generation's Jonas Salk."

"All this time and you still haven't figured it out," I taunted. I needed him to release me from the handcuffs and get me to the "others" Amelia had mentioned.

His smirk gave way to a scowl. "It's not easy to find immune subjects. Anyone can be immune; there's no telltale sign that's easily visible without examining for healed wounds from the dead-heads."

"You haven't even narrowed it down?"

He strolled right up beside the bed I was attached to in two giant strides. "Hold still." He ripped open a plastic package and produced a needle with a vial; he was going to take my blood.

"Fuck that!" I said out loud and shoved his descending hand away from me.

"I can restrain your other arm if you'd like. Or you could just let me take your blood and we can be on our merry way," he said. "Word of warning: you're not going to like the restraint option."

I sucked in a breath. *What do I do?* I was completely at their mercy until I found a weapon or got free.

"Just the one vial?"

"For now."

"Fine."

He held his thumb down just below where my forearm and upper arm met. When a vein began to bulge, he plunged the needle into my skin. I hissed from the sting. Blood spurted into the vial, my treacherous heart doing all the work. Once it was full, he removed the vial, and then the needle with a yank.

"You're not a bleeder, are you?"

"Shouldn't you have asked that beforehand?"

"You know, I don't think we're going to get along," he said, his eyes on the vial. He twisted it around in his fingers, as if looking for something inside.

"I can't imagine you get along with many people," I said, placing my free hand over the trickling wound the needle left behind.

Good thing I wasn't a bleeder, as he had asked. He stashed the vial in his pocket, then deposited the needle in a yellow box attached to the wall labeled with a biohazard symbol. At least they didn't reuse the needles.

"I'm going to unlock your wrist now. Try anything and you won't like the results," he explained slowly. I could have sworn he flexed when he said that. If immune people were so hard to come by, they wouldn't risk seriously injuring them, but I'd bet they had no qualms about using excessive force.

He leaned down and used a key to free me from my restraint. The cuff popped open and clanged along the metal bedframe when it fell free from my wrist. I pulled my left hand up and massaged the red ring the cuff had left behind.

"Get up."

I threw off the thin blanket and sat upright, finally noticing my attire. *They had redressed me!* Instead of my tank top and shorts, I was now wearing a plain white V-neck shirt and light-blue pajama bottoms. I felt so … violated.

I took a deep breath to calm myself and asked, "Where are we going?"

"You'll be joining the other immune subjects."

I didn't like the way he kept referring to people as subjects. As if he no longer saw them as humans, but lab rats.

He walked to the door, expecting me to follow. I stood up and wavered for a step before I was able to walk in a straight line. Whatever drug Wyatt had stabbed me with was out of my system, but my equilibrium was still off. When I finally got to the door, Josh ripped it open and motioned for me to go through. I went out ahead of him, not sure of what I would see.

It was just a hallway like any hospital one: the floors a scuffed yellowed color, the walls white and lined with hand sanitizer dispensers, and clinical florescent lights above. All the doors were closed as we walked side by side down the long corridor. A set of black doors at the end had 'Cafeteria' written above.

Josh rapped on the door with his knuckles. "Open up, it's Josh. I got a new one." The doors opened from the inside, two armed guards waiting for me on the other side.

My escort shoved me into the brightly lit cafeteria crawling with other similarly dressed prisoners. "Welcome to gen-pop."

Chapter 2

The doors were shut behind me. Josh stood on the other side giving me a sarcastic wave through the small window. I returned the gesture with my middle finger. The two guards each stood in front of a door, barely looking at me. They were dressed in black body armor that had the word 'SWAT' colored over, but you could still read the writing.

"So what now?" I asked.

"You find a spot and then sit," said the male guard on the left.

"Until...?" I made a rolling motion with my finger.

"Until we send you back to your cell," said the male guard on the right.

I felt like Alice trying to get information out of Tweedledee and Tweedledum. I laughed and they cast me a sharp look that said, "Don't try anything." This former mental hospital was going to turn me *mental*. With a sigh, I gave up trying to get anything from the two idiots and turned to face the cafeteria once again. Everyone was dressed in the same white shirt and blue pajama pants as the ones I was currently wearing. *Someone caught a sale at mental-patients-attire-R-US.*

My eyes landed on the windows as I scanned my surroundings, looking for a possible way out. I dashed over to them to find bars soldered onto the outside frame. This was starting to look more like a prison, not a hospital. Even if I smashed the glass, the bars would stop me from escaping. The windows on the other side of the room had been outfitted with the same security measures. Except for one of the smaller side windows; it was boarded up.

I could tell we were on the main floor. Green bushes and shrubs reached towards the bottom of the windows like curious fingers wiggling in the light breeze. Toward the back of the cafeteria was the kitchen, also guarded by one lone female guard. This wasn't where I'd be escaping from—but I *would* be escaping.

"A word of advice: don't try anything on your first day," said a guy off to my left. He had been watching me size up the joint from his spot at one of the bolted down, stainless steel tables.

"Maybe I was just admiring the lovely weather," I said.

"No one admires anything here. You had that look in your eye—we all did when we first got locked up." His eyes flashed to the guarded front doors.

I sat across the table from him in an uncomfortable steel chair—also bolted to the ground.

"How long have you been here?" I asked.

"Not a hundred percent sure. I didn't think to start marking the days until a while into my *stay*, but I'd say a month and a half," he answered.

His smooth tanned skin, black hair, and build made me think he was of Spanish decent. From his sitting position I couldn't gauge his height very well, but there was no way he was over six feet tall, maybe 5 '10. He also looked younger than me by a couple of years. He had to be twenty at most.

"Do you know how long this all has been going on?"

He itched at his cheek. "Not sure. Some of the longer term residents say they've been here for three months."

Well, at least they *had* long term people.

"I'm Bailey, by the way."

"Leo."

"So, Leo, what can you tell me about this place?" I leaned over the table toward him.

He let out a nervous laugh. "I don't know about any secret air ducts that can be used for a daring escape if that's what you're looking for." He glanced toward the front doors again.

"You looking for someone?" I twisted around to peer at the guards.

"One of the ladies, Rose, was taken for *testing* today and they haven't brought her back yet."

"How often do they take people?"

"Depends on what they are doing, but sometimes they do multiple tests a day and sometimes they don't need a subject for days."

"What kind of test?" I wasn't sure I wanted an answer.

He licked his lips, then pulled his left arm out from under the table. He stretched it out for me to see all the bite marks and scratches that had healed but left behind scars. It almost looked like he had been burned, there were so many.

"A personal favorite of theirs is trying to infect us while taking blood samples before and after."

"Before and after what?"

He gulped. "They bring in a dead-head to bite us." *Holy shit.*

"So what, they force you into a room with an infected until it bites you?" That sounded ... horrific.

"Pretty much. Once the *infected* bites you, they kill it and take your blood to compare. Oddly, they take good care of keeping the wounds from getting infected with regular germs—now."

"Now?"

"Someone died of blood poisoning a while back because they waited too long to treat the wound for the sake of their 'study.' Since then, they've deduced that they'll run out of subjects soon if they keep letting them die. The people running this place like to pretend they're doctors." He scowled at the last part.

"How many people have died since you've been here?"

"One lady died just a few weeks ago." He looked down at the table uncomfortably. I wondered what had happened to the lady, but I didn't think I wanted the answer at the moment. This was all overwhelming enough as it was. "Other than her, around seven people have disappeared—that I've noticed since I've been here."

I jerked my head toward the guards. "You ever see them kill a person?"

"No, they have guns but they don't use them on us. If someone gets rowdy, they get injected with drugs to calm them down or put in solitary."

"Jesus, this *is* a prison," I muttered.

"At least we get fed three times a day and are kept safe from the hordes of dead-heads or worse," Leo said.

When someone coughed, drawing my attention away from my questioning of Leo, I gawked around the cafeteria again. There had to be fifteen prisoners—sixteen if you counted the Rose person Leo had talked about. Most were keeping to themselves, a few clusters here and there. Various papers and books were scattered on the tables as well as game boards, and there was a small flat-screen in the corner surrounded by cushions and non-metal chairs. It was currently playing *12 Monkeys*—how fitting.

"So, how did you end up here?" Leo asked, claiming my attention again.

"I was betrayed." I couldn't mask the venom in my words. Ethan had *told* Wyatt about my scratches. I didn't think I could ever forgive him for this. *If I live through this, that is.* He had sold out his family to some crooked stranger. How could he have been to stupid? I didn't realize I was shaking until the metal table started to wiggle, the bolts loose.

Leo held up his hands. "Whoa, sorry. I shouldn't have asked."

I unclenched my vibrating fists. "It's all right. Not your fault."

"Well, I pity the soul who betrayed you. You'll be kicking their ass when you get out of here, right?" Leo shot me a grin. His teeth were perfect—he'd definitely had braces at one point.

"I'll be dumping him, that's for sure." No longer would I have to worry about leaving Hargrove because where I was concerned, Ethan was no longer my problem. But again, I had to get out of here first.

"It was your boyfriend? Damn, that's shitty."

I didn't want to talk—or think— about Ethan's disloyalty anymore. "So where are you from?" I asked. "You don't sound like you're from the south."

"I'm from New York. I was just down here visiting my grandma when everything went to shit. How about you? You're clearly not from here either."

"Canada. Was here for Mardi Gras with a friend."

"Looks like we're both miles away from home."

The guards moved away from the doors as they opened. Leo stood up, his eyes glued to the entrance. When they shoved through a larger-set male, Leo let out a gust of air and plunked back down on the hard chair. The tension in the air was practically visible, like the room had collectively held their breath. Once the man got to his feet and the doors closed behind him, that collective breath was released.

The man turned so I could see his face and I jumped up from my seat like Leo had. "Mac?!"

He stood deathly still before coming over to me, his slipper-clad feet shuffling the whole way.

"Bailey!" He gave me an enormous hug. "I wish I could say it was good to see you, but I wouldn't wish this place on my enemy."

We parted. "What are you doing here? You're not—"

His hand clamped over my mouth. "Shhh!" Then Mac steered me toward the nearest corner with his other hand on my back, away from Leo, whose face was scrunched after witnessing our exchange.

"Let's not make that information public," he whispered.

"Why would they think you're immune?" I said back in a hushed voice.

"Did you ever go back to the apartments?" I nodded and he continued. "When the mercenaries attacked us, I took a chance and bit myself and wrapped the wound quickly, then told them it was from an infected and that I never turned. They spared me." He was looking everywhere but at me. "I'm such a coward."

I placed a hand on his shoulder. "Mac, they were armed killers. You did what you had to in order to survive," I said, paraphrasing from the pep talk Darren had given me before.

"Doesn't mean I don't feel guilty. They brought me out through all the carnage. So much blood." He put his head in his hands. I noticed a patch of gauze taped on his forearm. People will go to extreme lengths to stay alive—a fact I knew well.

"How have they not figured out you're *not* immune yet?" I asked, trying to tear him away from his guilt-laced thoughts.

"Aside from Amelia, they aren't the brightest bunch. I've been acting out so they put me in solitary, and they don't usually use those in solitary for testing until they're able to handle being among the population. Something about needing healthy minds," Mac answered. "That's why I'm back in here; they're trying to make me a viable test subject again."

I had no idea how to help Mac—or myself. I knew nothing about this place other than what Leo and Josh had told me. Maybe once I got to see the daily routine, I could devise an escape plan. This hospital wasn't escape-proof, but seeing that it was known for being a mental hospital, I was willing to bet the security measures were better than most.

"Don't worry, Mac. We'll be getting out of here. And for the record, I'm really glad you're alive." I cast him a smile, which he returned.

"Thanks, Steve McQueen."

Chapter 3

Unfortunately, by the time supper was served, I had not yet escaped.

"This is practically gruel," Mac groused as he played with a blob on his tray.

All of the trays and utensils were plastic, and they even monitored to make sure everyone returned them when finished. Leo told us that they started doing that once a prisoner sharpened a plastic knife into a shiv and stuck it in the throat of one of the guards trying to get away—he didn't make it. *There goes my plan.*

One blond guy sitting with two other pale guys a few tables down kept glancing my way.

"What's the deal with blondie?" I asked Leo. I hoped there wasn't another threat I would have to deal with.

Leo scoffed. "He'll probably try to recruit you."

"What does that mean?" I asked, even more confused. Some kind of Jehovah Witness weirdo?

"Well since this is more of a prison, as you said, he's the obligatory white-power group leader."

"Ah." Even worse.

"Yeah, they're a bunch of *Mein Kampf* douchebags." Judging from the darker color of Leo's skin, they probably weren't the nicest to him.

"They tried to get me into the fold when I first got here, but after my outburst to get locked in solitary, they've kept their distance," Mac said.

"So just act crazy and they'll leave you alone?" I said. "Shouldn't be too hard."

Mac grinned. "You can be my cell neighbor in solitary."

We returned our plastic dishes. The lunch lady counted to make sure I had returned both my fork and knife. I would have to find another pointy object to use as a weapon. Two more armed guards joined us in the cafeteria.

"What's going on?" I asked. Were they expecting a riot?

"We're all being sent back to our cells—I mean *rooms*," Leo replied. "So they bring in more guards so they can take us two at a time."

I looked at Mac. "Will they be sending you back to the isolated cells?"

"I don't know," he whispered. He was busy picking at the gauze taped on his arm as he stared at the new guards.

They started calling names two at a time, taking them out in pairs. The two guards from before remained while the two new guards accompanied the two prisoners to their rooms. Eight trips later and I was all alone in the cafeteria with the armed help.

Don't panic. I could feel my pulse spiking as I started to wonder why I had been left by myself. They had even taken Mac with Leo. Every time I sat down on one of the table benches or chairs, I sat up a few seconds after and paced. I couldn't hold still. The doors opened and Amelia, the lady from when I first awoke, waltzed through. She walked over to me, the edges of her white lab coat swaying with her movement.

"Bailey, is it?" she asked.

"Yeah."

"Come with me. I'll show you to your room."

I followed her out of the cafeteria, a guard waiting for us on the other side. We walked back down the hallway and took a left past the room I had first woken up in. There were two other guards, dressed down in regular clothes and not SWAT gear, standing in the next stretch of hallway. As we continued down, faces peered out the small windows to each room. Amelia stopped at a door on the very end.

"This will be your room." She produced a ring of keys and unlocked the door. She motioned for me to go inside, but I remained where I was standing.

It was now or never.

I twisted around and bolted, turning the nearest corner only to run into another guard. I shoved her to the side and her arms flailed as she fell backward from the momentum. I could hear shoes slapping against the linoleum behind me, but I kept sprinting. There was an exit sign at the end of the corridor. All I had to do was reach the door. Throwing my hands forward, I slammed into the bar latch.

But the door didn't open so I ended up smashing my face into the metal. This was how bugs must feel when they hit a windshield. I whirled around to see Amelia and two guards looming toward me. I felt something trickle onto my lips so I wiped underneath my nose with the back of my hand. Blood. The impact must have made my nose bleed.

I moved to keep running down the next hallway, but I had reached a dead end. Empty vending machines and worn chairs surrounded me. The two guards raised their bulky handguns, but it was Amelia who stepped forward. I used my shirt to dab at the fresh blood running down my face.

"Please don't make this harder than it has to be."

"There's no way you're going to shoot me—if immune people are so valuable." I had no way of knowing this, but I couldn't show them just how scared I was.

"We won't shoot you with bullets, no. These guards are holding tranquilizer guns." She huffed impatiently. "Now you can either come with us willingly or we can hit you with a dose so you can no longer run."

I hung my head. There was no escape at the moment. I'd rather get locked up with my consciousness than be drugged up again.

"Fine," I gritted out.

One of the guards came up to me and grabbed my arm. They escorted me back to the cell Amelia was trying to stuff me into.

"See, we can be reasonable," Amelia said as she closed the door in my face.

I heard the lock click and watched her walk away down the hallway with the two guards. I ran my hands through my hair. This wasn't going to be easy. I shuffled to the tiny window past the beds on the right side, but it too had metal bars. My nose had stopped its mild bleed at the expense of my previously white shirt. It was now spotted with deep red blotches.

I didn't know how I didn't notice it before, but there was a woman lying on the second bed closest to the window. She was wearing a fresh white shirt and she was turned away from me, facing the curtain divider. This must have been a recovery room for patients. I cleared my throat, but the woman didn't stir. She was breathing steadily. Maybe she was doped up.

"Hello?"

No answer, but her breathing picked up. She had to be awake.

"So, it looks like I'm your new roommate. Bailey."

Still nothing.

"And you are...?"

Her body continued to rise and fall with her breaths.

"Fine. I'm just going to talk until you say something. So I'm new here. Never been imprisoned before, can't say I enjoy it. I take it you're immune too. Sucks to be us, huh?"

"Dear God, kid. Shut up," the lady growled in a thick southern accent.

She got up and turned to me, her brown eyes narrowed and glaring. Her bare feet hit the linoleum with a splat. She was tan—not as a result of being outside, but just as her natural skin color. She had to be somewhere in her forties—she had called me kid, after all. There were bandages wrapped around her arm and a distinct bulge under her shirt around the ribcage area.

"You injured?"

"What'cha think?"

"Those from the tests?"

She smiled, but it wasn't a nice smile. It was sardonic and nasty. "You'll be sportin' your own soon enough."

"I'm starting to see why you didn't have a roommate."

"Had one once. Irene. She hung herself with the sheets from your bed on the ceiling fan. Although, they've cleaned 'em since then," she snickered.

I sucked in a deep breath. I wondered if I could apply for room re-assignment?

Wait, Irene? Roy's wife?

"Tell me about Irene. Did she ever mention a husband or kids?" I asked, ignoring the lady's attempt at rattling me.

She stopped her snickering and shrugged. "Don't know, don't care."

"How long ago did she...?" I couldn't say it.

Roy was looking for a dead woman. He would be so heartbroken when he found out.

"'Bout three weeks. Couldn't take it no more."

"Take what? The tests? Being locked up?"

She shrugged again and I clenched my teeth. I wanted to take her by the shoulders and shake the answers out of her. She was being super uncooperative for someone who was being held against her will.

"You know, if you'd help me out a little, maybe we could come up with an escape or way out?"

"You think you're the only one whose thought 'bout escapin'? Trust me, people have tried and failed many times."

"So what, you going to stay in here until you die of old age or until your injuries finally kill you?" I jerked my chin at her wrappings.

She scowled. "Every new person they bring in has the same idea. Rally the troops and attack. But guess what kid, it won't work. So do yourself a favor and keep your head down."

She flopped back down on the single bed and rolled away, dismissing me. Escaping was never going to happen unless we all worked together. You'd think a common goal would unite people, but this lady and the white-power fools from the cafeteria seemed bent on alienation.

I walked away from the window and to my bed. I lifted up the blanket and sheets to check for nasty stains and bugs like I was at a sketchy hotel. If what the other lady had said was true, Irene had killed herself in here. Obviously they would have cleaned the sheets and bedding, but my terrible roommate had made me paranoid.

Seeing no other option, I lay down on top of the blankets and stared up at the ceiling, waiting for sleep to take me.

Chapter 4

I spent the whole night plagued with nightmares. I would open my eyes and see a dead woman hanging from the ceiling fan, then I would wake up realizing it was just a dream. I rolled onto my side and curled up into a ball, willing myself to get back to sleep despite the nightmares. But they kept coming. Sometimes it would look like she was mouthing words to me, but I couldn't make them out. The last time, however, it was clear. She had screamed, "Run!"

At that, I jumped out of bed, deciding that sleep was *not* going to happen. I started to pace until the lights in the hallway were turned on, shining into our room through the tiny window. It must've been time to move us to the common room. It was a lot of effort to keep moving people back and forth from their cells to the cafeteria, but like Mac had said, people needed to be right in their minds and socializing was a big part of that. Even real prisons knew that.

I watched people go by in twos with the guards right behind them, back to the cafeteria. After counting sixteen people, the movement stopped.

"Why aren't they taking me?" I muttered.

"Looks like you're gettin' the full-on welcome treatment, kid," the lady said from her bed.

"Don't move, don't breathe, and the dead won't bother you. But a word of advice, let 'em and you'll be released faster."

I refused to look at her, so I fiddled with the doorframe, picking at a paint chip. "What the hell does that mean?"

The locking mechanism to our door sounded, and Amelia's face appeared in the window.

"You're 'bout to find out. Good luck," was all she said by way of explanation.

"Do I need to remind you to not try anything again?" Amelia asked once the door opened. Her face was pinched tight, causing the glasses to ride up her nose.

She had a guard on either side of her. I didn't answer.

"Well, come on. You too, Rose."

Amelia looked past me to my roommate. She must've been the lady Leo was talking about. He could've warned me she was a *joy* to be around. Rose sat up and sauntered over to us. Her previously pristine white shirt was now as stained as my own. Blood soaked through from the bulge on her ribs. So she was injured pretty bad.

Amelia's eye's honed in on the blotch. "Come on, Rose. Let's treat that."

"How *kind* of you," Rose said, her voice sarcastic.

Amelia shoved one hand into her lab coat pocket and used the other to grab Rose's arm. Amelia steered her down the hall and before they disappeared into one of the rooms she turned back.

"Take Bailey to examination room 'F'."

The guards pulled me from my room and steered me down the hallway, but just before we reached the cafeteria, they had us hang a left down another corridor. The further we went, the quieter everything became. The noise level was low in the hospital, but this was deathly silent. Not even the florescent lights buzzed overhead. I nearly peed myself when something rammed up against one of the locked doors as we passed. An infected was snarling and banging from the other side, spittle coating the minuscule rectangular window as it got worked up. He was missing his front teeth like a little kid.

"Keep moving," one of the guards said as he gave me a little shove.

I started walking again, feeling more and more like a prisoner on death row. Every step brought me closer to some unknown examination room. My mind ran through all the stories I'd heard over the last twenty-fours and my heart sped up with each one. Examination room 'F' didn't sound like a fun place to be.

We finally stopped at the appropriately labeled door and the guards let themselves in. I dug in my heels as they tried to yank me into the stark white room. It looked like a rubber-padded cell used for the insane. I wasn't aware those were real outside of movies.

"You want us to sedate you?" one of the guards groused.

Facing whatever was coming next doped up sounded pretty good actually. Although I was pretty sure he was bluffing because if they wanted to run any kind of tests on me, they probably needed my blood to be clean, therefore *sans drugs*. Maybe I should mention the pot I'd smoked over two weeks ago. My system would test positive for a month at least.

With a final yank, I was thrust into the eerily empty room and the door slammed shut while I scrambled up. I ran to the door and tested the handle. Of course it was locked. I started to bang on the door with my fist. There was no tiny window to see out of.

"Let me out!"

There was no surgical equipment or operating table in the room; there was absolutely nothing. How did they expect to "examine" me? I gave up my fruitless banging in favor of checking the room. The walls were padded with rubber, and the only break was a mirror running lengthwise built into the left wall. The floor was made of uncovered stained cement with a drain in the middle of the room. My slippers slapped against the floor as I made my way over to one of the walls. I pushed with my hand, checking to see just how padded it was—about the thickness of a mattress topper. This was a room for crazies and I wasn't crazy. *Not yet.*

My heart dropped as the door opened. I fully expected Amelia to come through with some medieval torture devices, but I was wrong. A snarling infected was led through by a guard via a large animal control pole. The infected gargled and swung its grabbing hands in any direction it could, almost tripping over its own feet. The pole was *just* long enough to keep the guard out of the thing's arm reach.

I backed up until my butt hit the wall padding. They were going to lock me in here with that thing. The door would only be open for this one moment so I scuttled along the walls trying to keep away from the worked up infected. It jerked toward me, pulling the guard/handler further into the room.

"Stay where you are!" he yelled.

Fuck that. I reached the door and flattened it against the wall as I slunk toward the opening. No sooner was my foot in the hall than my face connected with the butt end of a rifle. I was knocked back into the room, falling flat on my ass. My hands flew to my face to find my nose bleeding again, but the pain hadn't yet registered. As the light cleared from my eyes, I started to feel the sting.

"Shit!" I hissed and tested my nose. It hurt, but nothing felt broken or bent at an odd angle.

I jumped up and rested a hand on the padded wall until the dizziness dissipated. I'd had the concussion before and I knew this was not as serious because my vision steadied quickly. The infected was thrashing again, clawing at the air to reach me. I watched the metal wire noose slacken around the infected's neck until the guard was able to lift it over the thing's head.

The guard didn't say anything as he bolted back out the door and shut it with a bang. Now free, the infected lurched toward me, but I shoved myself off the wall and into the opposite corner before it could reach me. It slammed into the padded wall so hard it bounced off and stumbled back a few steps.

Rose's *advice* played through my mind like a special bulletin report. *Don't move, don't breathe, and the dead won't bother you.* How was I supposed to do that when every instinct was screaming at me to run? I tried to slow my breathing but my body wouldn't have it.

The infected swung its head toward me and I stopped in place like a mosquito caught in amber. My legs ached to move; to run, but I had nowhere to run *to*. I was trapped in this padded cell with the enemy I'd been running from for months. The infected was no longer fooled and started toward me in a slow manner.

One step. Two steps. Three steps and it was less than a meter from me. *I can't do this.* I gave into my flight instinct and ran to the other corner. The thing followed my movements and came after me again. We kept going around in circles. I would let it get closer only to dodge around it and run to the opposite side of the room—it wasn't very effective.

For the fifth time, I passed by the red handprint I'd left from leaning on the wall after wiping my bloody nose. The infected was never going to get tired—but I would. My breathing was already spiking from the adrenaline and short bursts of running. Not to mention I hadn't eaten anything since "supper" last night. They were going to win. How far will they take this? Would they let it consume me? Or just bite me? I stopped in front of the door to listen for people right outside but I couldn't hear anything over the rasping of the infected in the small room.

"Shit, shit, shit, shit, shit," I muttered to myself as the thing launched itself at me again.

I leapt out of the way and it crashed against the metal door. For some reason, the back of the door wasn't padded like the rest of the room. The infected had landed so hard that when it fell backwards, I could see the bloody spot where it hit the door. Its forehead now had a small indent like someone had punched a hole in drywall.

My foot moved before my brain could tell it not to. I kicked at the infected's head but my slipper-clad feet didn't do much damage, so I kneeled down and grabbed the snapping head in my hands. There was nothing to use as a weapon. The room had been strategically cleared of everything. Not even a chair. Just the hard floor, so it would have to do. The fallen infected reached for me but I was no longer concerned with getting scratched. I wanted it dead. I lifted the head up so high that the shoulders lifted off the ground, and then I brought it down with all the force I could muster.

The infected's head hit the solid floor and tried to bounce back up. I used that momentum to raise the head again and bring it down once more. I let out a savage yell as I continually bashed the thing's head into the floor until it stopped moving. Its grabbing hands plopped onto the floor as the skull cracked and brain matter spilled out like a fallen container of cottage cheese.

I dropped the skull and scooted back until I hit the wall. I was breathing so heavy that I thought I might pass out. Gathering my knees, I put my head in between my legs and squeezed my eyes closed, blocking out the image before me. The room was now splattered from the carnage. Dark brown blood and brain matter had sprayed the otherwise immaculate, white room. No wonder the walls were padded with rubber—it was easy to hose off.

My clothes were a mess of my own blood and the infected's. Now I understood why they hadn't given me a clean shirt last night. I cracked open my eyes once my heart rate calmed down. The infected was truly dead. My eyes caught a brief glint of something reflecting the harsh light by the body of the infected. I quickly crawled over on all fours to the fallen corpse and stopped with my back to the mirror. The infected had been wearing ripped army-print cargo pants with giant pockets. Peeking out from one of the pockets was a black and metallic handled switchblade knife. The metal tip of the handle was what had caught my eye.

I heard the sound of the lock being turned, so I quickly grabbed the sheathed knife and stuffed it into the waistband of my pajama bottoms. I drew the drawstring tight to make sure it didn't slip out.

This time it was Amelia who came through first. She was scowling.

"That was our last dead one!"

She was angry? I was the one who should be angry!

"Fuck you! You threw me in here with an infected! What did you think was going to happen? Were you going to let it kill me?" I bolted to my feet and ran at her.

In those few seconds between standing and reaching her, I debated using the knife and ending her, but then I'd have to fight my way past the armed guards. Even if by some miracle I got past them, I still had no idea how to get out of the hospital/asylum. I assume one couldn't just stroll out of here—there would be keys required.

Instead I opted for my good 'ol fist. It connected with her face and Amelia went flying back, her glasses falling down to the ground. I couldn't stop the momentum and went flying forward with her. We landed on the floor in the hallway, but I recovered way faster than her. I kicked out and landed a hit a smidge above her stomach. She made an "oomph" sound and curled into a ball. Two pairs of hands shoved me to the ground and held me in place. I stopped my flailing.

"I'm good!" I yelled.

I didn't need them stabbing me with another needle. I couldn't afford for them to find the knife while I was out drooling on myself. They continued to hold me down while

Josh jumped over the fray to get to Amelia's side. He helped her to her feet, grabbing her broken pair of glasses from the ground in the process. She couldn't stand completely upright thanks to my Chuck Norris kick. I admit I got a little satisfaction out of that, and from the black eye she'd no doubt be sporting soon. The bitch deserved it.

She let out some kind of screech noise and went red in the face. "Take her to the solitary wing!"

I was yanked upright again, my head spinning from being tossed around like a birdie in a badminton game. Josh shot me a venomous look. It didn't look like I would be getting any BFF bracelets from this bunch. Not that I gave a shit; they threw me to the wolves—literally.

As the guards carted me passed Amelia and Josh I heard her barking an order at him. "Get everything ready. We need to capture a new dead one as soon as possible."

Chapter 5

My new cell was exactly that—a cell. Not that I had ever been in jail before, but I assumed this was what a cell would look like. A single cot was off to the side with a sink and toilet close by. There was no window to the outside, just a tiny one in the door showing the empty hallway. I was getting really tired of the minimalist accommodations.

My stomach growled, berating me for misbehaving and missing breakfast. Even the slop from last night sounded good. I patted by my hipbone where I still had the switchblade stashed. In all the commotion, it hadn't fallen out. Still had the ace up my sleeve—or down my pants to be more correct.

I laid down on the cot to plan. I couldn't just stab a guard and escape. There were too many of them and no doubt the exits would be locked up. I wrinkled my nose at the memory of slamming into the sealed exit door last night. My nose wasn't broken, but I was willing to bet there was bruising and maybe a black eye or two. Too bad mirrors were prohibited in solitary.

In order to get out of here alive, I would need the cooperation and help of the other prisoners. If we escaped as a group, we could overrun the guards. But the guards were armed, and even if the weapons were mainly for show, they might still shoot if swarmed. *Why had there never been a group escape attempt?* I mean there were only about sixteen people all together, but that was still better than only a few. Leo had never mentioned anything other than a single person trying to get out. If they all just worked together, they could get out— probably. I just needed to get back to the cafeteria. They were just locking me in here to try to exert their power; to break my will, but it wasn't going to happen.

I turned over on the cot and saw the tiny line markings in the paint. Someone had gouged hundreds of tiny tics into the wall, torn fingernail clippings stuck in some. I gulped and rolled back around. Would that be me soon?

They brought me lunch *and* supper; each time the guard brandishing pepper spray like I was a rabid drunk. It shamed me to admit, but I scarfed down the terrible food. I was starving and I would be no use without my strength. If they really wanted to break a person they would deprive them of food, which was kind of throwing me off. This place was confusing. They kept us here like criminals in jail, yet we weren't left to rot in a cell—unless we attacked them. They gave us food and clothes; the only torture was coming from the experiments and I was willing to bet they didn't count that as torture.

After being left for zombie-chow, I'd beg to differ. Facing the infected was scary enough, but facing them unarmed and stuck in a tiny space had been horrifying. I hoped whoever they sent out to collect a new infected was torn apart in the process.

My hateful fantasizing was interrupted by the lights going out. *Must be bedtime.* It looked like I'd be spending the night in here. I wondered how they were powering this place. There must be backup generators; all hospitals had them. But that was an awful lot of fuel needed. This place had been going for a few months, it had to be running on fumes by now. Maybe I could just wait it out. Once this place ran out of juice, escaping would be easier.

I spent the night dozing, too tired to toss and turn. This time I didn't dream of the lady hanging from the ceiling, but instead of being trapped in a kennel and then being released and chased. No matter how much I ran, I could never get away from the unseen thing chasing me. This place was going to mess with my head eventually.

In the morning, the guards tossed me a clean outfit to change into with my breakfast. Once I ate and they came to collect the tray, I complained about needing a shower before I changed into the clean clothes. I felt gross from stewing in zombie goo all night. The guards looked at each other like they didn't have a brain between them. One left to ask for permission and when he came back, they took me to the communal showers. No one else was in there, but I still felt awkward stripping down in a giant empty bathroom.

I quickly peeled off my stained outfit and washed my hair and skin with the toiletries laying around. Everything was communal in here. There was a pile of clean towels folded in the corner that I used to dry off before slipping into the clean clothes and tucking the switchblade into the waistband of my new pajama pants. I towel dried my hair as best as I could, but it was still wet, soaking the shoulders of my shirt.

Unsure of what to do next, I banged on the door. "I'm done."

The guards opened the door and escorted me to the cafeteria. Mac ran to me as soon as the doors slammed shut behind me.

"Holy shit, Bailey, you gave me a scare. I thought something happened to you!"

"Something did," I muttered, pointing to my bruised face.

We walked over to the table Leo was sitting at. Unfortunately, Rose was right beside him. She stared me down as I plunked onto the hard steel stool.

"What?" I barked at her.

"You didn't let it bite you. You goin' to regret that," she said and crossed her arms.

She winced when her arm pushed up against her wounded ribs. *Good.* Leo looked back and forth between us. As far as he knew, Rose and I had not yet been acquainted.

"They threw you in with a sick one?" Mac asked, his face going pale.

"How did you get out without a bite?" Leo asked before I could answer Mac's question.

"I bashed its head in." I jutted my chin out.

"With what?" Leo asked, his eyes narrowed.

"The floor."

"Hmm."

Our attention was briefly drawn to the cafeteria doors when Josh came through and talked with the guards. He was speaking to them so that his back was facing the populace. Together they looked around the room, his eyes momentarily locking with my own, and I could have sworn he shot me a smirk. Then without fanfare, Josh left back out the doors and the guards resumed their tough guy poses.

"What normally happens when they force you in with the infected?" I asked, starting up the conversation again.

"Once it bites or scratches you, the guards rush in and subdue the dead one—or kill it," Leo said.

"How would they know you're bit?"

"The window in the room is a two-way mirror," Rose said as if that was common knowledge.

"And how would you know that?"

"Been in a cop station a couple times in my day." I didn't doubt that.

It made sense, in a sick sort of way. They could stand behind their window all safe and secure while watching their patient get scarred for life in more than one way. I gritted my teeth. The people running this place were the crazy ones.

I leaned over the table. "We need to get everyone here on board for an escape."

Rose scoffed. "Good luck. Most people here either keep to themselves or their kind. Not much for socializin'."

I assumed she meant the obligatory white-power crew. Well they would just have to get over themselves if they wanted out of here.

"I'll go talk to them," I said.

All three looked at me like I had just claimed aliens were walking among us.

"Well, at least we'll finally get some entertainment 'round here," Rose said with a shit-eating grin.

When we escaped, I would have no problem leaving her behind. Locking eyes with her, I shoved myself from my seat slowly and walked over to the group of three white males sitting on the other side of the room. They stopped talking as I approached and eyed me warily. At least they didn't sport swastika tattoos. They did however have a bunch of gnarled scar tissue similar to Leo's arm. One guy even had the outline of a set of teeth in the apex where his shoulder met his neck. That must have been painful, not to mention hard to hide.

"Can we help you?" the biggest, blond one asked, his undertone telling me to fuck off.

"I was thinking we could help each other."

His eyebrows shot up and the three snickered. "What exactly could *you* help me with?" He eyed me up and down.

I breathed through my nose and ignored his lewd gaze. "I assume you don't like being locked up, but who knows, maybe you're accustomed to being in jail."

He scowled at me. "You better watch what you say. Those leaf-blowers ain't goin' to be able to protect you."

Show no fear. To their surprise, I sat down beside the big guy in the empty spot.

"You're telling me you don't mind being held prisoner by these psychos?" I asked, my voice *mostly* steady.

"What're you gettin' at, girl?" the guy with the longish brown hair and full beard asked from across the table.

"Escaping."

"We ain't workin' with no dead weight," the big guy said.

"Really? We're all on the same side here and we can fend for ourselves," I said through clenched teeth.

"Your face says otherwise." They all laughed.

My fingers touched at the bruising and swelling beneath my right eye and I glowered. "You should see Amelia before you judge me."

They stopped their snickering and the big guy gave me a different kind of stare. "I'll believe that when I see it."

I shrugged, feigning indifference. "Whatever, just think about it. We have the bigger numbers; if we work together we can get out of here."

"Yeah? Against *armed* guards?" the big guy challenged.

"I'm sure you prison savvy individuals can fashion a shiv or something." I didn't know if I was a masochist, but I was angling to get another black eye.

They regarded me in silence for a moment before the main guy spoke up. "Go back to your *group*." He waved his hand and turned from me.

I got up and walked back over to the others, trying to appear normal. In truth, I was fighting the urge to run from my first encounter with the Arian brothers.

"So when's the great escape?" Rose said.

I ignored her. "So looks like they're out. Care to help me round up the others?"

Mac looked at the entrance and back at me. "You're going to have to do it more discreetly or the guards will know something is up. Maybe try talking to people in the food line or when people gather around to watch a movie."

"Good idea." I hadn't thought of that. I didn't want to tip off the guards and foil our escape before it even happened.

"Okay, I have to ask. What are you even plannin' we do after we get people onboard? Just storm the guards?" Rose asked.

"I don't know. We need the numbers and someone whose familiar with the layout."

"George has been here the longest, so I'd start with him," Leo said. He discreetly stretched and pointed to the man sitting on the window sill in a house coat.

"We have no weapons," Rose said.

"Not exactly. It's not a gun, but I have a knife."

"How did you get a knife?" Mac asked.

"There was a switchblade in the pocket of the infected I took down."

"You just got a horseshoe up your ass, dontcha?" Rose said with distain.

"You keep being a bitch and you can *watch* me leave your ass behind," I growled. I was anything *but* lucky.

"Hey, hey, hey," Leo held out his hands. "We don't need to be turning on each other. Like you said, we need to work together."

I had no idea what had brought Leo and Rose to team up in here, but it sure wasn't their personalities. Or age. Leo could have been her son for all I knew except that he didn't refer to her as his mother. They both had tanned skin and black hair, but their features were wildly different. Rose had a more angled and skinny face where Leo had a rounder face and wider eyes.

We waited until we were called to line up for lunch before we talked to anyone else. I watch George saunter over to the line, his ratty housecoat swaying limply on his form. The belt normally used to tie up a robe was missing. I made sure I was next to him, butting past a girl around my age. She didn't even acknowledge that I had jumped ahead of her.

"George?" I whispered.

At first I got no reaction from him, even though I had spoken right beside him. I tapped his arm with my elbow to get his attention. He jerked like I had just stabbed him in the kidney with my concealed knife. His eyes were wide when he looked at me.

I held up my hands. "Sorry, didn't mean to scare you."

George tilted his head and made a gesture with his hand. I didn't know what to make of that so I continued on. "I heard you've been locked up here the longest." He made the gesture again and at the confused look on my face, he pointed to his ears and shook his head.

Oh God, he was deaf. *Thanks for the intel, Leo!* How did I explain this?

I talked really slowly—but softly—focusing on mouthing my words. "Can I eat lunch with you?"

He seemed to understand because he nodded. The lunch lady served us something that finally didn't resemble gruel. It looked like noodles and eggs. I led George over to where Mac was playing with his food. "Who puts powdered eggs with penne noodles?"

I assumed that was a rhetorical question, but eggs and pasta went further to fill a person up. George sat down beside Mac, so I sat across from him so he could see my words better. I just hoped that him reading my lips in the lunch line wasn't a fluke.

I didn't start badgering him immediately, instead opting to let us eat our exotic meal. Rose and Leo had sat down beside a couple others a few tables down and hopefully were discussing an escape with them.

George finished and looked up at me. I smiled as reassuringly as I could, although I was sure my bruised face ruined it. "George, can you understand what I'm saying?"

He nodded; I guess he could read lips. Mac's eyes widened as he set down his forkful of lunch. Apparently, he hadn't known George was deaf either.

I had to pick my words carefully so that George could answer. "How many months have you been here?"

George held up three fingers and then made a pinching motion, not allowing his fingers to meet. Three months and a bit.

"How well would you say you know the layout of the halls?"

He made a so-so gesture while rocking his head left to right. I was going to ask if he could describe it, but I managed to hold my tongue before those words awkwardly slipped out. That wouldn't work. And I was sure the chances of someone in here being able to translate sign language were nil. I looked around to see if anyone was watching our exchange. Most heads were down, either still eating or just minding their own business. My eyes landed on a pile of books tossed on the corner table.

I held up my index finger for George to stay put and headed toward the books. The selection was crappy, mostly used and discolored paperbacks you'd find at a garage sale in the fifty-cent bin. Good thing I wasn't planning to use them for reading. I just needed the paper inside for George to draw out some schematics for us to plan our escape route. Now I just needed a pen. There were no markers or pencil crayons, but there were wax crayons nearby. They took the "no sharp objects" rule very seriously. I scooped up the books with the widest pages and the darker crayons before heading back to our table.

The guards watched me with interest as I moved across the room. They looked so bored that maybe they were hoping I would start something to help pass the time. When I sat back down, they turned away from me, the one guard's chest deflating. *Sorry to disappoint.*

"What's that for?" Mac asked.

"I'm hoping George here can draw us a map."

I flipped through one of the books until I got to the couple of blank pages at the back, then passed it to George. When he looked up at me, I mouthed "escape" and "map." A smile spread across his face as he picked up one of the crayons and began drawing lines on the page. Mac and I held our breath as we watched him draw out various corridors. Eventually it began to look like a maze from all the lines, but that was more due to the cramped drawing space and dull crayon.

When George finished, he put down the crayon and gave me back the book. I looked it over. He had written "Cafe" to indicate the room we were currently in. According to the map, the main entrance was on the opposite side of the building. And guarded. He'd drawn a stick man beside it and any spot where he had seen a guard posted.

I smiled and patted George on the hand. He grabbed a different novel and scribbled something down.

I read his words and answered, mouthing each word so that George could see what I was saying. "When? I don't know. We need the right moment. Any kink in their schedule you know about?"

George scribbled some more before turning the page back to me. He had written, "When they send the guards to collect more of the dead ones. Less guards to worry about."

I frowned. We had missed that chance yesterday when Amelia sent them out after I killed their last test dummy. "That was yesterday."

George furrowed his brow as he tapped the crayon on the table. I turned to Mac as George thought on it and passed him the book. The guards were blocked from my view thanks to Mac and George sitting in front of me, so they didn't see us shifting the book back and forth.

"Is this the part where I have to stuff the map down my pants?" Mac joked as he examined George's drawing.

"Please don't do that," I deadpanned.

"What if the guards find it?"

"Can we take books back to our rooms?" I asked and Mac shrugged.

"You think his drawings are correct?" Mac asked.

We both looked at George, who was scribbling down something new. It wasn't like he'd heard what Mac said, but still, it was rude to talk about him while he was right there.

"Not like we have a bunch of mapmakers to choose from."

George shoved his book at me again, but before I could finish reading the words, the cafeteria doors opened yet again. This time it wasn't Josh. When Amelia came through with more guards, all the prisoners stopped what they were doing and turned to her, their faces masks of fury and horror. Some ducked their heads, trying to make themselves shrink into their environment. No one wanted to be the next name called.

Amelia's face looked as bruised as mine felt. I was getting good at punching people. The three macho guys I had talked to earlier definitely took notice as the blond leader looked from Amelia to me and back again. Now he would believe me. She continued to speed walk over to where I was sitting. *Jesus, not again.*

When she approached our table, her face was passive but something was lurking underneath that calm. I could see her hands twitching inside her lab coat pockets. Mac quickly slammed the book shut.

Amelia stood a foot from the end of the table and took a breath before speaking. "Mac, come with me, please."

I jumped up in my seat. "I thought you were out of infected?"

Mac stared down at the table, sitting ramrod straight. My outburst may have just made things worse.

"No need to concern yourself, you'll be coming too," Amelia said with zero emotion.

Mac looked up at me, confused. The others never mentioned them taking two at a time for the experiments. Having two of us against an infected would actually be better, so I was doubly suspicious. What the hell did she have in store for us?

Amelia jerked her head toward us and the guards sprang into action as if they were trained dogs. They grabbed both Mac and me in a tight grip and led us toward the doors. I looked back to see George slip the book into the pocket of his robe and give me a small thumbs-up sign, but his gesture didn't match the worried look on his face.

Chapter 6

We were brought back down the dark and quiet hallway that led to the room where I had been forced to kill the infected with my bare hands. I tried to catch Mac's attention without saying anything, but his gaze was firmly fixated on his feet. He was probably freaking out. He knew what was waiting for him thanks to the stories. Amelia stopped at the door beside the room I had been shoved in the day before.

"Put him inside. Bring her in here with me," Amelia ordered.

I pushed against the guard trying to pull me into the other room. "What are you planning to do?" I yelled. "I'm the one you want to put in there."

Mac's face was expressionless as the other guard opened the door to the padded room and gently pushed him inside. Mac wasn't resisting. He must have been in shock.

"Mac, don't worry, I'll get you out of there," I screamed, but I had no idea how I would go about that. I turned to Amelia. "I'm the one you want to punish, you bitch! Put me in there again!" I would survive a bite; Mac wouldn't.

"Bring her in here," Amelia said with force.

The guard resumed his attempt at trying to stuff me into the other room. I managed to wrench myself out of his hold and kicked him as hard as I could in the nuts. His armor didn't include a cup apparently as he sank to his knees, grasping at his injured junk and groaning. I ran like a linebacker and smashed straight into the other guard just as he was shutting the door to the padded cell. We flew to the ground and I tried to do the same thing to him as I did to the other guard, but he wasn't going to allow that.

The guard reared his feet up and shoved me back hard like a kangaroo. I flew back and to the side, slamming into the solid cement wall. My lungs froze at the impact, my breathing momentarily suspended. I struggled to get some oxygen and breath through the pain from the collision with the very solid wall. The guard who had kicked me had gotten up and grabbed both of my feet. I was dragged into the next room, still coughing up a fit as my lungs started working again.

The other room was small and skinny and dark. There was a desk attached to the wall and above it, the two-way mirror Rose had mentioned. They were going to make me watch Mac die. To them, he was immune and would suffer a simple bite. To me, it was watching an execution of a friend.

I was still lying on the floor and couldn't see through the mirror from my angle. I rolled to my side and tried to sit up.

"Try anything again, and Carlos will tranquilize you," Amelia warned. "But not enough to put you to sleep; just enough to keep you awake and lucid, but docile."

Carlos must've been the guard I had kicked in the nuts, because he gave me a sick sneer from his bent-over position, like he was already hoping I would try something. The other guard had moved his hands from my feet to my arm and yanked me to my feet. The man-handling from the guards was pissing me off. Next time, I would be angling to break some arms.

I swayed on my feet at first. The guard turned me so that I was now facing the two-way mirror. Mac was in the corner of the padded room on the opposite side of the mirror. He was standing extremely still, his eyes glazed over. They had tried to hose off the mess I'd left on the floor, but there was still a large, ominous russet-colored stain where the infected's body had fallen.

I had no choice, I had to tell them. "He's not immune," I said.

Amelia's head whipped from the mirror to me. "What did you say?"

"Mac isn't immune."

"He has a bite mark from an infected."

"He did that to himself when your murdering goons killed everyone in his group—including children," I spat at her.

She took a step back, her hand flying to her mouth. "Children," she muttered under her hand.

"Like you fucking care! You sent them! Now get Mac out of there!" I demanded.

She looked from me to the window a couple of times before swallowing. "I would have *never* sanctioned for children to be killed. Those mercenaries are godless heathens."

I didn't give a shit if she had some twisted morals where it was okay to subject adults to this torture, but couldn't handle the thought that children were harmed. Amelia was a monster; as bad as the infected in her own way. She was going to force me to watch as my friend met his end.

She lowered her head and nodded, her cold expression returning. "Carlos, tell them to bring in the dead one."

I knew right then that I would not be leaving this place until I made sure she was dead. Carlos stuck his head out the door and spoke to another who must've been standing outside. He came back in and closed the door, flicking the lock. The room was now completely dark except for the light coming in through the two-way mirror.

My heart rate picked up. "I told you he's not immune! What's the point other than to get your rocks off, you twisted bitch!"

I struggled to get to her. All it would take was my switchblade to her neck to end her. But the guard attached to me like a straightjacket. Carlos came over and yanked my arms behind me painfully and I felt plastic ties cut into my skin as he secured my hands. I tugged against them, ignoring the blood leaking down my arm from the plastic edges piercing my skin. I was helpless. I couldn't get Mac out of this and now I was going to be punished for it.

"Mac may not be immune, but that doesn't mean he won't aid our study. We can record and time the turning process to better understand how it affects non-immune people."

"You're killing him is what you're doing!" My voice came out cracked.

The door to the padded cell opened and a new infected was led through with the animal catcher rod. Mac flattened himself against the soft wall, his eyes wide. The wire around the infected's neck loosened and slipped over its head, and then the door was slammed behind it. Immediately the infected started toward Mac in the corner. Mac's head whipped back and forth, like he was trying to convince himself this wasn't happening. Just before the infected reached him, Mac ran around it like I had and then began a game of tag with the infected.

I tore my gaze from the window. "You can stop this right now." I tried a softer voice. "You're just as bad as the mercenaries if you let an innocent man die."

"I am *nothing* like them!" Amelia all but yelled at me. I had struck a nerve. "What I am doing will save the rest of our species. We just need more time."

A painful yell brought me back to looking through the mirror. The infected had sunk its teeth into the back of Mac's leg. Somehow the thing had fallen, but its hands and teeth reached Mac's calf. I lurched forward, my throat swelling with the urge to cry.

"Get them to remove the dead one," Amelia ordered and once again, Carlos opened the door and barked instructions to the person outside.

The padded cell door opened almost immediately. Josh walked through with the animal catcher rod with the noose portion slackened. The infected paid Josh no mind as he was busy chewing through the piece of Mac's leg he had bitten off. Like he was approaching a timid animal, Josh tiptoed toward the back of the infected. Once in range, he deftly dropped the wire metal noose over its head and tightened. He pulled up and back, and the infected resisted but still got up. Its arms clawed at Mac lying on the ground, angry that it had been denied the rest of its meal.

Josh started to pull the thing toward the door, but it veered off and slammed into the mirror. We jerked back as the mirror pulsated lightly from the contact. One more jerk and Josh managed to get the infected back out of the room. Mac scrambled away until he hit the padded wall, his leg leaking a trail of blood.

"He's going to die of blood loss," I said, my eyes blurring from the tears.

"Just keep watching," Amelia said.

Josh re-entered the room without the infected, carrying a medium-sized duffle bag. He proceeded to walk toward Mac and leaned down in front of him. Josh grabbed Mac's injured leg and spread it out, ripping open the torn pant leg. He reached into the bag and pulled out a wad of gauze and compression press. He tore into the bag and placed the press over the bite wound for a minute. Mac cried out in pain, his head knocking back with his eyes squeezed shut. *I'm so sorry, Mac.*

Then Josh took off the press and sprayed some disinfectant on the wound, making Mac yell once again. My own leg throbbed in sympathy. Josh put a clean compression press on the wound and fastened it by wrapping gauze around Mac's leg and tying it off. It made no sense that they were using medical supplies on a soon-to-be-dead man, but maybe they were expecting the turning process to take a while and didn't want their subject to die from blood loss first. Or maybe they were thinking that the disinfectant would slow the spread of the infection.

Mac said something to Josh, but we couldn't hear in the next room. Josh patted Mac's arm and got up and left, closing the door behind him.

Through clenched teeth I said, "So what now?"

"We wait and record."

Chapter 7

It was a stressful two hours. At first Mac seemed fine other than the injury on his leg. Within an hour he had developed a cough and we could see that the skin surrounding the wound had become grey in color, like he was already a corpse. His coughing increased and soon he was spewing blood with each hack. I let out a choppy breath. *He's not going to last much longer.*

The entire time I had been trying to slip out of my plastic cuffs, but all it earned me was a pair of cut up and raw wrists. The guards must've noticed, but let me keep trying, knowing I was just injuring myself more. Amelia had used our *quality time* together to fill me in on what they had discovered through their experiments.

"How long the virus needs to take over depends on if the host is alive or not. The virus has free run if the host is dead, because nothing is fighting it anymore. That's why those who die during an attack turn faster than those who are just bit or scratched. If it's a non-fatal attack, the time between initial infection and complete incubation in the patient is not uniform, but we have seen that the closer the bite or scratch is to the brain on the body of the victim, the less time it takes.

"The body is medically dead, but something inside the host reacts with the virus and the body seems to reanimate, defying the laws of science. What the virus reacts with, we're not sure. By running tests on the immune, we are trying to rule out what it could and couldn't be. We've had immune from many different cultures, backgrounds, blood types, age, gender, genetics, and we still can't narrow down what it is in you that renders the virus harmless."

"So ... I'm lacking whatever it is that the virus latches onto?" I asked, more confused than before.

Amelia nodded. "According to our findings, it would appear so."

Mac drew our attention back to the padded room when he collapsed onto his side, and with one last wheezing gasp, he stopped breathing. The tears that had been threatening finally fell. On one hand I was devastated to have witnessed Mac's death and to have not been able to help, but on the other, I was glad Mac was no longer being forced to suffer. *I may not have been able to save you, but I sure as hell will make Amelia, and everyone who's a part of this, pay!*

Mac laid still for a minute, then small tremors started in his limbs. His bitten leg jerked and his shoulder slid out from under him, sending him onto his back. It was eerie to watch a dead man start moving once again. That thought had never really sunk in until now. It really did defy all the laws of science. The convulsions wracking his body increased in their tempo, his limbs and torso now jolting all over the place as if he was having a seizure.

Amelia leaned forward, her face riveted on what was happening to Mac, not caring in the least that she was the reason behind it. God, I wanted her dead and even more so, I wanted to be the one to kill her.

The seizing stopped, and Mac laid still once again—but not for long. He stood up in one swift motion, his teeth gnashing together. All of the blood vessels in his eyes had burst, his pale blue irises sticking out among a wash of red. He got to his feet and ran at the door, smashing into it with substantial force.

"It's amazing how fast and strong the freshly turned are," Amelia said.

I was reminded of when Taylor turned and how quickly he had made a dash for John and then for Zoe.

Amelia continued my science lesson. "It's a good thing for us, that as their body decays, that speed and strength is diminished."

"Once they're turned, the body still decays?" I asked, my eyes not leaving Mac's form as he snarled and bashed into the door of the padded room.

"Yes, they're essentially dying. When they feed on the non-immune, they do appear to be receiving some kind of nourishment, hence why they don't just rot and fall apart immediately. But"—she looked at me through the corner of her eyes—"I have no idea how their anatomy works since they threw all we thought we knew about the human body out the window when they started coming back from the dead."

So they really knew nothing about this infection or how it worked. They were subjecting us to theses horrors for nothing because there would be no cure, at least not one these blind idiots would find. All these lives wasted.

I turned to face Amelia square on. "You think what you're doing here will make a difference but it won't. You're doing this for you." At that, I ran forward, taking the guard holding my arm with me, and head-butted Amelia. She let out a screech and fell back.

"That's it! Send her in there!" Amelia used the sleeve of her pristine white lab coat to wipe the blood trickling from her nose. Her bangs were tossed over her eyes, but I could see them seething with rage underneath. She wasn't used to being opposed so much. If she thought I was going to break, she had another thing coming.

Both guards gripped my arms and dragged me out until I was face to face with the padded room door again. I could hear Mac's corpse pounding away on the inside. A woman in full SWAT gear and a plastic shield was nodding at Josh. Josh opened the door, and before Mac could charge through, the woman with the shield bashed it into his face and shoved him backwards with surprising strength. Mac flew back into the room and I felt the plastic ties fall from my wrists. Once freed, I was pushed in next. The door slammed behind me as Mac's corpse got up. The small room smelled of rot and infected wounds and lemon Pledge.

Mac was too fast, and I barely missed being tackled by him as I fled to the other side of the room. I wouldn't be able to knock him down and bash his head in like the last one. He was too freshly turned. It was like facing a regular person—an insane person intent on ripping you to shreds. He let out a snarl and launched himself at me again. I would have to use his height and weight against him.

I stood still until he got close enough and then reared to the side, sticking my leg up. Mac tripped, but righted himself when he landed on the wall. *Shit*. This would only work when there was no wall to help him stay upright. I swallowed. There was only one way to do this. Mac ran back at me and I met him halfway, then dove at his legs. He fell over me and I tried to roll away, but his weight landed on my left side. I kicked out, trying to wedge him off of me.

He grabbed at my feet, pulling off the slippers in the process. I felt his teeth sink into my foot and then pain shot up my leg. I screamed and used my other foot to smash his head. His teeth let go and I scrambled out from under him as he was busy eating the chunk he had taken from my foot. My foot was pulsating with pain, but I had to force myself to ignore it.

I pulled the switchblade from my pajama bottoms and flicked the blade out.

"I'm so sorry, Mac."

He was lying on his stomach so I got to my knees and brought the blade down on the base of the back of Mac's head. When he didn't stop moving, I pulled out the blade and jammed it in at a different angle, toward the brain rather than just straight down. His hand that had grabbed me again while I was trying to stab him, fell off my leg and landed on the cement floor. The rest of Mac's body went lax.

I kneeled over his body for what felt like hours. My foot was throbbing; the nerve endings felt like they were on fire. The door creaked open and Carlos stepped through. He had a syringe in his hand. *Fuck that.* As soon as he was within range, I gripped the hilt of the switchblade tightly and lashed out in a sudden movement to take him off-guard. The blade landed in the inside of his upper thigh. Before he could react, I yanked it out and stabbed him again in the same area. I was hoping to hit the main artery there. Blood poured down my arm, leaving red tracks like a morbid tribal tattoo.

Carlos let out a very high-pitched scream and dropped the syringe as he fought me off. I felt nothing now except my need to exact revenge. The pain in my foot—and heart—was gone, replaced with a need to punish. He moved out of my range as I went in for a third stab, so I missed, the blade hitting the messy, blood-coated floor. It was hard to tell how much blood he was losing since his pants were black, but judging from the amount on the floor, I had hit my target.

Carlos retreated back into the corner of the room as his hands pressed to his wounds. His eyes met mine, and they were shocked and scared. Now he knew how it felt to be powerless. Josh and the other guard stormed the room. Josh ran to Carlos and the guard came at me. I stood fully, and took a swipe at the guard's face. He reared back, the blade waving in front of him uselessly. I charged forward, but he kneed me in the gut and I crumpled to the ground. He stepped on my hand until I released the knife. It was either let it go or have him break my hand.

Once I let go, he kicked the knife away. I was too busy fighting the pain in my stomach to stop the needle that was jammed into my arm. The pain started to ebb as the drug kicked in. I felt delirious and couldn't stop the laughter from bubbling through my lips. I didn't need to see their faces to know that they were horrified. Then all I could see was the stained cement floor come closer and closer to my face, before I saw nothing.

Chapter 8

When I woke up, my first thought was about how surprised I was that they hadn't killed me. My next one was that my foot really hurt. I opened my eyes to find that I was back in my solitary cell. I wiggled my injured foot, and then panic took over. Rearing upright, I pulled my left foot to me to examine the wound. They had cleaned it and dressed it in mounds of gauze. Slowly, I undid the white wrappings to find that when Mac had taken a bite of my foot, he had taken my pinky toe as well. *Oh my God, I'm missing a toe.* I stared at the red and angry patch where my toe should have been. Somehow this wound was more of a shock than all my others, and I didn't know why.

I hastily rewrapped and tied off the gauze and tried to ignore the fact that I was now missing a body piece. It was shallow to care so much about a toe, but I couldn't shake the shock. I gave my cheek a slap.

"Get ahold of yourself," I said out loud.

My hand went to the waistband of my pants to find the switchblade gone. *Right, I had to use it. On Mac.* I chewed on my lip to help distract myself from crying. Mac was dead and it hadn't been a quick death either. He had suffered.

"Stop this!" I hissed at myself. This train of thought wouldn't help me get out of here.

I had no idea how long I'd been out for. They had managed to bring my limp form to solitary, clean and dress my foot, and even Carlos's blood had been wiped off of my skin, so it had to have been at least a few hours. The lights were on in the hallway, so it must still be day time as well.

I swung my legs off the bed and tested out putting weight on my injured left foot. It hurt, but I needed to be able to run. So I got up and tried walking around. As long as I kept the brunt of the weight on the inside of my foot and mostly on the heel, the pain wasn't as bad. Although I looked super gibbled when I did that. I rubbed at my eyes. This was not ideal for an escape because my running speed was now hindered. *Shit.* I went up to the small window and looked out as much as I could. There was a guard posted to the left of my room. I guess I was now considered a high-risk prisoner.

The fluorescent lights flickered above me and out in the hallway. The guard posted at my room shoved himself off the wall and looked around as if he was worried. I didn't think we had ghosts to worry about, but running out of fuel for the generators was a very real threat. He relaxed and leaned back along the wall. I was about to bang on the door when the lights went out fully. The room was close to being pitch black thanks to the fact that there was no window to the outside in here. Emergency lights flickered to life in the hallways.

The guard was now gone. I craned my eyes to try to see further down the hallway. He wasn't there either. He must've taken off and with him, the keys to my cell. *What if they abandon the place and leave me in here to rot?* I needed to escape, but how? I frantically looked around the room. There was a toilet and sink and cot. That was it. I yanked off the single mattress to get to the sparse metal bedframe. It was simply four metal slats on legs, interconnected to form a rectangle.

I leaned down and examined the corners. It took some arm strength, but I was able to disconnect the one. I stood up with the one end of the slat in hand and pulled until it was free of the other connected corner. This would hopefully work as a lever to wedge open the door. I peeked out the small window to the hallway to see two guards go running by, their forms more like shadows moving in the low emergency lights.

They paid my room no heed. I stuffed the flattest portion of the bedframe piece into the apex where the doorframe and door met and then heaved. The slat slipped out of the apex and fell to the ground, slipping out of my sweaty hands. I let out a huff of air and wiped off my hands on my pants, then tried again. I strained against the slat, trying to leverage the door away from the frame. This was an old hospital. The frame wasn't made of metal or whatever you usually saw in newer hospitals—it was still wood. If all the breaking and entering I had done over the last few months were any indication, this would eventually work; it just needed some elbow grease.

I set the metal bedframe piece down to catch my breath from all the exertion. My usual amount of strength was zapped from the stress and lack of calories. This might end up taking a while. Once I got a second wind, I jammed the metal piece as close to where the door lock was as possible. The door creaked as I shoved the rod. The door gave an inch on the frame, but didn't open.

The sound of gunfire stilled my efforts. *Holy shit.* What was happening? Were the others using this as their chance for escape? Were there infected? I needed to get out—now! Using my entire body to put pressure on the lever, I heaved. The door flew open and I fell to the floor as the lever had nothing more to brace itself on. I jumped up with the metal piece in hand—it would have to do for a weapon. When no one came rushing to my room, I looked out to see the immediate hallway empty.

The emergency lights were few and far between, making it hard to see fully. I stayed low and crept down toward the direction of the cafeteria. Another couple of muffled gunshots had me stop and duck. They were coming from somewhere inside the hospital. I kept moving until I hit a crossroads. I peeked around the corner to see a bunch of commotion. It was hard to make out, but it looked like the group of prisoners in the cafeteria had stormed the doors and were fighting off the other guards. Should I try to use them as a distraction and try to escape myself? Or should I try to help them and gain some allies for the escape? My choice was made for me when the skirmish made it further down the corridor, almost reaching me. A couple of pajama-clad prisoners bolted past me. We locked eyes, but they kept running.

One of the guards chased them, then lifted their rifle and shot the escapees dead. Their bodies fell face-first to the ground. My mouth flopped open. How could they just mow down the immune people they had collected?

The guard was within my range, but he hadn't seen me hiding around the corner yet. I paused with shallow breaths, waiting for him to reach me. When I saw the tip of his rifle to my right, I waited just a little bit longer for him to take two more steps until his head was in my view. Then I lifted the lever, brandishing it like a spear, and jammed it into his neck. It wasn't very sharp, but the force still made the metal pierce his tender neck.

He dropped his assault rifle as we crashed into the opposite wall of the hallway. His hands flew to his neck as I yanked out my makeshift spear and he collapsed on the ground. I avoided the guard's eyes as I grabbed the rifle and slunk back to my vantage point around the corner. The rifle wasn't a model I was familiar with, but it was semi-automatic judging from the way the guard had shot the two immune people.

It was armed, but I didn't want to fiddle with the magazine release to check to see how many bullets were left. I would have to take my chances. I propped the frame piece against the wall and slipped around the corner again to see the unmoving body of the fallen guard. His neck was still leaking blood like a dying pump. I supposed I should feel bad about that, but I couldn't muster any remorse for killing a guy that had shot two unarmed people in the back. Keeping low, I approached the riot. The other guards weren't shooting their guns; instead they were fighting in hand to hand combat against the prisoners. I spotted Leo just as he took a hefty fist to the face. Rose jumped on the offending guard's back and began punching him. The guard spun around to dislodge her and she slid off of him and onto the floor.

He raised his own assault rifle like he was about to bash her brains in with it, but I pulled my trigger before he could. The rifle jerked in my arms, but I still managed to hit the back of his right shoulder. The guard crumbled to the ground and suddenly all eyes were on me. *Shit.* The remaining guards wrestled to free their own weapon, but the other prisoners weren't going to let them.

The leader of the tough guy, white-power crew steamrolled one guard, and I winced as I swore I could hear the sound of something snapping. I used the distraction to run to Leo and help him to his feet. Rose had gotten on top of the guard I had shot and was pummeling him with her fists. The guard raised his one good arm to fend her off, but she was still managing to land hits.

I wasn't paying attention as I hurried over to help Rose and almost tripped over something. I looked down to see another dead prisoner. Her neck was twisted at an odd angle with her face turned to stare at the carnage. I grabbed a handful of Rose's shirt and yanked her backward. She fell off of the guard, her fists flying all over the place. It would have been comical in another life. Once she was clear of the guard's body, I aimed the rifle.

"No, don't!" he yelled, trying to sit up. I ignored his protest as I pulled the trigger.

He fell back to the ground, dead, with a bullet hole between his eyes. At this close of range, I wasn't going to miss even if this wasn't the AR-15 I was familiar with. Both Leo and Rose stared at me with their mouths open.

"Still got one more!" a strained voice boomed behind me.

I whirled around to see the big guy struggling with the last guard. I lifted the rifle to shoot, but it clicked empty. The prisoner let out a harsh breath as if saying, "Fine, I'll do this myself I guess." He punched the guard again and again until the guard went slack. I didn't know if he was dead or not, but I didn't care. All that mattered was that he was out for now.

There were only about eight of us left standing. Among the group was the white-power leader, Leo, Rose, George, myself, and three others—two girls and a guy. This was hardly enough people. The tough guy ripped the rifle from the guard he had just punched the shit out of and popped out the magazine.

"It's empty," he growled, and tossed the pieces back at the fallen dead or unconscious guard.

That explained why they weren't simply shooting everyone. They had no ammo. Rose checked the rifle of the guard I shot and it was the same thing—out of bullets.

"These were practically for show the whole time!" Rose yelled.

"We need to get moving," I said. "Who knows where the rest of them are at."

Rose looked me up and down through narrowed eyes, as if she were seeing a different person. "Didn't think you had it in you." In some weird way, it sounded like I had just earned her respect. Leo, however, eyed me warily. "Where's Mac?"

I bit my lip. "Amelia killed him." Leo didn't ask anything more.

I turned to George, and mouthed "map." He reached into his housecoat pocket and produced the book he had scribbled in. We all huddle around him as he flipped it open to the back where his hand-drawn schematics were. The tough guy saw us and hurried over.

"What're we lookin' at?"

"George drew us a map from memory," I said.

"And how the hell would he know somethin' like that? He's retarded!"

"He's deaf, not stupid, you asshole," I hissed.

The guy shot me a look, but quickly turned back to the map.

"How are we going to get through the locked doors?" Leo asked as he cradled his sore face.

"Pat down the guards," I instructed. We checked the pockets of all the fallen guards, but only one had a set of keys on them—the one that I had skewered with the bedframe piece. Thankfully, no one felt the need to comment on what I had done. I set down my now empty rifle and picked the metal rod back up.

"Think these are the ones we need?" Rose asked, holding the keys in front of her face.

"We don't really have a choice, now do we?" the tough guy replied, then turned to me. "Pass that here." He held out his hand for the only weapon we had.

"No way in hell," I said. "Find your own damn weapon." He took a step toward me so I held the piece of frame like a bat.

He stopped and took a step back. "Fine, then you get to be in the lead."

"That's fine with me," I said. At least if I was in the lead, they couldn't leave me behind should my missing toe slow me down.

I turned to face George, making sure he could see my mouth. "Where to next?"

He turned the book on its side, then pointed straight. Rose gave me a nod, like she was confirming George's instructions. I swallowed; my nerves were shot. I had no idea how this was going to turn out. One literal wrong turn meant death.

Stamping down my unease, I started in the direction George had pointed. We moved at a slow pace, looking around us.

One of the female prisoners gasped and clamped her hand down on her mouth when we passed by the fallen bodies of the two prisoners the guard had shot. The others had to prod her along, making them fall a few yards behind us. George tapped my shoulder and pointed to the left, indicating that we had to turn that way when we came to the end of the hallway. One of the emergency lights wasn't working, so the crossroads that we were slowly approaching appeared darkened and uninviting.

"You hear that?" the tough guy asked.

I was about to ask if that was a crack at George when my ears picked up the sound of rasping and growling. We peered around the right corner to see a group of infected—some crouched, tearing into a fallen body.

"Run!" I yelled and we bolted left, away from them.

A bunch tore themselves away from the feeding frenzy to pursue us. The other three prisoners were too far behind us and the infected cut them off. The one girl screamed, and they bolted back toward the cafeteria.

"We have to go back for them!" Leo stopped to yell.

I grabbed his arm and yanked. "They're on their own now, we need to move!"

Leo looked from me to the crowd of approaching infected, his brows drawn. With his head down, he finally starting moving again. The tough guy had already bolted to the end of the corridor and was currently body slamming the emergency doors on the left. We sprinted to him, putting some more space between the infected in the hallway and us.

I halted long enough to tell him, "They won't open," and then kept following the hallway as it turned to the right.

Our escape was foiled as someone had closed and bolted shut the two giant metal doors at the end of the corridor. As a group, we slammed into it, but they didn't open. Rose quickly tried to cycle through the keys on the ring we had lifted off of the guard. I looked around. We were in a waiting area, with a small office with a giant plane of glass allowing people to look in.

"None of these are workin'!" Rose cried out.

"The sick ones are almost at the bend!" Leo added from his post at the corner.

I turned in circles trying to see a way out, but there was none. Unless the metal doors opened, we were trapped. Tough Guy tried body slamming the office door, then gave that up in favor of kicking it down. The door shot open with his last kick, and we all stared at each other, frozen.

"Come on!" He waved us over.

We piled into the small office just as the infected made it around the corner we had come from. The door's lock was broken thanks to the rough entry, so Tough-guy leaned against it. We watched through the window, as the infected swarmed the small waiting area and began banging on the glass and door. I let out a humorless laugh. We were really up shit creek now.

Chapter 9

"Shit, shit, shit," Rose muttered to herself.

The keys jangled in her hand as she fidgeted. Thankfully, she hadn't dropped the keys—not that we could use them at the moment.

"This is what we get for followin' a cripple," the tough guy said as he strained against the door he was keeping closed.

I shot him a look telling him to shut up, then turned to face George. I held out my hand for the map and he placed the pocket book in my hand. After flipping to the back, I realized his map didn't reflect the double metal doors we had run into. I wanted to scream, but I couldn't really begrudge George. After all, he had drawn the schematics off of memory alone. But it was still really disappointing.

The door groaned and the big guy was shoved forward. Leo quickly ran and slammed against the door to help keep it closed. Hands scraped and banged along the glass, sending me back to the time we were in Wal-Mart and the infected had burst through the two sets of glass doors and we were powerless to stop them. At least in here, they would have to somehow climb over half the wall to get through the glass window.

"What do we do?" Leo asked.

I threw my hands in the air, the metal frame piece in my hand hitting the roof. "I don't fucking know!"

Instead of staring at me, their gazes were all on the roof. The metal rod had lifted up one of the roof panels.

"Think it'll hold us?" Tough Guy asked.

I set down my bedframe piece and grabbed the desk chair, rolling it underneath the exposed panel. George held onto the back of the chair to stop me from rolling away as I climbed up. My head poked through the opening and dust instantly assailed me. I had to crouch back down to hack up the particles in my lungs until my eyes watered. Using my shirt, I covered my mouth and nose and tried again.

Without the main lights on, I couldn't see a thing. I reached up and tried to use the beams to hold myself up to test how much weight they could take. When I didn't come falling down, I lifted myself higher, but I didn't have the upper body strength to lift my entire body that way. My arms gave out and I crashed back down on the chair, almost falling off as the chair swiveled from the impact. George gave me an apologetic look.

"Give me a boost," Rose demanded as she shoved the chair out of the way.

George and I kneeled, each taking one of her feet. Together we heaved and lifted Rose up like a couple of cheerleaders doing a routine. Rose was small, so it wasn't so much of a strain. If we had to do this for the big guy, I didn't think we would get him very far. The weight we were holding eased up as Rose crawled into the space above the roof tiles. She peered down at us through the panel opening.

She teetered back and forth as she tested her weight. "Seems okay. Can't see worth a shit, though."

Gunfire, closer than before, echoed over the sound of the infected outside the office. We needed to get gone right now.

"Push that desk over," Tough Guy commanded.

George and I dragged the heavy desk over to the door. We shoved it as close as we could while Leo and Tough Guy's bodies were still bracing the door.

"One, two, three!"

On three, we pushed the desk up against the door just as they moved out of the way. It opened a couple of inches from the pushing on the other side, but was quickly closed as we got the desk in place.

"This won't hold for long." Tough Guy stated the obvious.

His words were emphasized with more automatic gunfire. If they found us in here, we would be easily picked off—if they got past the horde of infected, that is.

"Lift me first and I can help pull you guys up," he said.

It took the three of us to push the big guy up to the ceiling panels. His legs flailed as if he was swimming as he shimmied into the small space. He couldn't kneel like Rose was, so he stayed on his stomach and lowered an arm.

Next, Leo and I hoisted George up. He was suspended between the ceiling and the floor when gunfire started outside the office. I let out a yelp as a bullet pierced the office window, and Leo and I ducked instinctively. They hadn't gotten a good grip on George, so he came crashing down with us. He landed with an "Oomph," on top of us. I groaned in pain from the impact. George may not have been big, but it still hurt.

Automatic fire continued, spraying the window with blood and holes. We crawled under the desk braced against the door and pushed it over to use like a shield. The gunfire seemed to be concentrated at eye level, not floor, so I hoped they didn't start shooting randomly. A door and desk could only hold so much.

Finally, the glass gave way and shards fell to the ground. A couple of dead infected slumped over, impaling themselves on the larger, still attached glass around the edges of the window. Blood ran down the wall underneath the window, pooling and spreading like it was still searching for us.

The gunfire had stopped and I let out the breath I had been holding, only to suck it back in when I heard people speaking. My ears were ringing from the spray of bullets and my blood pounding like a drum, so I couldn't even make out if it was a female or male voice, just that there were words being spoken. Leo jerked a finger toward the bedframe piece in the middle of the room. I shook my head. They would see us for sure if someone moved right now to get it. I was hoping that whoever was out there would keep moving now that they had taken out the horde.

He licked his lips and ignored me as he dove for it. I grabbed at his shirt as he moved, trying to hold him back. He swatted my hand and turned to mouth, "Let go." I mouthed back, "No." Even George was shaking his head and had latched onto Leo's leg to drag him back. Leo gave up and slunk back to our hiding space, his chin jutting out. *Please move on.* I snuck a peek at the roof, but Rose and Tough Guy were nowhere to be seen.

My heart lurched as the voices got closer. *Please go away, please go away.* I squeezed my eyes closed, not wanting to see my death coming. Leo's hand found mine and he latched onto it, gripping it tight. After everything, was this how I would end up going out? It seemed so ... unfair. I'm sure that's how most people felt when staring imminent death in the face.

"Ho-ly shit, Bailey!"

Chapter 10

My body refused to move at first as my brain processed the voice I had just heard. "John?" I got up and my eyes landed on that familiar, worn cowboy hat and a face I'd thought I'd never see again.

John smiled as he stuck his head through the broken office window. "Thank God we found you!"

I took a hesitant step forward. "How?"

"When you went missin', we knew somethin' had happened. We *questioned*"—John's eyes narrowed—"Wyatt. He eventually caved and told us where you'd been taken."

Us? I looked further out the destroyed window to see Ethan. I stiffened as he cast me a sorrowful smile, his rifle pointing at the ground.

"Bailey, I—"

"I don't want to hear it!" I yelled.

His mouth fell open and he stepped forward, about to say something, but I cut him off again, "Don't you fucking dare," I hissed through clenched teeth. "I don't want to hear your excuses."

Ethan stopped in his tracks and looked down at the carnage-coated ground. John held up his hand. "Hey, hey, let's save this for later, okay? We need to get outta here first."

Ethan must have told John about his betrayal.

"Who's that?" Rose demanded from the ceiling space.

John's head flew up to spot Rose's face poking out of the empty panel space.

"My name's John, ma'am," John said as he tipped his hat.

I almost rolled my eyes. John was right, though; we needed to put everything aside so we could escape. Leo and George had gotten up while we were talking and were staring at our saviors.

"How'd you get in?" Leo asked.

"We broke into the basement and shut down the generators, then made our way upstairs," John said.

"Did you run into any people shooting at you?" I asked. Maybe they had taken out the rest of the guards.

"A few."

Tough Guy jumped down from the ceiling panels, rolling and swearing as he hit the floor. Leo helped Rose down while George and I removed the desk from the door. Once we opened it, John shouldered his AR-15 and rushed to give me a hug. When we let go, he looked me up and down. "You injured?"

"My foot is." I left out all the other various sore spots from all the fighting with the guards. I had a nice bruise on my stomach from being kneed by the guard earlier, and I was sure John could see my black eye.

"Can you run?"

I nodded. "I'll be fine."

"You wouldn't happen to have any spare weapons on you, would ya?" Tough Guy interrupted.

"Just the one."

John pulled a handgun from his waistband and passed it to me. It was my Beretta. I ejected the magazine; it was full.

Tough Guy leaned down and picked up my discarded bedframe piece. "Guess you won't be needin' this then."

"All yours," I said.

We walked out of the office, jumping over the piles of infected. Amelia's men must have grabbed a bunch on their last round-up trip. Bet they were regretting that now.

"This way," John instructed. "We can leave the same way we got in."

We followed him down the corridor and took another left. The emergency lights were beginning to go out as whatever tiny reserves they were hooked up to ran out.

"We need to go back to the cafeteria and get the others!" Leo said. "We have guns now; we should be able to take out the rest of the infected."

John looked at me and I nodded. "There were a few more who got separated from us during the escape attempt."

Never one to leave people behind, John didn't need to be coaxed into it. Ethan was very unsubtly glancing my way, trying to catch my eye, but I refused to look at him as we made our way back to the cafeteria.

There was a layer of infected trying to get into the cafeteria doors. They must have barricaded the doors because the infected were getting nowhere. John and Ethan raised their weapons, but I held up my hand.

"If you can hear me, move away from the door!" I yelled, hoping they weren't using themselves to barricade the door like we had to do in the office.

Of course my yelling brought the attention of the infected from getting through the doors to us. One by one, they started towards us, giving up on the cafeteria doors.

"Good job, genius," Tough Guy muttered.

John and Ethan easily took out the infected with their rifles. When the gunfire stopped and the bodies laid still, we ran to the cafeteria doors.

"It's us," Leo said.

A face popped up in the small window and went from terrified to relieved. It was the girl who had stopped mid-escape. Not the smartest choice. We heard rustling from the other side before the double set of black doors opened.

"Thank you for coming for us!" the girl cried and launched herself into Leo's arms. He patted her back awkwardly before saying, "We gotta keep moving."

John led the group of us back down the winding corridors to the basement stairs. All of the guards were somewhere else, except for the few that John and Ethan must have shot. There were bullet holes and blood smears across the wall leading to the stairs. It looked like the guards had ambushed them as soon as they got to the top.

Ethan took the lead with a flashlight and descended down the stairs. I made sure everyone had gone through before I took one last look around. One of the doors down the hallway had light peeking underneath. Since all the hospital lights were out, there had to be someone in there with their own light source. I didn't know how I knew it, but every part of my brain knew it was Amelia in there. And I wasn't going to leave this place with her still alive.

"Bailey, come on!" John hissed.

I looked back at him. "You guys go on. I'll catch up."

The edges around John's mouth tightened. "You gotta be shittin' me. We ain't leavin' without you after comin' all this way to get you!" He was less than pleased.

"John, do you think there are some people out there who deserve to die?" I asked. I had to make John understand.

He lowered his gun and adjusted his hat. "I believe there are some, yes. But I also believe we don't get to make that call."

It was just like with Byron. I had wanted to kill Byron, but John had wanted to let the town decide what to do with him— to be fair. The thing was, none of this new world was fair. If it was, I wouldn't be here in this hellish hospital, and all of our dead friends would still be alive. John's son would be alive. I would be with my family. We wouldn't have to fight for our lives over and over again. If I could help relieve this world of something evil, then I would. I would make it fair. And nothing was fairer than Amelia dying.

"I listened to you about Byron, but I won't this time. She has to die," I said, then bolted down the hallway before John could try to stop me. I got to the door where the light was shining below and twisted the knob.

Inside Amelia was sitting at a desk, staring intently at the framed photo in her hand. There was a giant wind-up flashlight propped up on her desk shining towards the ceiling. She didn't even look up. I was expecting a fight, so I stood in place, unsure if I could shoot her if she was just sitting docile and unarmed.

"Shouldn't you be long gone by now?" she said, continuing to peer at the picture.

John appeared behind me, finally making Amelia raise her head. "You've come to kill me, yes?"

"What did you expect?" I spat. "You killed Mac and who knows how many more. You've imprisoned and tortured the rest of us." I pointed my gun at her.

She calmly set down the photo on her desk. It was of a young boy in a soccer jersey smiling for the camera. His jet black hair was a little too long and was a perfect match to Amelia's. She didn't say anything to counter the accusations. Instead, her hand went to her lap and raised back up with a revolver in it. John shoved me to the side and raised his rifle. I quickly moved out from behind him and re-leveled my gun at her head.

"Now ma'am, there's no need for this. I'm just gonna take Bailey and leave. No more bloodshed."

Amelia's chest deflated as her eyes landed back on the picture. A tear slipped down her bruised face before she opened her mouth and squeezed the trigger. Her head flew back, then her dead body slumped forward landing on the desk, blood leaking onto the framed picture. Both John and I stood frozen as the smell of the discharged revolver and rust filled the small room.

Amelia had seemed so steely and unbending. I wasn't expecting her to kill herself. I had been expecting a fight. My mouth opened to say something, but I couldn't remember what

I had wanted to say. All the anger I'd had moments earlier vanished and I now felt worse than I had before. I felt sick— and cheated somehow. She was dead; did it matter at whose hands she had met her death?

"Glad you came back?" John was angry, something I rarely saw.

I didn't want to fight with him so I just exited the office and went back to the top of the basement stairs. John followed behind me, not saying anything more. We descended the stairs and John clicked on his own flashlight. The others must've kept going. John maneuvered around me and led the way. There were no emergency lights on down here, making the flashlight beam our only source of illumination. I bumped into a tin canister, letting out a huff. Like I needed more bruises.

We passed by a giant red tank connected to a bunch of equipment. I sniffed as the smell of gas became overpowering. The floor was coated in the liquid, so I used my shirt to prevent me from inhaling the fumes.

"We cut the main gas line to cut the power," John explained. "We probably should've thought that out better." He was using his hat to cover the lower part of his face, making his words muffled and hard to hear.

Natural light began to fill the area as we continued on and fresh air pushed out the gasoline smell. We rounded a corner to face a dead-end except for the smashed basement window. I wondered how Tough Guy had fit through.

There was a tin canister propped underneath the window. I climbed up and shoved myself through the small window. I turned around and gave John a hand as he shimmied through. The fresh air was a pleasant relief to my burning lungs. Gas fumes were terrible to breathe in. We stood and peered around, looking for the others. I couldn't see them, but I could definitely hear Rose and Tough Guy arguing. John and I followed the sound around the corner to see the group flush against the side of the building.

"There they are," Leo said as we approached the group.

Rose and Tough Guy, who were previously in each other's faces, now turned to regard us.

Ethan rushed from the front of the group to us. "Where did you guys go?"

I refused to talk to him so I walked around him to the others. I could feel his eyes following me but I kept walking towards Tough Guy and Rose who were at the forefront.

"What are you guys fighting about?" I asked as I peered around the corner.

There were infected randomly milling about the courtyard and beyond, like cows in a field grazing. As I was about to turn back to the others, the front doors to the hospital flew open and two guards poured out. One of them was Josh. I crouched down and motioned for the others to do the same.

"She killed herself, man, there's nothing left!" one guard shouted at Josh. They must have stumbled onto Amelia's body right after we left. They were heading towards the only truck parked in front.

"We can't just leave everything. All the research! We were so close, I know it!" Josh screamed back, his voice an octave too high.

"I ain't going back in there, man."

"Yes, you are," Josh said as he pulled a gun on the guard.

"You ain't going to shoot me, you need me," the guard sneered.

"I need to make sure you keep your mouth shut." And Josh shot the guard in the head.

The guard fell to the ground as the gunshot echoed through the area. Shit. Now the aimless infected would be heading our way. We needed that truck for a quick getaway. I was sure John had brought a vehicle, but would have parked it away from here to avoid detection. We might not be able to get to it when all the infected started to converge on the hospital.

Josh leaned over the body and started rummaging through the guy's pockets. He straightened up with the keys in his hand. If I was going to do this, I had to do it now. I jumped up and bolted around the corner, leveling my gun at Josh. He twisted around, his mouth wide. Before he could react, I squeezed the trigger and Josh landed dead next to the guard. I ran up to them and searched for the keys, hoping I would find them in the overgrown grass around the bodies.

"Damn, girl," Rose said as the others caught up to me.

"What? We needed the truck," I said briskly. My hand ran over the key ring and I scooped them up. They had a little bit of blood on them.

"I hated that guy," Tough Guy said as he kicked Josh's dead body. "He always made sure they brought in the biggest dead ones for me."

John's eyes narrowed. "What do you mean *brought in*?"

"I'll explain later," I said, hoping maybe he would forget. I didn't really feel like relaying what had happened so soon after. "We need to move. I assume you guys parked your vehicle nearby?"

"Follow the entrance path down and take a right. We're parked under some trees for cover," John said. I knew he would have been smart about it.

"Everyone hop in," I said, pulling open the driver's side door.

John got in the cab and everyone else piled into the bed of the truck. It was tight, but they all fit. I started the truck and reversed just as the first line of infected reached the hospital. The slow girl screamed as one infected groped at them. Ethan took it out with his rifle and told the girl to be quiet. I straightened out and tore down the path as fast as I could with a full load of people in the back. I didn't want anyone to go flying out. I snorted out loud at the thought, and to his credit, John didn't bat an eye. He was probably getting used to my weird quirk.

I spared a glance out the rearview to see Tough Guy batting down every infected he could with my old bedframe as if he were a frat guy bashing mailboxes. He was grinning widely. I couldn't hold that against him; it actually looked like fun. Man, I really was becoming unhinged. I'd have to worry about that later.

I slowed and rounded the corner to the right as John kept an eye out for their vehicle.

"There." He pointed toward an area where there was an abundance of green.

We came to a stop and John and Ethan jumped out to uncover our other mode of transport. Rose jumped out of the back and climbed into the passenger's seat.

"You ridin' back with 'em?" she asked.

"No," I said. I had no desire to be stuck inside a vehicle with Ethan right now.

"Well then, I dibs ridin' upfront."

I was about to argue, not wanting to have to spend who knew how long with Rose in a confined space, when John knocked on my window. I rolled down the window with the ancient hand roller.

"We brought a large SUV so we can take some of the people in the back," John said. "I take it I won't be able to convince you to ride with us?"

I shook my head and John sighed. "All right. Well, stick close then and honk if there's any reason you can't keep goin'."

George and the three we had liberated from the cafeteria piled into the SUV, while Tough Guy and Leo remained in the back. I could tell that the younger girl who had thrown herself at Leo didn't want to leave him, but he convinced her to go with John and Ethan.

Leo slid open the back window to the truck cab and said, "You sure we can trust them?"

"Of course," I said. "You're little girlfriend will be fine." *Wow, that sounded bitter.*

Leo bristled at my comment. "Wasn't the younger guy the *boyfriend* who betrayed you?" he pressed on.

I turned and glowered at him. "I trust John with my life and if..." I paused. "...if Ethan does anything else like that again, I'll kill him myself."

Chapter 11

My cold words had shocked me, but I forced my expression to remain stern. Even Rose had seemed stunned with my words as her eyebrows shot up comically high on her forehead. Leo seemed to accept my answer and settled down for the ride back to Hargrove.

Oh god, how was that going to go? I hadn't gotten a chance to even think about Hargrove. Wyatt, Grant and Oscar were the reasons I was abducted. *How had they even managed to* get *my body out of Hargrove without anyone seeing?* I would have to solve that mystery later.

John mentioned earlier that they had *questioned* Wyatt. What else had they done? They couldn't expect me to be okay living with Wyatt and the others in Hargrove. Either they would have to go or I would.

"So, did that kid really betray you?" Rose asked, breaking me from my concentration.

We were currently barreling down a residential road. It was obscenely dirty judging from the dirt being thrown up by John's SUV. No doubt Tough Guy and Leo were choking on it in the back.

"He told the crooks who used to be in charge about my immunity," I admitted.

"*Used* to be in charge?"

"They were covering for a psychopath who was murdering people. Now they're no longer in charge."

"What happened to the psychopath?"

"He was exiled."

Rose made a scoffing sound. "Should've killed the bastard. Ain't no room in this world for a person like that."

I nodded in agreement.

"What happened to the others? The people who used to be in charge?"

"They're still there—as far as I know. John didn't get to tell me everything," I said.

"You gonna *exile* them too?" The way she said exile made it sound like she was definitely against that plan.

"I don't know. We have to get there first." Maybe I'd come up with a solution by then, or maybe we'd all be eaten alive by then. "By the way, where were you before you got taken by the mad scientists?" I asked.

Rose barked out a laugh. "Mad scientists. That does fit those assholes." Then Rose peered out the window, her face away from my view. "I was pretty much on my own—easier that way. I'm startin' to see that wasn't the best plan." I wasn't sure I heard that last part correctly.

I couldn't believe what I was about to say, but I knew I had to say it. "You can stick with us if you want."

"I don't need your pity," she muttered into the window.

"Fine, just offering."

She turned to me. "What about the others?"

"They can stay too. I'm not promising it'll be some paradise or anything." I was suddenly transported back to when Darren and I were trying to convince Colin to come back with us. Great, I really had become the type to take in strays. When did that happen?

"We'll see," she said with her nose very much in the air. I rolled my eyes. Her ego wouldn't let her say thank you.

We sat in silence for a little while longer until she asked, "So what's the cowboy's deal?"

I scrunched up my face, not liking where this was going. "What do you mean?"

"He ... with anyone?"

I wanted to lie and say he was gay, but she would eventually see through that. I sighed.

"Not that I'm aware of."

John hadn't seemed to be romancing any of the ladies at Hargrove, but then again, I wasn't with him twenty-four hours a day. And he was a man. Ugh, I didn't want to think about this. He was like a father to me.

Rose seemed placated with my answer and peered out the windshield at the SUV in front of us. Perhaps I should tell John that Rose was bad news. I accidently hit some debris and the truck lurched over the lump, tossing the guys in the back like a pancake in skillet. They hit the bed with a thud when they came back down.

"What the fuck are you doin', girl? Watch the damn road!" Tough Guy bellowed.

Both Rose and I looked at each other and burst out laughing.

"It ain't funny!" Tough Guy yelled.

And of course we laughed even harder. I had to wipe away the tears in my eyes so I could see the road. Wouldn't want to accidently toss them again.

"Did you ever catch his name?" I asked Rose.

"It's some hillbilly name like Cletus or Adolph or somethin'," she said and we started laughing again.

I would probably have to learn his real name eventually if he was going to say at Hargrove. I couldn't just call him Tough Guy forever. We both stopped joking when we passed by a building that had its side spray-painted with the mercenaries' hand and eye symbol. I heard Tough Guy spit at it as we passed.

"We gotta keep an eye out for those bastards," Rose said.

The only time I had actually seen the faces of the mercenaries was when they had tried to abduct me at the apartments, and now they were both dead. Then there was the time they had shot up John, Roy, and I while driving, but again, they were dead. The only living ones I'd had contact with were the one on the radio and the ones who brought me to the hospital—but I had been unconscious for that trip. I wouldn't be able to recognize one unless they wore their pendants with the hand and eye symbol or, you know, a shirt saying, "Hey, I'm a mercenary."

"Would you recognize any of them?" I asked her.

"Only the ones that ambushed me," she said, her voice harsh. "But I'll tell you what, if I ever come across 'em again, I'm killin' 'em all."

I didn't verbally agree with her, but inside I was agreeing. Like hell they would be capturing me again. Not that they had someone to turn the immune over to anymore. The hospital and their messed up experiments had died with Amelia.

"I went back to kill Amelia," I admitted.

"So that's where you disappeared to," Rose said. "Please tell me that bitch got what she deserved."

"She killed herself."

"Damn, wasn't expectin' that," Tough Guy said, making us both jump.

His face was right outside the open slot in the cab back window.

"By the way, my name ain't Cletus or Adolph. It's Lucas," he huffed.

I tried really hard not to laugh that he had been listening to us the whole time, even as Rose poked fun at him. Rose was currently fighting it too as she chewed on her thumbnail with the corners of her mouth upturned.

"She's really dead?" Leo asked, shoving Lucas to the side.

"Shot herself in front of John and I, so, yeah."

"Good," Lucas said while nodding. Well maybe he was nodding, it might have been from being bounced around in the bed of the truck. "Good that she's dead, I mean, not that you had to see that."

I lifted a brow at that. Maybe Lucas was learning to play nice with others. Stranger things had happened. He muttered something and settled back into a seated position with his back against the cab.

"I'm sorry for what I said earlier," Leo said. "I shouldn't have brought up your boyfriend."

I waved it off. After all, I had kind of started that. "It's fine. You can stop calling him my boyfriend, though."

An awkward silence fell over everyone as no one knew what to say next. I had meant what I said. Ethan was no longer my ... anything. *What about Chloe?* My anger shifted to panic as I thought about Chloe. She was a little sister to me now, in every way that mattered. Could I just leave her behind? It wasn't her fault her brother was a dumbass. She would be devastated if I left and there was no way she would leave Ethan. Shit.

Chapter 12

Hargrove looked the same as I had left it. I half expected it to be up in flames when we got back; civil unrest having taken over inside. But no, it was still intact with guards at their posts. John stuck his head out the window and they opened the gate for us. I was suddenly very conscious of my attire and condition. It was obvious we had been through the ringer at the hospital. I hoped that Wyatt would have to see—not that he would care in the end.

We got out of the vehicles, the new additions sticking close to me, unsure of the approaching crowd. The slow girl ran over to Leo and latched onto him. George gave me a curious glance and I gave him a thumbs up. John walked over to me.

"Could've mentioned that guy was deaf. I was talkin' to him for a good ten minutes before one of the others informed me he couldn't hear," John said.

"Not like I had time to facilitate introductions, you know," I pointed out. But I knew how John felt; the same thing had happened to me. "Speaking of that, what did you guys do with Wyatt and his crew? You can't expect me to stay here with them."

"I wouldn't do that to you. We have 'em locked up in the condo we used to hold Byron. There's a guard posted at all times till we decide what to do with 'em."

"Do I get a say in that?"

John pursed his lips. "Depends on what you want to do with 'em. Would you hold Ethan to that same punishment?"

I held eerily still. "He told you then?"

"He told me he made a big mistake in tellin' those guys about you bein' immune before you and Chloe even showed up. Before he knew they were bad news."

"Well he did tell them and I got punished for it. He can go to hell." My fists were shaking again. I didn't care if he felt bad. He shouldn't have betrayed my secret regardless of whether he thought Wyatt was a good guy or not. That wasn't for him to share.

John placed a hand on my shoulder. "I ain't goin' to tell you to forgive him, but you have to deal with him. You got others besides him to consider."

As if he had summoned her with his words, Chloe came running up to us. She looked at Ethan, then swung her head around until she saw me, then ran straight for me. I braced myself for the impact, but my stomach was still sore from the punt I had taken. I let out a pained sound and Chloe loosened her grip.

"I'm so glad you're okay!" she said, looking up at me.

"You injured worse than I can see?" The ever-watchful John asked.

"Just some bruising," I said, trying to sound blasé about it.

"What happened?" Chloe asked, still not fully letting go of me. I cursed Ethan again for putting me in this situation.

I gently pushed Chloe off. "You know me, just getting into some fights."

John's eyes narrowed. "You should get that looked at."

"By who? The guy who helped send me off?" I said harshly. "Maybe he should have to look me over, so he can see firsthand."

"No, Oscar is locked up as well. Crystal was unofficially shadowin' him, mostly after Sheri was shot. She can have a look," John said.

"I'm not the only one," I said, motioning to the others we had brought back. Rose was injured for sure, and I didn't know if any of the others needed something looked at.

"All right everyone, follow me," John barked at us.

We walked together to the medic center, Chloe hanging on me the whole time.

"There she is," Chloe said.

I turned to see what she was talking about. Zoe stopped just before me and looked me over. Tears filled her eyes, and she gently gave me a hug.

"Oh my God, I thought I'd never see you again. Those asses wouldn't let me come with them to find you!" She pulled away and shot an accusing glance at John. He looked away. "How injured are you? What happened? Who are these people?"

I held up my hand. "Whoa, one at a time."

She shook her head. "Never mind. I'm just glad you're back," she said with a smile. "Did John tell you about what they did with Wyatt and the others?"

"Being held prisoner?" Just now I saw the irony in that.

"After John worked Wyatt over."

I looked at John for confirmation, but he was already ushering the rest of the group into the makeshift medic center.

"He told me he questioned him," I said.

"Well, that too. If John hadn't done that, Wyatt might never have broken down and told us what happened. Unsurprisingly, the town didn't object to using force," Zoe said.

I couldn't imagine John doing that. Me, yes—but not him. My eyes threatened to water as I felt a sudden rush of emotion. John cared enough about me to put aside his own set of rules in order to find me. That's what family did. I discreetly wiped at my eye.

We walked into the condo and it was a rush of activity inside. Crystal was running around and Sheri was writing furiously onto a clipboard. She looked up and shot me a grin.

"Glad to see you're back."

"Thanks."

"Now go to the operation room so Crystal can examine you."

I did as I was ordered. After ten minutes of poking and blood pressure taking, Crystal finally gave me her diagnosis.

"There's no internal bleeding that I can tell, but you're going to have to keep that foot injury hella clean to avoid infection." She took off to the medicine cabinet on the wall and came back with a tube. "Antibiotic ointment. Apply this twice a day and use clean wrappings every time."

I took the tube from her outstretched hand. "Thank you. So you think my stomach is okay?"

"Yes, if you had any internal damage, it would have made itself known by now and your blood pressure is normal. Considering what you've just been through, that's a medical miracle."

I smiled at her joke, but it wasn't sincere. Such a little thing as being hit in the stomach could've killed me if it had landed in the right area. Humans were so fragile ...

I thanked Crystal again and left. I made sure to tell the others to head to my condo once they were done being looked over. We would hash out the living arrangement details after that.

Once showered and changed and my foot re-wrapped, I walked into my condo living room to be greeted by Roy and Amanda in addition to everyone else. We said our hellos all while in the back of my mind I was fighting with the right way to tell him about his wife. Maybe I could have Rose do it? I sighed internally. That would be cowardly, plus Rose had no tact. I was saved from my conundrum when the door opened to reveal the others done with their examinations.

"Please tell me I can get a shower in here," Rose said. "And some clean clothes."

We split them up into some of the empty condos and gave them spare clothes to change into. Everyone was happy to be rid of the hospital pajamas we had been forced to wear. I was considering burning mine in a metal garbage can later. It would be therapeutic.

By the time everyone was rounded up and squeaky clean, it was time for supper. We showed them the clubhouse where the food was served and tried to give them the shorthand tour along the way. Most weren't listening, too hungry to care. My own stomach was growling under the bruises. We got our food and sat down with some of the town people introducing themselves periodically.

"Damn, this is much better than the gruel they served at the hospital," Leo said between huge bites. Rose grunted in agreement. "Even Mac would've approved."

Roy and Chloe's heads shot up. "Mac was there?" Roy asked.

Everyone was looking at me now. "He pretended to be immune to avoid ..." I looked at Chloe. We had never told her about what we had found at the apartments, "... leaving the apartments. But the mercenaries still handed him over to the hospital group. He was bitten and turned while we were there."

Roy looked down at his plate and Chloe looked like she was about to cry. Amanda already was. This was turning into a great supper. It made me even more apprehensive about telling Roy what I'd found out about Irene. My appetite had taken a nose-dive, but I still forced myself to finish my plate. I needed the nourishment, even if it felt like a lump was sitting in the pit of my stomach at the moment.

John tried to steer the conversation towards the newcomers, asking them about where they had been before they were taken. Most came from rag-tag groups like ours, except for Rose, who had preferred to be on her own. And Lucas refused to participate.

"Can we stay here?" the slow girl asked.

Turned out her name was Brittany. She was sitting right beside Leo and looked like she would rather give up her food than her spot.

"Of course," John said. "We could always use more hands around here."

Brittany smiled and nudged Leo with her elbow. He was too busy eating to notice. A pair of hands slid over my eyes.

"Guess who?" Colin's voice said from right behind me.

"The creepy clown from IT?" I joked. "Or a least some guy with the same hair?"

"Please, that guy wished he had hair like mine," Colin scoffed as he removed his hands from my eyes. I sat up and gave him a hug. "All right, Mom. That's enough, you're embarrassing me in front of my friends!"

I rolled my eyes. "Still a brat, I see." I looked him over. He looked as tired as I remembered him. I would have to have a talk with him about what Oscar had revealed, but in private.

"Nice shiner," he said.

"Thanks."

After supper, most people just wanted to get some sleep that wasn't in a cell. Brittany practically dragged Leo to the condos. I shot him a wink and he turned red in the face. Rose followed after them, muttering about how she wasn't looking after no baby.

Another round of hugs from my friends ensued and I finally had to shove them away in the name of sleep. I was exhausted.

The next day I woke up disoriented, still half expecting I'd be unable to leave the bedroom. I was giddy when the doorknob unlatched, and I walked into the living area with a smile on my face. It faded when I spotted Roy reading an old paperback, sipping on a cup of coffee. I had to tell him about Irene.

"Mmm, coffee," I said as I made myself a cup of instant. "Where's Amanda?"

"She went with Chloe to help with collecting eggs. Why?" Roy asked.

I sat down at the island on a stool. "I have something to tell you about Irene."

The cup fell from Roy's hand and shattered on the fake hardwood. Black coffee spread over the light flooring like it was devouring it. He ignored his mess and asked, "What is it?"

His eyes bore into mine, shrinking my confidence. I had to tell him, but I really didn't want to. Didn't people say ignorance was bliss? I took a deep drink of my coffee. It burnt my tongue a little on the way down.

"She had been at the hospital," I said slowly, carefully. Obviously she wasn't here now and that had to tell him how the rest of the story went.

"You saw her?" He got right in front of me.

"No, I didn't." I placed a hand on Roy's shoulder. It was tense. "Rose told me that she died before I arrived there."

Roy seemed to collapse on himself, and he had to put a hand on the counter to balance himself. "You ... you sure it was her?" His eyes were unfocused.

"Rose said her name was Irene. And you said the mercenaries took her because she was immune and that hospital is where they dropped all the immune off at."

"Maybe it was a different Irene," Roy mumbled.

I didn't say anything, I just let him soak up the news. Instead, I grabbed a handful of paper towel and cleaned up the coffee he had dropped.

"It might not have been her," Roy said suddenly, and I jumped from the startle.

"You can talk to Rose. She was Irene's roommate. Maybe she can describe how Irene looked and then you can be sure." I'd have to get to Rose first to tell her not to mention that Irene had hung herself, though.

Roy bobbed his head. "Which one was Rose again?"

"How about I take you to her?" I suggested.

"Okay." Roy looked so small and defeated.

I chugged the rest of my coffee and led him to Rose and Leo's condo. There wasn't much choice because Roy stood at the door like a puppy waiting to go outside. It was sad to see him look so lost. I was fidgeting the whole walk over, while Roy moved like his legs were made of stone. Was telling him the right thing to do? It would save him from risking his life for a ghost, but maybe hope that she was alive was what kept him going. I wanted to pull out my hair from the stress.

I knocked on their front door and Rose answered quickly. She had her own full cup of coffee in hand and wore a big smile.

"Can't remember the last time I had coffee. It's heaven!" Rose exclaimed.

"Uh, can we come in?" Rose must have sensed my mood because she turned off the happy face and let us in. "Rose, can I talk to you for a second?" I pointed to the hallway.

She nodded. I turned to Roy and told him to hold on for a minute. He barely acknowledged me.

When we were out of earshot, Rose said, "He slow or somethin'?"

"No, that's Irene's husband."

Rose's mouth fell open. "No shit? Why'd you bring 'im here?"

"He doesn't quite believe that it's the same Irene as his wife, so can you describe her to him?" I said, then quickly added, "without mentioning how she died."

"If he asks, what should I say?"

"Make up something. Like she died in an experiment, so he knows she's dead, just not by her own hand."

"All right, but truth has a way of gettin' out," Rose said.

"Yeah, but he doesn't need that right now," I insisted.

We walked back over to Roy. "So what can I do for you, Roy?" Rose said.

I glared at her for using such a casual tone. She knew exactly why we were here.

"What did Irene look like?" Roy asked in a small voice. He wouldn't look up from the floor.

"She was a brunette with iron straight hair, I think," Rose said, "um, she was about as tall as you." Rose pointed at Roy and then had to stop to think. "Ah, she had been bitten on the left hand. She'd cry about her kids all the time. She mentioned an ... Amanda?"

At that Roy let out a sob and Rose flew back like she had been shoved. She gave me a pleading look that said, "Get him out of here." Roy continued to cry and I placed a hand on his back. This was awkward. Despite the looks Rose was giving me, I let Roy cry it out. There were no tissues so I gave him a hunk of paper towel from the kitchen to cry on.

It was odd to see a grown man sobbing uncontrollably, but I wasn't going to hold this against Roy. I felt like I had just pulled the rug out from under him. Like I had just destroyed his hope. I should have just let him keep searching for her... Roy sniffed a couple times and looked up. He opened the front door and took off in a brisk walk. I followed after him afraid that he would do something stupid. He walked back to our condo and all the way to his room.

I watched from the hallway as he threw his bags about. Finally, he found whatever he had been looking for and sat down at the bed. It was an old photo. I slowly approached him and peeked at the picture. It was of their family. Roy and Amanda and one adult female and another young one.

"That's a beautiful picture," I said quietly.

"It was from last Christmas," Roy said. "How am I supposed to tell my daughter?"

"I don't know, Roy," I said. I'd had a hard enough time struggling to tell him. "You can tell her when you're ready. It doesn't have to be right now."

"You're right." He continued to stare at the photo. "Maybe then we can have a little service for Irene."

"That's a lovely idea. I'll help with whatever you need," I offered.

Roy looked up at me. "Thank you. Do you mind if I have a moment alone?"

"Of course." I wanted to tell him to not do anything stupid, but I held my tongue.

I left him alone and closed the door behind me with a small prayer that he would be okay.

Chapter 13

The rest of the days was like trying to herd cats. It was impossible to find everyone as they had taken off exploring Hargrove before we could gather them. Henry and the other elected council people were currently coming up with options on how to deal with Wyatt and the other two. When I had first gotten dressed and joined everyone, Henry had made a point to come up to me.

"I just wanted to say how sorry I am that you had to go through what you did," Henry said solemnly.

It was nice of him to say, but really he had no idea what had happened. He was only judging based on our injuries. Not all injuries were visible.

"Thanks," I said. "But speaking of that, what do you guys intend to do with Wyatt?"

"Not sure yet, but we'll come up with some ideas and let everyone have a vote later." He briefly laid a hand on my shoulder and smiled, then took off back to the condo where their meeting was being held.

I had a sinking feeling that they would all be exiled like Byron. One person didn't stand a chance out there by themselves, but if all three got to leave together, they would more likely survive—which would defeat the purpose of the punishment.

Trying to ignore my unease, I continued walking to the clubhouse for breakfast. Maybe some of the newcomers had ended up there.

Indeed, most were inside eating. Rose stopped me as I was leaving the buffet line.

"That guy Roy okay?" she asked.

"I don't know. He just found out his missing wife is dead, so no. But I don't think he would do anything stupid. He's still got one daughter to care for."

"Bailey, this place is great," Leo said as he approached us.

"Now it is," I said.

"What're we expected to do here?" Rose asked.

"Well, if everyone hadn't taken off this morning, we would have explained. Everyone will either pick a job or be given one—eventually."

"I saw some small gardens. I'd like to volunteer for that," Rose said.

I held up my hand. "I'm not the one to talk to about that." I put my hand down slowly. "Actually, I'm not sure who decides that now that Wyatt is out. Probably the council?"

"Some help you are." Rose smirked.

"Hey, I'm sure I could put in a word and have you cleaning up after the farm animals if you'd like."

Rose's smirk faltered. "Really funny."

I waggled my eyebrows and headed towards the table John was at. He was currently trying to slowly mouth something to George while Chloe and Amanda watched curiously. When I approached the table, George turned to give me a smile and wave.

"Hey George, how are you liking it here?" I asked slowly.

He took a bite of his breakfast and gave me a thumbs up.

"I was tryin' to explain the job situation to George," John said. "I also tried explainin' it to that guy Lucas, but he just brushed me off and left the clubhouse with his food."

"Yeah, he's not the friendliest person I've ever met," I said as I took a seat and faced Amanda. "Has your dad come in for breakfast yet?"

She gave me a puzzled look. "Yeah, he's right there." She pointed to the long food line. Sure enough, Roy was waiting in line. He must have come in after me. I sagged against the back of my chair. Thank God he hadn't done anything stupid. Now John gave me a strange look, which I waved off.

We finished eating and sent the girls off to their little school lessons. John started rallying up the newcomers and telling them to meet at the front gate when they were finished. I guessed he would be giving the orientation.

It took a good hour, but everyone eventually sauntered over to the front gate, except for Lucas. That wasn't a surprise. I would have to hunt him down later.

John got right into it. "All right everyone. By now you've had some time to see a little bit of Hargrove and as you're probably already aware, most people have a job. What I want you to do is to spend the day lookin' around even more and see if there's a job you'd be interested in. Once you come up with a few ideas, we can run 'em by the council."

There were murmurs, especially from Brittany who insisted that she and Leo get the same job. Leo didn't look pleased with her declaration.

"What if we already know what we wanna do?" Rose said, cocking out a hip.

"Then I say still take the day," John said firmly.

Rose stared him down, but eventually gave in. When the newcomers dispersed to follow John's orders, he walked up to me.

"That Rose lady is sure ... somethin'," he said absently.

"Nope."

John tilted his head to the side. "What?"

I shook my head. "Never mind." I was being petty. "How long do you think the council will take?"

"They've turned into a bunch of indecisive bureaucrats, so the rest of the day," John groused. "We've gone from one guy making quick, but bad decisions, to a bunch of random people takin' forever to come up with good solutions."

"The price you pay for democracy, I guess. Speed," I said.

It turned out John was right. The council had spent the entire day debating on the outcomes to vote for. The vote was held in the clubhouse during supper to ensure people got a vote. They even let the newcomers have a vote. When it was all said and done, the majority again voted for exile. More than a few huffs were given when the announcement was made.

The decision was to send them out, one by one, starting in the morning. They were not to be given any food or water, though. Rose came up to me with a scowl on her face.

"What if they come back with weapons and such?"

I didn't like the outcome either. How had they spent an entire day debating this? Too many people trying to get their opinion in and heard.

"I don't know, Rose." I sighed. "I don't like it either, but it's what the majority agreed on."

"They should just shoot 'em in the head."

"You gonna volunteer for executioner?" I said.

"You seem like you'd be a good fit." I froze at her words.

"Fuck you," I snarled and walked away from her.

Was that how she saw me? I only did what I had to in the hospital to escape. *Except for going back for Amelia.* That had been personal, but I was never given the chance to kill her as she had taken her own life. I had only killed when it had been necessary. Or was that just something I told myself to make me feel better about it? What about the guard I had stabbed repeatedly? Or the one I had killed while he begged for me to not shoot him?

I had wanted to kill Byron, but John had stopped me. If John hadn't been there, I probably would have killed the murdering asshole. In the end, would Byron and I be that different? He killed for his own sick enjoyment.

Did I enjoy it?

The fact that I had to ask myself that, sent a shiver up my spine.

Chapter 14

I spent the rest of the day avoiding people and drowning in my own head. Obsessing about how many people I'd killed and how easy it had become was starting to take a toll on me. I rubbed at my eyes and propped down in the lawn chairs behind my condo, continuing to stare at the tall brick fence separating us from the outside. It was getting dark as the sun set for the night.

Using the bricks as a distraction, I started counting them. I gave up at number eighty-seven as the dark thoughts crept back in. I'd lost count of how many people I'd killed. When had it become easy to shoot a living person? Maybe this was why John had stopped me with Byron. He knew it was a slippery slope. At first it was people who had deserved it, but then what happened when the area of 'deserving it' went from black and white to grey? Would I eventually end up killing someone I shouldn't?

I stood up and kicked over the chair I had just vacated. This was painful to think about. I decided to go for a stroll as most people would be tucked away in their condos by now. Maybe that would help distract me better than counting had. I knew I wouldn't be able to sleep right now anyways. I felt wired, like I had slept too much the day before and thus couldn't sleep tonight. I used to do that in university. Sleep from midnight till noon and then that night was hell to try to sleep.

Everything on the street was quiet except for the few sounds of bugs. After a few more paces, my ears picked up on something that wasn't the noise of crickets, but sounded like banging doors. I followed the noise up to the back portion of the clubhouse, which was where the kitchen was housed. Taking my gun from my waistband, I inched up close to the window. After what happened with Wyatt, I was never going to go unarmed in here again. I'd learned my lesson—never let your guard down, ever.

Someone was rooting around in the cupboards with a flashlight. The beam bounced to the window and I ducked down to avoid whoever it was seeing me. Staying crouched, I snuck around to the back door which was wide open. I crossed the threshold and stood still to listen. Judging from the rustling, they were off to the left. I took a deep breath and rounded the counter.

"Hold still!" I yelled.

The figure dropped their bag and it crashed to the floor. Tin cans rolled out and smacked the bottom of the counters. They were trying to steal our food. The flashlight pointed right at me.

"Bailey?" It was Lucas.

I didn't lower my gun. For all I knew, he had a weapon too. "What are you doing, Lucas?"

He didn't respond right away, but instead reached down for his bag.

"Uh-uh," I said. "We didn't invite you hear so you could steal from us."

He straightened back up without his sack. "I'm not stayin'. I just need a little food to get me started."

"You got somewhere to go back to?" I asked.

"No," he said with a hint of venom. "I just ain't stayin' here."

"Why not?"

"I don't belong here."

I lowered my gun, but still kept it in hand. "Why do you think that? Everyone's been pretty welcoming to you guys."

Even with just the flashlight, I could see the smirk on his face. "Yeah, it's kinda creepy. Ain't no people this nice in the apocalypse."

"I ... agree, but now that Wyatt and his goons are going to be out of the picture, this place is going to get a lot better," I said. It was funny how much Lucas sounded like me when I'd first arrived in Hargrove.

"Whatever. Keep your food." Lucas rushed past me to the back door but I grabbed onto his arm.

He ripped his arm out of my grip and turned to scowl at me. Even through his shirt fabric, I could feel the gnarled scar tissue from the infected bites.

"Don't do that again," he grated through his clenched teeth.

I held up my hands. "I won't. I just think you should stay, that's all."

"Yeah? Why's that?" he challenged.

"You said it yourself, you don't have anywhere else to go. It's a death sentence out there when you're by yourself."

He took a few steps so that he was right in front of me so I could see the elevator eyes he was giving me. "That the only reason?"

He was trying to be lewd to throw me off. I poked his chest with my finger. "Please, when has being a dick ever actually kept people out? It never works for me."

His head knocked back. "You a therapist or somethin'? Or do you just enjoy goin' 'round spewin' advice?"

"I'm very far from being prepared to deal with other people's issues. I can barely handle my own shit, but I just happen to do the same thing as you."

We stood staring each other down for so long that I thought we'd be there until the sun came up. I was getting tired of the intense silence so I finally spoke up.

"I'm going to level with you. Me asking you to stay is for purely selfish reasons. Right now we need as many competent people as we can get. Could you stay for just a little while longer until the unrest settles?"

He looked around the kitchen as if searching for a reason to say no, then let out a huge sigh. "Fine, but it's only temporary. And you have to let me take a few things when I do leave."

"Sounds fair." I held out my empty hand and we shook on it. "Now put that stuff back." I pointed to the sack lying on the floor. I helped him to make it quicker and then made sure he left the clubhouse kitchen.

Lucas nodded at me and took off for the condo he had been assigned. I had no idea if he would keep his word, but I hoped he did. I put my Beretta back into my waistband and headed back towards my condo to try and turn in for the night. I didn't want to deal with anymore crap today, especially after my existential crisis. But of course the universe had other plans for me. When I got back, I found Ethan sitting on the steps.

He had a lantern beside him and when he looked up, I could see the pain in his eyes. I debated running away, but that would be a stupid move. I knew we would have to eventually hash this out—I just didn't want to do it right now.

"I really don't want to do this right now, Ethan." I scowled. I tried to get past him but he blocked my way.

"Please, Bailey," he begged. "I need you to know how sorry I am."

"There, you've said it, now move."

He took a deep breath. "Not until we talk this through."

I shocked both of us when I shoved him backwards. His arms flailed but he didn't fall or move out of my way.

"Move."

"No."

Then I punched him in the shoulder. He grunted, but didn't do anything. He kept his arms dead at his sides.

"I will make you move," I threatened.

"I'll willingly move if you just hear me out."

"There's nothing to hear, Ethan! You sold me out!"

He winced at my words. It was more of a reaction than when I had hit him.

"I had no idea, I thought they were good guys!" he finally said back.

"Fuck you. I *told* you they were bad people, but you didn't listen! And it wasn't your secret to share. Go absolve your guilt somewhere else." I stabbed my finger into his chest.

His hand wrapped around mine gently, but I yanked it free.

"Bailey, I'm sorry."

I was about to yell some more when I picked up the heavy scent of smoke.

"You smell that?" I asked, taking a step away from the stoop. Ethan stuck his nose in the air and sniffed.

"Somethin's burnin'."

We rushed into the street. One of the condos near the front was engulfed in flames and a bunch of smaller fires littered the area by the gate.

"Go find Henry and the others!" I yelled at him, already sprinting for John's condo.

Chapter 15

We weren't equipped to deal with a large scale fire. This would burn Hargrove to the ground. And those bunches of smaller fires had me worried that it wasn't an accident. I was almost at John's condo when a loud crash echoed from the front. I turned in time to see the front gate explode with sparks flying into the night. A truck came barreling through. The guards began shooting at the encroaching truck as it skidded to a stop. Men burst from the back and began shooting at our guards.

My heart stopped as I ducked when the gunfire erupted. This would draw people into the street, right into the danger. I ripped my Beretta from my waistband and ran the rest of the distance to John's condo. The door flew open before I could reach it. John ran through with an M-16, ready for action.

"Don't shoot," I said while ducking further.

"Bailey? What's happenin'? Is that smoke?" John asked in a rush.

"We're under attack!" I yelled.

Chloe and Zoe chose that moment to appear outside.

"What's goin' on?" Chloe asked, sleepily.

"Zoe, take her back inside and hide!" John ordered, and they fled back into the house.

"What do we do?" I asked.

It would only be a matter of time before they made it this far into Hargrove. More automated gunfire bounced off the walls and echoed down the streets. People were already emerging from their homes. I waved at the closest ones, silently telling them to go back inside.

"We need to get to the armory before they do," John said.

Together, we kept close to the front of the condos and avoided being out in the open as we made our way to the building we used for the armory. My hands were shaking from the adrenaline rushing through my system. I wasn't prepared for something like this. No one in this town was. It was going to be a slaughter if the invaders didn't stop. Not to mention the big gaping hole they'd left in their wake where the infected could now get in.

Had Ethan gotten to Henry and the others? Oh God, what if I had just sent him to his death? I was mad at him, but I didn't want him dead. The gunfire stopped for the moment. I could hear a male bark orders that sounded like he was telling them to fan out. John pulled out a ring of keys and quietly inserted one into the deadbolt. Slowly, he turned it until we heard the deadbolt retract and we scurried inside, immediately shutting the door behind us.

"We gotta get as much guns and ammo out as we can," John said, leading the way to the back bedroom being used as an armory.

The front door handle rattled and John grabbed my arm yanking me to the side, using the hallway to cover us. He took off his hat and peered around the corner. I hadn't realized I was holding my breath until I had to take a deep breath to avoid passing out. It was different when it was just me that I was accountable for. Now I was worrying about everyone else. I couldn't stand to lose another friend.

"Ethan?" John hissed.

I relaxed a measure. I hadn't sent him to his death after all. Ethan joined us in the back along with Henry and his new wife.

"You had the same idea too, huh?" Henry said.

"Yeah, we need to make sure they don't get our weapons. You see how many were out there?" John asked.

Ethan shook his head. "Just saw the ones that came out of the truck. 'Bout five that I could see."

More gunfire sounded from outside and we all heard the screams. I swallowed over the sound of my heartbeat thrashing in my ears. They were getting closer.

"Open the door!" I yelled.

John used another key on his ring and opened the armory. There wasn't much left as our supplies had been dwindling. Especially after Wyatt no longer could sell people off to the mercenaries. Everyone got to work grabbing as much as they could. There were a few gun bags that we stuffed to the brim. I tried to lift one, but it was pretty damn heavy.

"I got that." Ethan swung the bag onto his shoulder with a grunt.

I knew now was not the time to argue. In this case, his strength outweighed by stubbornness. Instead, I grabbed a smaller bag and packed it will as many ammo boxes as I could and shouldered a loaded AR15. Now that I could actually use.

Something came crashing through the front window, shattering the glass. We all ducked, expecting to be under fire, but instead a slow smoke began to fill the condo. It was so strong that my eyes and throat started to burn. John used the butt of the automatic rifle he was holding and smashed out the back window.

"Get out, now!" he yelled, then broke into a coughing fit.

We tossed our bags out into the backyard and then dove through one by one. John was the last to come through. Once his feet hit the ground, he hunched over and continued to cough.

"What the hell was that?" I asked, my own lungs having finished spasming.

"Tear gas," John croaked out.

"Shh," Ethan whispered.

I didn't have time to react to Ethan's command before two of the armed mercenaries rounded the corner. I scooped up my AR15 and flicked the selector switch to fire. John was much faster than me and let out a burst of bullets, knocking down the two mercenaries.

"We need to move," John commanded.

We grabbed our haul and ran through the connected backyards to get to John and Ethan's condo. More gunfire erupted from the streets in front of the condos. I could see the muzzle flashes as we passed between condos. Were they just picking off people as they saw them? That's what they had done back at the apartments. Not one person had been left alive. I refused to allow that to happen. I wanted to stop running and just start shooting at any one of the mercenaries I could find. But I wasn't Rambo; that would just get me dead. We needed a plan of attack.

We rounded the condo and burst through the front door. Henry and his wife kept going down the condos, trying to hand out as many weapons as they could. I wished them luck and slipped inside behind the others.

"It's us," John boomed. After a second, Zoe and Chloe appeared around the corner. Chloe ran up to Ethan and hugged him.

"What's going on?" Zoe asked, her eyes wild.

"Take this," John said, handing a shotgun to Zoe. She grabbed it and pumped the fore end, chambering a round. I was a little impressed. Even I didn't know how to use a shotgun. Her secret redneck history was clearly coming in handy.

"The mercenaries have busted through the front gate and are shooting people in the streets. They started a bunch of fires as well," I answered.

"How do you know they're the mercenaries?" Zoe asked.

That was a fair question; I'd just assumed it was them because it matched the other horrible things they had done.

"Doesn't matter who it is. Gear up, cause we gotta take 'em out," John said as he pocketed an extra magazine for his gun.

I rooted through my ammo bag and passed out the ones I thought would match. Turns out I had given the wrong ammo to Ethan for his rifle, so I let him check the bag himself. Zoe picked up a box of shotgun slugs and stuffed a bunch in her pockets. This looked very much like we were about to go to war.

Ethan kneeled in front of Chloe and handed her—butt first—a small revolver. "This is not a toy. Remember all the times I took you shootin'? I need you to use everythin' I taught you if one of those men come anywhere near you."

With her face serious, Chloe nodded and took the gun from him. She popped out the cylinder and checked that there was a round in each chamber. The situation had never been bad enough before that we had handed her a loaded gun. Again, I couldn't believe I was about to do this, but I sent out a small, silent prayer. *Please let us live through this.*

"All right, Zoe and Chloe, you're goin' to stay here tucked away and if anyone you don't recognize comes through that door, you shoot 'em. You understand?" John looked them both in the eyes until they nodded, then whirled on us. "Ethan and Bailey, we gotta avoid bein' spotted for as long as we can. We still got some guns to pass out so first stop is to get Roy and Amanda and bring 'em over here. You got that?"

Both Ethan and I nodded. I felt very much like a solider at the moment. I'd feel a little bit better if I was wearing a bullet-proof vest, though.

We gathered our bags, making sure they weren't so heavy that we couldn't move easily. With our weapons armed and at the ready, we left the condo one by one, John taking the lead. I gave one last look back at Chloe and Zoe before shutting the door behind me and walking into a battlefield.

Chapter 16

Dead bodies lined the streets. All that I could see were causalities of Hargrove and not any of the mercenaries. I could hear screams coming from inside one of the nearby condos and then more flashes of gunfire.

"Move!"

Keeping low, we bolted across the street to my condo. The fire that had engulfed the condo by the front gate was now spreading to the one next to it. The blaze was so great that it was like a midnight sun, lighting up the front half of the cul-de-sac.

"Shit," John whispered.

I drew my eyes away from the intense flames and shifted them to my condo. The front door had been bashed in. I gripped my AR15 tighter and ran in, briefly registering John telling me to stop. There were heavy footsteps in one of the back rooms. I tiptoed to the edge of the living room, using the wall to flatten my back against. I took a shaky breath and waited until I could hear the person better. It sounded like they were opening and closing doors. Probably looking for hiding survivors to shoot. Were Amanda and Roy already dead? Or were they still in here somewhere?

John and Ethan flattened against the wall beside me. I didn't bother to look at them as there would no doubt be a couple of angry expressions waiting for me. Whoever was in there opened one of the drawers in my dresser. I knew it was mine because it rubbed and made a cringe worthy squealing sound every time I opened it.

I rushed around the corner and burst into my room. The man was caught off guard as he fumbled to lift his gun. Unlucky for him, I had mine ready. I let off two rounds, both landing in his chest. The man flew back, knocking into the dresser and almost toppling it over. I quickly ran to the other side of the bed and kicked away the gun he was toting. He was coughing profusely. The light shining through my window illuminated the blood dribbling down his lips with every breath.

I hadn't killed him instantly with my shots.

"Who are you guys?" I asked, suppressing the urge to shoot him right then and there.

He coughed and tried to smile, but it came out as a grimace. "Fuck you."

"Fuck me? You just invaded our town and killed innocent people. So no, fuck you!" I growled, putting a bullet in his head.

"Interrogations are for after we've dealt with the threat. Now keep movin'," John said through clenched teeth.

We checked Roy and Amanda's room, but there was no sign that they were in there. The whole condo was free of blood, so I assumed they must have gotten away. While we were still inside, I tucked the sheathed hunting knife I found in my room into my waistband. I could use all the weapons I could get.

"Where are they?" Ethan asked.

"Dunno, but we gotta move onto the next condo." John waved us on.

Outside there were two mercenaries heading our way. They starting firing when they saw us and we bolted off in different directions to avoid the spray of bullets. I dove into the bushes on the right and returned fire once I could right myself. This caused them to focus on me. Bullets ripped through the foliage and despite myself, I let out a scream. Staying low to the ground, I crawled further away from them with the goal of using the side of the condo as cover.

Hot pain sliced through my right calf and I gave a harsh yelp. I dragged myself up and against the side of the condo, putting a hand to my leg. It came away wet with blood. I tore my attention away from my injured leg when someone crunched down on the bushes I had vacated. I reached for my gun, which in my panic was still lying on the ground.

I fumbled to reach the knife concealed in my waistband, but I didn't need it as the back of the man's head exploded and he fell forward dead.

"You okay?" John asked as he ran up to me.

"I got hit."

John kneeled down and examined my leg. I let out a hiss as he poked at the wound.

"There's no bullet in there. It just grazed you." John stood up. "You goin' to be okay to walk?"

"Yeah, just hand me my gun." I pointed to where the dead guy had fallen. John reached underneath the guy and pulled out my AR15.

"Never lose your weapon," John chastised me.

"I was a little occupied," I murmured as I took my gun back.

I tested out some weight on my leg. With a missing toe and now this, I was really gibbled. I'd probably be just holding them back.

"Maybe you should just stay here," John said, clearly thinking the same thing.

I looked around. "Where's Ethan?"

"He's not behind me?" John's eyes went wide. "We killed the other mercenary and then went after the other guy shootin' at you."

We ran around the fallen mercenary and out onto the street, but I couldn't spot Ethan. My leg protested the entire way.

"He wasn't shot, was he?!"

"No, he said he was fine and that he'd be right behind me," John said, running his hands down his face.

"Come out, come out where ever you are!" an unfamiliar voice yelled through the streets. "I suggest you listen or the country boy gets it!"

My heart lurched. They had Ethan. Further down the street where the voice had come from, there was a mass of figures. They appeared like black shadows against the fiery backdrop that had now taken over more than three units.

"What do we do?" I asked.

"They want somethin' from us," John said ominously. "Or they'd have killed us by now."

"I *will* shoot the guy if you don't come forward with your hands in the air," the voice prompted.

I looked at John and saw the same look on his face that he had when Taylor had died. He was out of options. We both were. If we just started shooting, they'd definitely kill Ethan.

"Now!" the guy prompted.

We shouldered our guns and walked up to them with our hands in the air. I was sweating through my shirt from the mix of fear and heat rolling off of the fire that was gaining ground. On the bright side, the terror reduced the pain in my leg to a mere pinprick. John was holding his head high, not looking the least bit scared. I tried to imitate him but as we drew near, it became impossible.

They had Ethan on his knees with a gun pointed right at his head. He gave me a look that was hard to place. Somewhere between an apology and a goodbye. My throat swelled as I tried to swallow. Would the last thing I said to him be telling him to fuck off? That's not how I wanted it to happen.

The man who had yelled for us wasn't the one holding the gun, instead he was standing proudly in front of the rest of mercenaries. There were six right here, but who knew how many were still slithering from condo to condo. They converged on us and relieved us of our guns—including the Beretta I had stashed in my waistband and my ammo bag, then backed up and trained their own guns on us.

"Smart move," the guy said. "Now don't try anything stupid."

"What do you want?" John asked, wasting no time.

"It's pretty simple. We've come for Wyatt. He's been ignoring us lately and that doesn't make for very good business." The guy tsked.

"He's no longer in charge," John said.

"Where is he?"

John jerked his chin up front. "Being held in that condo." John paused. "Or he was. They might have left for fear of bein' burned alive."

The leader of the small group barked orders for two of the men to go and fetch Wyatt—just Wyatt.

"Well, while we're waiting, you can answer my other question. What happened at the hospital?"

My hands trembled slightly as I prepared to answer. John gave me a small shake of his head, telling me to stay quiet. The leader turned his attention on me, his narrowed eyes looking me over.

"I might have use for you if you tell me. Natural blondes are rare these days." The nasty grin on his face made me want to slice it off with my hunting knife.

If they knew how much of a hand we'd had in shutting down that place, they might just kill us right here. I'd have to be very careful with my word choice. The leader wiped the sweat from his forehead. The heat from the fire could be felt even this far away from it.

"Amelia's dead," I said.

The grin melted from his face. "They were a major business partner of ours. Now what are we to do with the immune?"

The guy took a step towards me and I held my ground. My anger was starting to overtake the fear. These people attacked us because they could no longer do their shady dealings? They were going to pay, somehow. I just had to figure out that part without risking them shooting Ethan—or us.

"Found 'em!" one of the returning mercenaries yelled.

The leader gave me one last hard look and then turned to see. The two were practically dragging Wyatt, who was screaming and wailing at the same time.

"Grant and Oscar were one of us!" Wyatt yelled hysterically. I guess that meant they had shot the others, including the guard.

"There is no *us,* shithead," the leader spat.

The two released Wyatt and he flopped to the ground, then they returned to pointing their guns at us. The leader walked up to Wyatt and punted him in the ribs. Wyatt let out a wheeze, curling into the fetal position.

"I was going to ask where you've been"—the leader looked back at us—"but I already got the answer to that."

Wyatt kneeled and latched onto the guy's boots. "Please, Shawn. Don't kill me. I can be one of you guys."

The leader let out a sound of disgust. "I'm not Shawn; he had more important things to do. But he does send his regards." The guy kicked out at the groveling Wyatt and he fell back to the ground. "You could never be one of us, but that crazy bastard you sent us sure fits right in."

"Who?"

"Oh, he's around here somewhere looking for a particular ... skirt," the leader said with a smirk. "You'll be seeing him soon."

John and I shared a look. Who the hell was he talking about? The only crazy person I could think of was Byron ... *No.* He'd come back for Zoe. My breath started to come faster as I fought the urge to hyperventilate.

"What?" John whispered.

"Byron," I barely said back. "I think he's looking for Zoe."

John stiffened. "There, you got what you came for," he said, trying to move this along.

The leader sighed. "Well not entirely, but this is a good start." He pulled out a pistol and shot Wyatt right in the street. His body shuddered once and then spread out until he was lying stretched on the pavement.

"Now that he's dealt with, that leaves you, Blondie," he said, walking over to me.

Ethan dove for us, but one of the mercenaries grabbed him and bashed his head into the street. He pulled Ethan up, revealing a bloody, but angry face. Ethan struggled some more so the one guy used the butt of his rifle to smash the back of his head. Ethan slumped forward, unconscious, back to the ground.

I lurched forward, but the leader stopped me by pointing his gun at me. "Uh-uh. He's fine, just a little bump, that's all. Now, explain what happened at the hospital."

"They're all dead. What more do you need to know?" I gritted through clenched teeth.

"I wanna know who *did it*." He enunciated the last two words, like he was worried I was slow.

"They did it to themselves," I said back slowly.

The guy scowled, not having liked my answer, and stepped closer to me, the gun still pointed at me. John bounced back and forth on his feet, looking like he was getting ready to strike. They'd shoot him and me if he did that.

"I want a better answer than that. Who killed Amelia?"

"She killed herself," John answered for me. "Shot herself right in the head when the place fell."

The leader soaked in the information. "Too bad. I kinda liked that cold bitch."

"Uh, boss. There's some dead fucks headin' our way," one of the goons said.

"You two, go take them out," the leader instructed with a wave of his hands.

They took off to the front gate where infected were sneaking in. The fire was higher than the stone walls and was no doubt attracting the infected like a star in the dark night. Not only was this place going to be burned to the ground, infected would eventually overrun us. *There was no safe place anymore.*

The leader turned back to me, but before he could say anything, a familiar voice yelled, "Bailey. John. Down!"

We flew to the ground just as shots erupted overhead. There were so many, it was impossible to pinpoint where they were coming from. The leader and the others returned fire, but it was clear they couldn't see where it was coming from. One of the mercenaries got hit and went flying back. The others scrambled to get out of the range of fire. The leader pointed his gun down at me, ready to pull the trigger as he ducked and dodged the impeding bullets.

I heard what could only be described as a war cry sound out from my left. It even got the leaders attention. I looked to see Roy running and screaming like a madman from the sidewalk, shooting off an automatic gun. John grabbed my arm and yanked me back. Together we scuttled away as bullets ricocheted off the spot on the cement we had just vacated. Roy couldn't aim worth shit.

The leader turned just in time to be impaled by Ron's assault, but he still managed to fire a few rounds from his own gun.

I screamed as I watched Roy jerk to the side, having been hit by the mercenary. Roy's automatic fire stopped and both bodies fell to the ground.

"Roy!" I yelled, running over to him.

He had been shot twice, once in the shoulder and the once in the stomach. He was gurgling and talking incoherently. The other gunfire faded into the distance as I focused on finding the wounds and trying to stop the bleeding.

"Roy, hold on!" I pleaded.

I ripped open his shirt and shredded the bottom of it. Using the balled-up fabric, I pushed it on the stomach wound that was gushing blood. The shoulder shot wouldn't be fatal, but the stomach one would be if he didn't get help immediately.

John looked him over. "We need Crystal."

"Go find, her," I said and when John didn't move, I screamed, "Now!"

"You need a weapon," John said, half sitting, half standing.

"I got Roy's, now go find her!"

John nodded and took off for the medic center. Please let Crystal still be alive. She needed to save Roy. I turned to look down at Roy, who was paler than I had ever seen him. He had naturally darker skin, but even that had faded as he continued to stain the street with blood.

"Hold on," I said, my eyes tearing up.

His whole body jerked as he coughed up a mouthful of blood. He was rasping something, but I couldn't make out the words. I placed an ear close to his mouth.

"A ... man ... da."

"You're going to be fine. You'll see Amanda soon," I said, trying and failing at keeping the panic from my voice.

"Wat ... ch h ... er," he said between struggling for air and trying to expel the blood.

"Of course," I promised.

He closed his eyes.

"No, don't do that Roy. Keep your eyes open!"

I tried to move his head from side to side to keep him awake, but the only response I got was fluttering behind his eyelids.

"Roy, stay with me," I pleaded as the tears leaked down my face.

The fluttering stopped when Roy gave one last rasp, then his chest went still.

"No ..." I mumbled. *Not another friend.*

Chapter 17

I stared numbly at Roy's dead body. He had just died saving me. Why did everyone have to die? I turned to the goon leader but he was very much dead. I wished he hadn't been, and that I'd had the honor of doing it. I was shaking with my anger and need for revenge. The fighting and shooting in the street had stopped. Either people were dead or they were ducking for cover out of sight from the street.

"What dis here?"

I froze at the dialect, instantly recognizing the voice.

"Now turn 'round slowly, cher."

I dove for Roy's gun and whirled around, pulling the trigger. It clicked empty. A big, toothy grin spread across Byron's face as he straightened himself from his ducking position.

"Now dat no way to say hello."

"You fucking led them here!" I screeched.

"Naw, dis bunch wanted Wyatt and I needed a ride," Byron said. His eyes landed on Roy. "Sorry 'bout yer friend." He paused. "Speakin' of dem der friends, where's dat pretty one of yers?"

I grinned back, looking very much the psycho. "Like I'd ever fucking tell you." I would never sell out a friend.

Byron frowned. "Dat no good, cher. 'Cause den I don't need ya."

"Why did you kill Darren?" I blurted out. Half because I needed to know, half because I was stalling.

"He got in da way; dat Asian friend of yers is sure pretty. I ain't normally one for killin' guys." His eyes crinkled as he smiled wistfully. *Sick fuck.* "Now girlies on da other hand ..." He trailed off.

He raised his gun and time seemed to stop. This was it. I was going to be blown away by a serial killer of the apocalypse. After everything, I was going to be executed in the streets.

"I don't think so."

Byron and I turned in time to see Zoe shoot off the shotgun she had aimed right for him. The blast was deafening. Small metal pellets impaled Byron and he flew back a good couple of feet. Not to be half-assed, Zoe walked briskly over to Byron and shot him again at close range. His feet actually flew up in the air from the impact. She turned to me covered in specks of blood, hatred in her eyes. I wondered if she had heard what Byron had said.

"You okay?"

I nodded. I wasn't sure I could speak over the ringing in my ears. Shotguns were *really* loud. She ran over to me and offered me her hand. I took it and she helped me to my feet.

"Oh my God, Roy," she said, her hand cupping her mouth. She looked at me. "Amanda?"

I shook my head to dispel the bells chiming in my head. "I don't know. We need to find her. What about Chloe?"

"She's fine. Some of the others came into our cabin for safety and they're all tucked away hiding. I heard all the gunshots and decided to help."

"Thank you, Zoe."

She smiled, but it wasn't a happy smile. "I'm just glad you're okay. Not sure how I feel about shooting him, though."

She hefted her thumb toward Byron, but refused to actually look back at his dead body. I didn't blame her. She had gotten her revenge on Byron for killing Darren, but it was a type of revenge that changed a person. Haunted them long after it was over.

"What do we—?" Zoe was cut off by the sound of rasping.

We turned toward the front gate to see an army of infected heading our way. Fuck. As if the mercenaries hadn't been enough, now we had to fight the infected.

"Ethan!" I screamed, having momentarily forgotten about him.

We ran to Ethan's unconscious form and tried to rouse him. He let out a moan, but didn't wake up. That guy had whacked him hard. I frantically looked around, my eyes landing on a fallen mercenary. He was the one who had stripped me of my guns and ammo bag. I reached into his waistband where he had tucked away my Beretta. I tried not to think about where I was reaching.

I pulled out my gun. The guy hadn't even flicked the safety on. He was lucky he hadn't shot himself in the nuts. I also grabbed back my AR15 and ammo bag, slinging them over my shoulder.

"We need to move inside somewhere," I said. "Grab his arm and we'll drag him."

Together we each grabbed one of Ethan's arms, and dragged him to the nearest condo. His head lolled to the side and I got a good view of the bloody spot where he had been hit. He more than likely had a concussion. *Welcome to the club.* He was in for a major headache when he woke up.

I opened the door and we lugged Ethan over the threshold, immediately shutting the door behind us. The first wave of infected reached Wyatt and the mercenaries' fallen bodies and went into a feeding frenzy, momentarily distracted. *Oh God, Roy ...* His body was still out there. We didn't have time to move him too. *I'm so sorry, Roy.* I turned from the window, unable to watch my friend get devoured.

I raked a hand through my hair. "We can't kill that many with the guns we have."

"Need an extra pair of hands?"

I jumped at the voice. "Jesus, Rose. Don't do that," I growled. We must have ended up in her condo.

"He all right?" Leo jerked his head at Ethan, who we had placed on the floor.

"He got knocked out," I said.

"He's bleedin' all over my floor," Rose groused.

"Then fucking help me dress his wound!" I was fried at this point. If anything else happened, my sanity would finally snap.

Rose shot me a look, but grabbed a roll of paper towels and bent over Ethan. She placed a bunch of wadded up ones on his head and pressed.

Leo ran to the front window. "Holy crap, that's a lot of dead ones. How'd they get in?"

"Someone bulldozed the gate," I answered. "You guys get any of the guns Henry was handing out?"

"Yeah, got one between us," Rose said.

I took the gun bag and AR15 off my shoulder and passed the weapon to her. "You know how to use one of these?"

"I grew up in the south. Of course I know how to shoot a damn gun."

"Don't you need a weapon?" Leo asked.

"I'm much better with my Beretta."

I crouched over the gun bag and began rooting for some more 9mm ammunition. I ejected the magazine in my gun and filled it up, pocketing as many bullets as I could. If I carried around the bag out there, it was one more thing for the infected to grab at so I would have to leave the bag there.

"You're not going out there," Zoe said firmly.

I was still crouched over the bag when I answered. "How else are we going to kill them? If we start shooting from in here, they'll just swarm the building. We need to stay on the move as we kill them."

"Then I'm going with you." I could tell she wasn't going to take no for an answer.

"Us too," Leo said.

"No, you need to stay here. Ethan is still unconscious."

"You're kidding. You want us to stay and protect the guy who turned you in?" Leo sounded half angry, half surprised. "You should've left him out there!"

I took a deep breath through my nose. "I wasn't asking."

Everyone looked at me like I had grown a conjoined twin in the last few seconds. I grabbed a box of shotgun slugs and shoved them at Zoe. She took them and reloaded her gun, then pocketed all that she could fit.

"I'm going to leave the ammo bag here. If they try to get in, shoot them. You should have enough rounds here to kill all that wander over here if you need it."

I went to the windows and peeked out. The infected must have finished their ... meals. Most were up and about again, while a few remained crowded over the fallen people—intent on cleaning the bodies down to their bones. I gulped as I thought of Roy. *There won't even be a body to bury.* I would give myself time to dwell on that later.

"Zoe, stay right behind me. We're going to try to lead them back out the gate. Whatever you do, don't stop moving," I instructed.

Zoe nodded. I must have sounded sure, but inside I wasn't. This was a long shot and who knew how many mercenaries were still out there. All I knew was that if the infected converged on one condo, they would knock it down, and Ethan was still unconscious in this one, so we really didn't want their attention to swing this way.

I took another deep breath and opened the front door. *Here goes nothing.*

Chapter 18

We bolted left, toward the opening where the front gate used to be. The infected saw us running almost immediately. Zoe let out a yelp as one made a grab at her. I turned and shot it.

"Use your gun," I prompted.

I should have made her stay inside. She wasn't ready for this. She bit her lip and straightened up, pointing the gun ahead of her. With her covering the back, we made our way down the sidewalk. It was getting brighter the closer we got to the raging fire. More than three condos had been swallowed and soon it would make its way down the rest of the street. I just hoped that it didn't reach Rose's condo before we could round up the infected.

We were popping off rounds, mostly hitting our targets. Zoe could take out more than one at a time with her shotgun. I, on the other hand, had to spend a few seconds aiming each time to avoid wasting bullets.

The infected really seemed to be focusing on Zoe. Any that came at me seemed to give up on me when Zoe was within range. One snuck past me as I focused on a different infected.

"Zoe, look out!" I screamed as I whirled around.

The thing flew at her, but she was faster than I gave her credit for. She jumped out of the way, causing the infected to fall to the ground. I lifted the foot with all my toes and brought it down on the growling head. As soon as I hit it, I released the mistake I had made. I fought the urge to yell as pain shot up my leg. I had forgotten about the gun graze wound.

At least I didn't need to do that again. I had caved in its head with the one hit. It must have been really decayed.

"Keep moving."

We returned to back-to-back formation, taking out the infected. The heat from the fire was oppressive, which gave me an idea. For some reason the infected wouldn't get close enough to the fire on their own. Perhaps we should give them a push in the direction—perhaps literally. It wasn't an elegant plan, and it meant we had to get close to the flames, but it might work.

"Zoe! The fire!"

"What?" she yelled, still focusing on the invading infected.

I had never faced so many infected at once. For a brief second, I felt like a cowboy in an old Western. The adrenaline was pumping through my veins and it was better than any high I had ever felt. I knew I should be scared, but ... I wasn't. Was that the adrenaline or was it something else? Had I finally cracked?

"Let's push them into the fire!"

She finally turned to look at me. She nodded, but her expression was tight. I didn't need her approval of the plan, I just needed it to work. We gave up going back-to-back and both sprinted toward the inferno. Sweat coated my skin as we got dangerously close. The flames were wriggling in the air like worms breaching dirt. They were getting fatter as they ate away at more of the condos.

We stood our ground. I grabbed the closest infected by the scruff of its already torn shirt and tossed it into the flames beside me. It caught on fire instantly, not letting out a sound. It tried to get up, but the hotness of the fire burned its rotten body faster than it could move. Before it could get up, it sank to the ground. It had worked.

"Zoe, don't touch them. Use your gun to bat them into the fire," I said.

"What? Your way's easier!" she yelled as she took an unsure step backward. The infected had caught up with us.

"I'm immune. You're not. Keep them away from your limbs."

The shotgun in her hands trembled slightly, but she still managed to club an infected that had dared to approach her.

I grabbed at another that had forgone an attack on me in an attempt to get to Zoe. *Just like the old days at the bars.* I whirled around to get momentum and threw infected into the fire. *Well, maybe not* just *like the old days.* The thing was still waving its arms as it went down. The clothes caught fire first, then the rest of it followed.

It was starting to smell as we managed to usher a bunch of them to their fiery deaths. My hands were soaked with perspiration, making it a bit difficult to grab at the infected. The last one I had tossed didn't make it in as far as the others because of the pile of burning bodies we had created. It managed to escape the flames and walk back out. It was literally burning alive so I couldn't get close to it without being burned.

Zoe saw this and ran at the burning infected with her shotgun in hand. She smacked it in the head, sending embers flying into the air like a damp log in a campfire. The thing flew back into the flames, finally lying still when it added itself to the pile. I was going to thank her when the fire crackled and exploded as it hit something inside the condo. I barely had time to cover my face when we were tossed back from the pressure.

I scrambled up and helped Zoe to her feet. I felt around my person, making sure I wasn't on fire.

"You're good. Although, if we still have eyebrows after this, it'll be a miracle," Zoe said.

Paranoid, I touched at my brow to make sure I still had hair there.

"I think we've done all we can with this." I looked around at the fallen infected who had been tossed by the explosion and the others that were currently being cremated. "It's getting too dangerous to be near the fire."

Gunfire went off inside the clubhouse across the street, drawing our attention. Zoe and I shared a look before running to the other side of the road. Zoe went to shoot at an approaching infected, but her gun clicked empty.

"I need to reload!"

Zoe was frantically reaching into her pockets to get to the last of her ammo. I fired at the infected she had been aiming at and it went down, but now my own gun was empty as the slide of the gun popped back. I steered her into the clubhouse as she shoved the slugs into the chamber. I thought shotguns could only hold two rounds, but I guess her model was a newer one as she loaded more than two rounds of ammo.

She was done in time to keep away the nearest infected. They were blasted into pieces, and some of those pieces had managed to rain down on us. I wiped away at the zombie chunk that had landed on my shoulder. The old me would have freaked out, but now it was nothing more than an annoyance.

I had no idea who was shooting inside the clubhouse, but we needed to get off the street so I could fill up my magazine. I motioned for Zoe to get low. In our crouching position, we approached the clubhouse door. I opened it a smidge, but didn't see anyone in the immediate area.

"Where were the gunshots coming from?" Zoe asked as we snuck in.

I shut the door quietly behind us. There was no one in the main mess hall, but all the lights were off so I couldn't be sure. The inferno outside was coming through the windows, making the shadows inside look like they were dancing. It was unnerving. And not to mention making it difficult to spot bodies.

"Maybe they're in the kitchen looting," I whispered back to Zoe.

Still crouched, we stuck to the walls and made our way to the back. My foot hit something and I fell over, landing on top of whatever it was. I pushed myself up with Zoe's help and we stared in horror at the almost headless body lying on the floor. The mercenaries had blown the person's head off—or at least had tried.

Carefully, I continued over the carcass. I could actually *hear* Zoe swallow as she passed over it. Whoever was back there was not getting away, not if I had anything to say about it. Once we got up to the door leading to the kitchen, I held my breath so I could listen. There was rustling and footsteps, but no one was saying a word.

"You ready?" I murmured to Zoe.

She looked terrified, with her eyes wide and her mouth set in a grimace.

"You stay here," I said.

I could probably do this myself. Just point and shoot at everything. Easy.

She shook her head. "Like hell I'm letting you do this by yourself."

"Zoe, look, I don't—"

The door to the kitchen flew open. I tried to shoot my Beretta but it was kicked out of my hands as I was still in my crouched position. I went to dive for it but something connected with my head with such force that a blinding light exploded behind my eyelids. I couldn't even let out a scream as my brain didn't know which way was up and which way was down at the moment. My shoulder landed on something hard, my brain barely coming-to to register that I had fallen over. The pain was paralyzing. Like the worst headache you'd ever had in an instant. I wanted to vomit from the agony.

I struggled to clear my vision but the images in front me kept swirling, adding to the need to throw up. I clamped my eyes shut and when I opened them, all the bodies were in a different position in the room. It felt like I was watching a film through a pair of kaleidoscope glasses. Nothing felt real, more like a fever dream.

One very large guy ran at Zoe, who had backed away from me. She pulled the trigger, but the guy grabbed the barrel and yanked it to the side just before it went off. The pellets flew up into the air uselessly. He relieved Zoe of her shotgun and used it to whack her upside the head. She fell to the ground limp and the guy scooped her up, throwing her over his shoulder.

"I told you it was girl voices," said another man.

He leaned down and grabbed Zoe's shotgun. He started coming towards me, but was stopped as the guy carrying Zoe said, "Leave her. We need all the ammo we can to get out of here."

"I wasn't goin' to shoot her. We can bring her too. You know Shawn likes his blondes."

If my body had been working properly, it would have shivered.

"You see all those undead freaks out there, dumbass? You need your hands clear to take 'em out since I got mine full," the big guy said. "Now. Leave. Her."

The guy gave me one last look before joining his large friend. I tried to reach a hand out to stop them, but my arms wouldn't work. *Zoe!* I screamed inside. I blinked and they were gone, leaving me to fight the blackness invading my vision.

Chapter 19

A rough pair of hands shook me awake. "Bailey!"

I swatted them away.

Just five more minutes ...

Piece by piece, my brain started to boot up. I sat upright and yelled, "They took Zoe!"

My hands flew to my head as the throbbing made itself known. "Ugh," I groaned as I started to sway. A pair of hands steadied me. How long had I been out for?

"You should stay lyin' down for a minute," John said. It was his hands holding me upright.

"I'll be good in a second," I said, the swaying already starting to stop. The headache was still there, but my vision was clearing rapidly.

John gave me a slow smile. "Of course you will, but pushin' yourself ain't good for anyone." His smiled faded and his eyebrows drew together. "I thought you were dead. We saw the headless body over there and then you on the ground."

Why *wasn't* I dead? I knew the big mercenary had said to save the bullets, but it was nothing for them to kill a person. Probably best to not overthink it.

Beside John were Rose, Leo, and Lucas. But no Ethan, and they were supposed to be watching him.

"Where's Ethan?"

"Your *boyfriend,*" Leo said with distain, "is being watched by the girl who looked us over and two little girls."

I sagged in relief. At least he was with Crystal and Chloe—safe. As much as I was pissed at him, I still cared for him.

"How long was I out for?" I asked.

"No idea, but it's only been like forty minutes since I left you to find Crystal," John answered. I couldn't have been out for more than ten minutes then.

"How many fingers am I holdin' up?" Rose said, shoving her middle finger into my face.

Leo swatted her hand away. "That's the last thing she needs."

I blinked, in too much pain to yell at her.

"We need to take you to Crystal. You think you can stand?" John asked.

"With some help." I held out a hand and John grabbed it.

Slowly, he helped me to my feet. I stumbled a bit, but Lucas put a hand on my back, preventing me from falling back to the ground.

"Thanks," I said.

Lucas just grunted in reply. I half expected him to bolt during the invasion. It was a welcome relief to see him still here.

"Now, there's still infected out there and the fire, but the remainin' mercenaries took off," John said.

With Zoe. I hung my head. I hadn't been able to save her, and now she was who knew where with those monsters. First Darren's death, and now this.

"Except for the one we caught," Rose added.

I lifted my head.

John shot her a glare and she looked to the floor.

"What do you mean you caught one?" I asked. "Alive?"

"Yes, but before we deal with him, you need to see Crystal so she can look at your head," John said carefully.

"He could tell us where they took Zoe!" I said, trying to walk on my own. There was no time to lose. The longer we waited around, the further she got away.

John held me in place. "Crystal first. He ain't goin' anywhere, Henry will see to that." His voice darkened when he mentioned Henry.

"What do you mean?" I asked.

"They're holdin' him prisoner for right now. They killed Henry's wife right in front of him."

At least they hadn't taken her. I shuddered, thinking of why they wanted Zoe. I would find her if it was the last thing I did. She would do the same for me.

"Fine, let's go to Crystal," I said.

As we left the clubhouse, everyone had their guns at the ready. John had scooped up my Beretta but refused to give it back to me until Crystal had me checked over. He was worried that I might accidently shoot him or someone else in my dizziness.

Guns fired all around me, making me wince. I wasn't as bad as John had thought, but the loud noise was making the headache worse. I'd had a concussion before, at the apartment, and this wasn't the same. This time everything cleared a lot faster. I could see and I was steady on my feet—well as steady as one could be while missing a toe—as soon as I had woken up. I really wanted to get to that mercenary so maybe I was telling myself I was in better condition than I actually was.

I stared at the flames. The fire had almost engulfed half of Hargrove by now. The first condo that had caught fire was now reduced to a smoldering heap while the flames moved on, intent on finishing the job.

"Don't worry," John said, noticing where I was looking, "we evacuated all the condos on that side of the street."

"Where is everyone?" I asked hesitantly. I knew that wouldn't be a pretty answer.

John made a face. "Everyone who's left is either in the medic center or gatherin' supplies for leavin'."

"How long do you think this place has before the fire completely takes over?"

"I dunno, but the sooner we're outta here, the better. The mercenaries trashed most of the vehicles with fire as well so we only got two workin' trucks."

Shit. "Will everyone fit?"

"There ain't many people left," John said.

We had reached the medic condo and burst through the front door. Half the people in the waiting area jumped. It looked like an evacuation center. There were people spread out all over the area, some in blankets, some standing, some sobbing quietly. It reminded me of all those months ago when we went to the school emergency center.

I did a quick tally and came up with fifteen people. The mercenaries really had done a number on Hargrove. I spotted Colin's blue hair tucked away in the corner of the room. When he saw me, he started to get up so I motioned for him to sit back down. He gave me a hurt look, but complied. I didn't need him getting involved in what was coming after the examination. John latched onto my arm and dragged me to one of the back rooms. Crystal was inside, patching up a lady's arm. She looked over at us.

"Oh, God, what now?"

"Bailey here needs you to look at her head," John said.

Crystal had the lady jump down from the stainless steel table and sent her back out into the waiting area. Everyone looked at her as she passed.

"She bit?" Rose asked with narrowed eyes.

"No, another bullet wound," Crystal answered.

She motioned for me to come over and I complied. The sooner we got this over with, the sooner I could get to questioning our POW.

Crystal began poking and prodding at my head. I winced as she touched a particularly sensitive spot. She shined a light in my eyes and had me follow a tongue press with my eyes.

"I'm not gonna lie, Oscar never taught me much about head wounds. I'd say if you can see and walk straight, you're okay?" She didn't sound very sure.

Too be fair, she wasn't a trained medical professional like Oscar had been. I got down from the table.

"But I think Ethan does have a concussion," she continued.

"Where is he?" I asked.

"In the next room."

I hurried out of the room we were in and busted into the next room over. The condos only had two rooms each so I knew he had to be in there. Ethan was lying on the hospital bed, throwing up into a small pail. Chloe was playing the part of helper, and I spotted Amanda sitting on the only chair in the room, staring at her feet. She looked up and when she saw me her eyes went wide. She got up and looked around at the others behind me.

"Where's my dad?"

I bit my upper lip. I kneeled down to her level and she instantly teared up. She may have been young and naive, but she wasn't stupid. Amanda latched onto me, almost sending me to the floor from my kneeling position. I hugged her back as she cried.

"I'm sorry, Amanda. Your dad was a great man. We will all miss him," I said in a quiet voice.

I gently pushed her from me, then guided her back to the chair. She sat and continued to sniffle. I felt bad for her, but there was a mercenary to get to. By the time I approached the bed, Ethan had put down his bucket and was peering at me through half closed eyes.

I put a hand on Chloe's head and ruffled her hair. She pushed my hand off.

"I'm helpin' nurse him. Crystal said to," Chloe said with intent, as if she was worried I'd tried to tell her otherwise.

"Good, looks like he needs it," I said.

I looked at Ethan and he flashed me the thumbs up. Now that I'd seen he was relatively okay, I turned to John. "Where are they holding the guy?"

John looked around the room before answering. "I'll take you to him."

He led me, and the others, outside and to the condo next door. John rapped on the door with his knuckles. It slowly opened just enough for a face to appear. It was Henry.

"We need to talk to him now," John said.

Henry looked back inside the room before letting us in. The mercenary's hands and feet were bound and he was lying on his side in the center of the floor. His face was battered and bloody, but he was conscious. It looked like Henry couldn't wait. There were two other Hargrove people inside. One was Sheri, who gave me a grim nod, and the other was one of the men on the council whose name I couldn't remember. He looked just as pissed as Henry.

"Jesus, Henry. I thought you said you'd wait for the rest of us," John muttered.

"Yeah, well this one had a mouth on him," Henry spat.

The mercenary began to stir, a sick smile on his face. "Still pissed 'bout that little wifey of yours, eh?"

Henry clenched his teeth so hard I thought they were going to shatter. He ran over to the restrained mercenary and punted him in the stomach. The guy let out a wheeze and curled in a ball. Henry wound up for another, but I intervened.

"Stop!" I commanded.

Henry shot me a glare, but lowered his foot back to the ground. "Did you not hear him?" Henry was gesturing wildly at the guy.

"I need him to be able to talk." I walked over and kneeled down beside the mercenary.

"Where would they have taken my friend Zoe?" I asked. Out of the corner of my eyes I saw Sheri clamp a hand over her mouth. Henry and the other guy stood there with their brows drawn.

He cracked a smile. "She pretty?"

I couldn't blame Henry for beating the guy up first—I wanted to—but I had a feeling it wasn't going to work. The mercenary finally opened his eyes. Well, eye—the other one was swollen shut. I watched his good eye look me over.

"I'm surprised they didn't take you. Shawn loves 'em blonde."

John was beside me in two heavy footfalls, and with a scary look on his face. "What'd you say?"

I held up my hand to John. "Answer my question. Where is she?"

"She could be anywhere, 'specially if she's pretty."

"That's sick!" Sheri yelled, pushing herself off of the wall.

"Life goes on, sweetheart. Dead walkin' around or not. Some businesses just outlast everythin'," the mercenary said, this time without a smirk.

"Where's your hideout then?" I asked.

He snorted. "I ain't gettin' out of here alive, so what's the point in tellin' you?" He looked around at all of us, challenging us to say anything different. His one good eye widened.

"Well, I'll be damned." He grinned at his joke. "Switched teams did ya, Lucas?"

We all turned to look at Lucas who was standing in the background. Rose very obviously shifted away from him.

"What the hell is he talking about?" I asked, bolting to my feet.

Lucas ignored me and flew over to the mercenary. The ground creaked every time his boot-clad foot hit the flooring. "After ya'll sold me out for bein' immune, yeah, I reckon I did."

Lucas had been a mercenary. John and I shared a concerned look. He sidled up to me and placed my Beretta back in my hand. I gripped the butt of the gun tight and flicked off the safety just in case this got messy. Lucas had a fully loaded weapon. If he decided to start shooting to help his old buddy, I would be able to retaliate.

"You know it was nothin' personal, just business, right?" The mercenary was trying to play Lucas's past.

"Yeah, nothin' personal," Lucas said flatly. He lifted his gun and shot the mercenary twice.

"No!" I yelled, lurching forward. He was my only option for finding out where they had taken Zoe!

The mercenary gurgled for a few seconds before he stopped moving—and breathing. Sheri let out a squeaking sound and turned away. I whirled on Lucas and punched him square in the face.

"You asshole! I needed the info he had!"

I launched myself at Lucas again but John caught me around the waist and yanked me back. I struggled as I watched Lucas right himself and massage his jaw. He glared daggers at me, then took a step forward.

"Try somethin', I dare you," Rose said with her gun pointed straight for Lucas. Leo followed her lead and leveled his own shotgun at Lucas.

The room was tense. No one said a word or moved for a few moments as everyone tried to catch up with what had happened.

"You good?" John asked me, still holding on.

"I'm good," I said and he released me. I looked between Lucas and the dead mercenary. Lucas used to be one of them; maybe he knew where their hideout was.

I got right in Lucas's face. "You killed my only lead. Now you're going to take me to the mercenary hideout, whether you like it or not."

Lucas opened his mouth wide, but Rose spoke before him. "You best do what she says or you're not goin' to like what happens next." She still had her gun trained on Lucas.

His jaw shifted. "What's in it for me?"

"Well for one, Rose won't shoot you right here for being one of those scumbags," I said.

"I haven't been with their crew in over four months," Lucas growled. "They're the reason I was in that hospital."

"Think of it as revenge, then. If you take me to their compound, or wherever they hide out, you can get them back for handing you over. Hell, I'll even help!" My desperation was showing as my voice rose with each word.

"Bailey," John said, sounding as if he was warning me.

"They have Zoe and you heard what that guy said!" I barely suppressed a shiver. *My poor best friend.*

Sheri walked over to us and pointed a finger at Lucas. "Were you ever part of whatever they do to the girls?"

"No," Lucas said with conviction. "They have different ... branches? I was with the crew who rounded up immune people."

"Pretty ironic, eh?" Rose quipped.

Lucas scowled at her and she just smirked. I was glad she was on my side. I couldn't tell if Lucas was telling the truth or not, but right at that moment it didn't really matter. I needed his intel to get to Zoe, and we could always take care of him later if it turned out he was lying. It was a cold way to think; I was well aware of that.

"You going to take me there or not?" I prompted.

Lucas looked around at all of our faces and whatever he saw there, had him say: "Fine. I'll lead you there, but only so I can take out Shawn *myself.*"

"He's their leader, right?" I asked.

Lucas made a scoffing sound. "I guess you could call him that. He's the worst one of 'em all. Started the whole thing. He's the one who ordered me turned over to the hospital."

"You came in pretty beaten up at the hospital. He do that to you, too?" Rose asked.

"Some." And that was all Lucas said about it.

Chapter 20

Rose and Leo had agreed to keep an eye on Lucas while everyone else prepared to evacuate Hargrove. The remaining two trucks were loaded with whatever supplies we could scrounge up. It was decided that kids and the injured would ride inside the cabs while the rest would ride in the truck beds. It was going to be majorly squished.

Colin made a fuss when I told him he would be riding inside the cab as well. I grabbed his arm and steered him off to the side, out of earshot.

"Before Oscar turned me over, he told me you were sick," I said quietly.

Colin's nostrils flared as he crossed his arms. "I don't know what you're talking about."

I sighed. I had a feeling it would go this way. Colin was too stubborn. "Look, I haven't told anyone else—that's up to you to do. All I'm saying is that it's not good for you to ride in the back of a truck all night. Your immune system already has enough to deal with." Colin opened his mouth but I held up a finger. "Plus you're fifteen and technically still count as a kid and therefore, you ride in the cab. Suck it up."

I walked away from him before he could argue further. I would bind his arms and legs and toss him inside the truck if I had to.

The uninjured adults were armed and shooting at the infected still sneaking in while they loaded up the kids and wounded. The fire had crossed the street to the other condos, ensuring that we all had no choice but to leave. Crystal had to be practically torn from the medic center. She grabbed everything that hadn't been bolted down just before the fire took it over. My own condo had long since burned, taking everything of mine with it. All I had were the clothes on my back and my Beretta. Even my trusty axe was lost to the flames. I shouldn't complain, I was still alive, after all. That was more than most people had. Most of Hargrove's population had been decimated. Even kids hadn't been spared. The mercenaries were a plague and whoever they didn't get, the infected tried to.

I triple-checked to make sure Chloe and Amanda—and Colin—were inside one of the truck cabs with Ethan. I had once told Roy that my babysitting days were over. Looks like he proved me wrong—I now had Amanda to look after. I rubbed at my eyes. We were all exhausted from the hellish night and it still wasn't over. We had no idea where we were going. Obviously we couldn't all just head to the mercenary compound right now.

We would need to find some place we could temporarily secure and unload everyone. Once we re-grouped, then the able and willing would come with us to the compound to find Zoe and as I suspected, exact revenge. Lucas wasn't the only one with a grudge.

John was currently talking with Henry over a spread out map on the hood of our escape vehicle. They were trying to find a muster point within driving distance that we could fortify for the night. We had extra canisters of gas, but if we had to keep driving around to find a place, those would soon be gone.

As I approached them, I aimed and shot my Beretta, taking out an infected that had made it through the others protecting the trucks. John turned to see the thing drop and turned back to give me a curt nod.

"We need to get out of here before we're overrun. Or use up all our ammo. Or we're burned alive. Take your pick," I said grumpily. This evacuation process was nowhere near as fast as it should have been.

As if to emphasize my words, one of the condos down the street exploded. We ducked as pieces of flaming boards and glass flew into the street. There were screams from the people around us even though it was a relatively small explosion and we were out of range.

"Must've hit the fertilizer and feed shed," Henry said.

John stabbed a finger at a spot on the map. "We're thinkin' we need to move away from the middle of the city for tonight. This is an industrial area so there should be less infected to worry about. The further we head east, the less city we'll touch."

Should be. Nothing was ever certain.

"All right, let's go," I said.

Henry took the wheel of one truck, while John took the other. I hopped into the back of the one John was driving. Ethan was in the front seat with him, while Amanda, Colin, Chloe, and one other young boy were squished into the back seat. Rose and Leo joined me, forcing Lucas in with them. He didn't even look at me as he sat down on the cold truck bed. He just stared back into the inferno making its way through the entire cul-de-sac.

"Anyone see George?" I asked, looking around to spot him.

Rose shook her head. "They got 'im."

I paused for a moment before asking Leo, "What about your friend? What was her name ... Brittany?"

"There's no sign of her. The other two we escaped with were shot but she wasn't there," Leo mumbled as he stared at his feet. Rose put a hand on his shoulder.

I had a sinking feeling the mercenaries might have taken her like they did Zoe, but now wasn't the time to say anything. She hadn't looked any older than sixteen...

A couple other survivors joined us in the back of the truck and then I pounded on the top, telling John to go. The truck lurched forward, rocking us in the back, then went out through the spot where the front gate used to be. We all looked back at Hargrove as we left it for the last time. The flames were twice as tall as the brick fencing, reaching toward the night sky. It looked like a volcanic explosion.

I shoved a bag full of supplies to the side so I could lean on the edge of the truck bed. It was very uncomfortable back there with all the people, supplies and constant moving about as the truck continued. Infected instantly started toward the vehicles. It was dark so we had to keep the headlights on to see so we would be getting plagued with infected for the whole trip.

"Only take out the ones closest to us. This is all the ammo we have," I ordered.

The armory was the first thing we cleaned out when we'd started to evacuate. We had about two full duffle bags of ammo, but if everyone kept popping off rounds, they would be gone sooner rather than later.

To my surprise, people listened. They focused on the immediate threats that were banging and scraping along the sides and reaching into the back. John wasn't going very fast because he was busy maneuvering to avoid hitting the infected gathering in the beams of the headlights. He veered to the left, almost tossing Rose out the vehicle.

"Watch your drivin'!" she yelled while shaking her fist at the cab of the truck.

I started to laugh and she shot me a venomous look. Stifling my laughter, I returned to taking out the infected but not before I caught the small grin on Leo's face. I squinted into the headlights behind us. The second truck was following us with their lowest lights on, but they were still bright on the eyes.

The further we got away from Hargrove, the less infected we encountered. After an hour, we could no longer see the flames over the rooftops.

"How long do you think it'll burn for?" Leo asked.

"Depends if it spreads past the brick fence or not," Rose answered.

"You think it'll continue and burn down the rest of the city?" Leo kept going with his questions.

"Depends if it rains or not," Rose said.

"What direction are we heading?"

"Mostly east."

"Do you—?"

"For Christ's sake, shut up!" Lucas said.

"Just trying to make conversation," Leo muttered.

"Don't worry 'bout the Nazi mercenary," Rose said while patting Leo's knee. "He don't know how to be 'round normal folks. Bein' raised to appreciate Hitler will do that to a person."

Lucas narrowed his eyes at her and if she was intimidated, Rose didn't show it. Instead she gave him a sarcastic smile.

"Better watch what you say, leaf-blower," Lucas growled.

"That the best you got?" Rose countered. "I woulda thought they taught you some more creative ways to be racist at Hitler school."

Lucas's gun had been forcefully taken from him right after the mercenary incident. He was now weaponless, and kept eying Rose's rifle. She was practically wagging it in front of him like she was daring him to try. Lucas shifted in his spot, making her clutch her rifle tighter. He smirked at her and she glowered at him.

"Enough," I said with a weary sigh.

I was too tired for this shit. And I'd had enough of Luca's racist comments. He was lucky I wasn't willing to waste the energy to pop him one—again.

They both looked at me and I challenged them to argue with a stern stare. Rose huffed and returned to looking out for infected, while Lucas regarded me for a second longer than necessary before returning to stare blankly out the side of the truck bed.

After another twenty minutes of driving, with the occasional infected to shoot, the truck slowed down. The brakes for the second truck squealed as they were forced to slow down behind John. Slowly, John took the truck over a set of railway tracks, causing those of us who were in the bed to be tossed up.

The buildings were starting to get further and further apart—and bigger—unlike in the city where everything was crammed together. There were still infected to deal with but John had been right; it looked like there were less in this area. John slowed the vehicle and pulled to the side of the street.

"What's he doin'?" Rose asked no one in particular.

John got out of the truck and turned to us in the back. "I think this place is as good as any."

We looked to the side to see a tacky castle-themed motel situated at the beginning of the industrial area. Kind of an odd place for a motel. It had fake decorations to look like stone walls and towers. There was even a ditch filled with stagnant water that ran around the front by the "draw-bridge" gate to look like a moat. It looked like the kind of place where you slept on top of sheets and pushed a chair up against the inside of the door.

The sound of Rose's gun going off brought me out of my critiquing. This place would have to do. I turned to John.

"How do we get in?"

The front gate was shut, and after a light investigation by John and I, we discovered that it was also locked. There was a small black pad on a stand beside the driveway that looked like you needed a fob or a card key to get the gate to open. Too bad there was no electricity to make it useful.

"Care to give me a boost?" John said, pointing to the top of the iron gate.

"Looks like you'll get tetanus from those tips," I muttered.

"Just don't drop me," John said.

"How about you pop me over?" I suggested. "I'm smaller."

I really had lost a lot of weight in the last months. I didn't think I had ever been this skinny in my adult life; too many Big Macs to eat back then. John looked from me to the gate with his lips twisted.

"Fine, but just focus on gettin' the gate open, then we'll search the place together."

I nodded and he kneeled down to give me a boost. Carefully, I pulled myself up and lifted a leg in between the pointed tops of the gate. I managed to get up to straddle the gate and then I looked down on the other side. It was a long way down without help. I took a series of short breaths to prepare me for the jump. I lifted my leg over so now they were both on the same side and slid down while holding onto the top of the gate.

The ground was hard and I hissed as my ankles—and foot and calf—burned from the impact. I leaned against the surprisingly solid gate until the stinging stopped. I had forgotten about my other injures.

"You okay?" John asked.

"I'm fine." I peered back through the other side of the gate at the two trucks. Everyone was watching me. Great, nothing like pressure to get a person moving.

Tearing my eyes from the front, I looked around the inside. No vehicles were parked in the small parking lot. There were no infected wandering around the asphalt courtyard either. They must have locked this place up tight after the infection took over. That boded well for us.

There was a small office to the left with frosted and barred windows. As I approached the office door, I noticed a small sticker saying the cashier had no more than fifty bucks on them. *Definitely a homey vibe around here.* With my Beretta pointed straight ahead, I pulled on the handle with my free hand. It didn't open. I scanned the ground around me, my eyes landing on a small patch of green. There were tiny flower beds surrounding the office. All the plants had long since died from neglect but the decorative rocks would prove useful.

I grabbed one that was painted to look like a lady bug and used it to smash the glass by the door handle. The glass shattered and I cleared away the jagged edges with the rock.

"Bailey!" John whispered just loud enough for me to hear him from the front gate.

"I'm fine, just had to break the glass," I whispered back harshly.

Unfortunately, there were still metal bars to get past. I felt around the inside of the door as much as the metal screen would allow. My fingers ghosted past what felt like a deadbolt. I strained as I pushed my fingers to grasp at the latch. After a few failed tries, I finally managed to flip it and the deadbolt retracted. I smiled briefly at my triumph and opened the door.

The broken glass crunched under my feet as I entered. It was dark and dingy inside without the long fluorescent lights to make the tiny room look even more like a place you didn't want to be after dark. There was a pamphlet display in the corner and that was it. No chairs or pictures on the walls. The scratched up counter was a hideous coral color with boot scuffs along the entire bottom. Behind the counter was a closed door, and all the room keys hung on tiny hooks. They still used physical keys here.

I approached the side of the counter where you could access the back and let myself in via lifting up the counter. It banged closed behind me. I held my breath, waiting for something to come rushing to the front. After a few beats, nothing moved or stirred. Tucked away on the employee side of the counter were shelves filled with papers and binder. I quickly tried to sort through them to see if anything popped out about the gate. The only thing that caught my eye was the large black flashlight that looked like the ones police used. The heavy ones that could beat a person in a pinch, if need be. I grabbed it and flicked on the switch. The yellowed beam illuminated the dirty floor.

Turning away from the mess, I aimed the flashlight at the back door. Did I dare open it? It was probably some sort of employee area. There could be something back there that I could use. I swallowed and tried the knob. It was unlocked. The hinges creaked as I pushed the door open. With the flashlight and my gun in the lead, I started inside. The air was stale from being closed up for so long.

It was a tiny room, with a seating area that consisted of a worn couch and mismatched armchair and then a kitchenette off to the side. A skinny door labeled 'bathroom' was immediately off to my right. I slowly opened the door, but nothing was inside. It was about the size of an airplane washroom. I moved onto the kitchenette portion. There was an apartment sized fridge, sink and a hotplate that looked like it came from the seventies. I opened the fridge only to slam it shut again with a gag. Everything inside had gotten way past its expiration date. I breathed through my mouth until the smell cleared.

The tiny worn couch was facing a wall with an old tube television and a cork board plastered with papers. I walked up to the board. One poster outlined the importance of guest privacy. Another one was a procedure for cleaning a room when housekeeping would find a weapon or drugs. *Lovely place.*

My eyes landed on one that was the emergency protocol for the gate not working. *Bingo.* I ripped the sheet down and walked back out of the small room and the office. John was pressed up against the gate. His shoulders sagged when he saw me.

"What took you so long?"

I lifted up the sheet. "Had to find instructions."

According to the paper, there was a latch release that unlocked the gate. I examined the gate until I found the large lever and yanked on it. There was a rusty sound of gears moving. The gate fell slack from the one wall. We grabbed onto the bars and pulled. The gate retracted from the one side and disappeared inside the building along the tracks as it opened.

John jumped back in the truck and led them inside. Once they were parked, we reclosed the gate using the rest of the instructions and locked it back up. I handed the sheet to John. He folded the paper and stuck it in his coat pocket.

"We better keep this safe," he said, patting the outside of the pocket. "Now, did you find any keys?"

"Inside. I figured we should probably scout out the rooms before we start handing out keys," I said.

Chapter 21

I showed John the office and together we grabbed all the room keys. There were twenty in total, all labeled with the room numbers. We didn't need our people spread out until we could secure the area, so no one would be getting their own rooms tonight. I handed a couple of keys to Rose and Henry for them to search, while John and I took the rest to do a quick sweep. People were starting to get to the point where they would sleep anywhere. I knew I was. Hell, I could probably sleep out on the cracked parking lot right about then, even with being a light sleeper.

Other than at the gate, we couldn't see the outside of the motel courtyard. Most people had vacated the vehicles to stretch and were regarding the place with curiosity. A couple of people went up to the pop machine to see if they could shake a few cans loose, but the noise had John telling them to stop.

The sun was starting to come up, orange and pink light reaching over the top of the castle-themed motel. Chloe and Amanda looked dead on their feet with their eyes half closed. Some people were still streaked with blood and soot from Hargrove. Our group looked like the survivors of a bomb blast.

"Clear!" Rose yelled from across the courtyard.

"She needs to be quiet," John muttered.

"I think she only has one setting," I joked, but it was lost on him.

We examined our first room. There was no one inside judging from our quick sweep—we even checked under the beds. There were two of them inside covered in coral and green comforters to match the decor of the office. I waved Chloe, Ethan, and the others over.

"You guys can take this one," I said.

Chloe and Amanda plunked down on the bed by the window, not even bothering to remove their shoes they were so exhausted.

"Where are you goin' to stay?" Ethan asked.

His head was wrapped in white gauze, making his hair spike up in the middle.

"I'll let you know once we get everyone in a room," I said.

"I don't have to stay with them, do I?" Colin asked through a yawn.

"The last thing we need is for people to be spread thinly while we're still checking the place out. Suck it up for one night," I said grouchily.

Colin looked from me to the bed and the bed won the contest for his attention as he wandered over to it and collapsed. I gave Ethan a curt nod and continued on with John to inspect the other rooms that we had keys for.

All rooms were clear. There wasn't a soul staying at the motel. I had a feeling this was more to do with the cheap atmosphere than the infection. Business probably wasn't good beforehand. We stuffed four people in each room with double beds to make sure we were easily accessed should something come up.

Lucas was still our prisoner at the moment so I volunteered to share a room with him. John said he would be staying with us too, and then Rose added her name to the rooming list. This was going to be a fun day of trying to sleep. Leo was mad that he had ended up with Henry and two others in the room beside us. He also didn't appreciate that I made him play messenger boy by going to tell Ethan which room I was in.

The supplies were packed into our room so that we could monitor the usage. We fed everyone before they went to sleep and it made a noticeable dent in the food we had managed to scrounge up during the evacuation. It would maybe feed the twenty mouths for one more day in total—two if we really rationed.

I mentioned this to John.

"We'll worry 'bout that once we've had some sleep," he said.

I pulled back the covers to examine the sheets.

"Seriously? That's the last of our problem," Rose said jumping into the bed, forcing the blanket out of my hand.

I scowled, but gave up on my inspection. She was right. Sleep trumped clean. We had locked the doors and Lucas was already under the blanket, snoring lightly. I pulled off my shoes and laid down. My eyes closed and sleep came surprisingly easy.

I was stiff when I woke up. I was still facing the same direction I had been when I went to bed and in the same position. Everything cracked when I rolled onto my back. Rose was gone, but the other bed was still full. I heard rustling in the washroom and a flush.

"Whoa, it works." I heard Rose say.

She walked back to the bed and noticed that I was awake. "If you need to use the toilet, you gotta get some water first."

I cleared my throat. "How's it still working?"

"You don't need power to run toilets that don't flush anythin' upwards. It runs on a syphonin' action, but you need to refill the back of the tank everythin' before you push the lever," she explained.

"You sure know a lot about toilets." I laughed. I don't know why that was funny. Toilet humor wasn't supposed to be funny past eight years old. I blamed it on being tired.

She glowered at me. "You kids these days don't know how anythin' works." She crawled in bed, her back turned away from me as she muttered about ignorant kids.

I bit my lip to refrain from laughing more. Now, how would we get that much water? I gave up on my wonderings as I fell back sleep.

John woke me up a few hours later. "Bailey, you gotta get up."

My eyes flew open, and then I groaned. "I feel like a bus hit me."

"We *all* feel like that," Rose said from her perch on one of the chairs in the corner. Lucas was looking bored in the other chair across from her. She was leaning over the round table looking at some papers.

I ignored her and asked John, "What time is it?"

"Somewhere 'round three in the afternoon."

I grumbled and pulled myself out of bed. John handed me a granola bar and an opened water bottle.

"I'm not hungry right now," I said, pushing the offerings away.

I was still feeling sleepy and a bit disoriented from the night before. *Zoe's missing.* My brain wasn't going to let me forget; not that I wanted to. I just didn't want to think of all the horrible things that could be happening to her right now. My stomach was starting to go from indifferent to upset as I thought about my best friend. If only I had done something different in the clubhouse. If I had just been able to get off a shot before I had been smacked in the head, maybe I could have saved her from being taken.

"You okay?" John asked, dropping to a knee in front of me. He placed a hand on my forehead. "Do you feel nauseous? You were whacked in the head pretty good yesterday."

"Don't throw up in the bed," Rose added, not even looking up from the table.

I clenched my hands in my lap. "I'm fine," I said curtly.

John frowned and shoved the water bottle at me again. "Just take a sip at least."

Grudgingly, I took the bottle from him and had a small drink. I picked up the granola bar John had set on the bed and tried nibbling it.

"You need to get that down, we got some big plans today," Rose said, finally looking up from her papers.

"You don't even know if it'll work. I ain't doin' shit until you prove it to me," Lucas said.

Rose glowered at him. "As long as you don't go stompin' 'round, it'll work."

"What are you talking about?" I asked. I looked to John for an answer.

"For the record, I don't like Rose's plan, but if it works, we could have more food by the end of the night," John said, avoiding my eyes, "And Bailey's only goin' if you can prove it works like Lucas said." John pointed at Rose for the last part.

"You're a bunch of wussies," Rose muttered. "Fine. Let's gear up and head out, then I'll show you."

"Okay, I'm even more confused," I said.

"Rose here thinks immune people can move among the infected without bein' attacked by 'em," John said, sounding completely unconvinced.

"It's true," Rose said with conviction. "I'll show you all."

She got up, grabbing one of the papers on the table with her. It was a map. Rose stormed out of the room, leaving us to squint into the midday light after she left the door open.

"You think it'll work?" I asked.

If she was right, I could move among the infected. All the times the infected passed me over for someone else sprang to mind. Like when I was fighting off the horde with Zoe. Or when I was trapped in the basement where Riley had found me. The infected chained to the wall stopped coming after me once I had stopped moving around, and then went for Riley's partner the minute they were in range. It was starting to add weight to Rose's claim. But then again, there were infinitely more times where I had been running for my life while infected chased me. I wasn't convinced. John was right; she would have to demonstrate first.

I went to use the bathroom, then stopped. "Did you guys find any water for the tanks?"

"Yeah, the ice machine had lots of water. There's a bucket of water in the bathroom for you to fill the tank," Johns said.

Thankful that they had found water, I used the bathroom and then met the others back outside. Most people were out in the courtyard talking. Some were still in their rooms with the doors wide open so we could see them. Rose was jamming some rounds into her rifle. Henry was shooting her weird looks, but let her continue. The guns and ammo bags were open in the middle of the group. As I approached, John handed me a box of 9mm.

"Load up your Beretta."

I took the box from him. It was pretty light.

I filled up my magazine and pocketed another fifteen rounds. I could really use a spare magazine like John had for his automatic rifle.

"I ain't goin' out there without a weapon." Lucas crossed his arms.

John reached down into the pile and handed Lucas a crowbar. "Here."

Lucas yanked it from John's grasp with a glare. He knew we weren't going to give him a gun, but a melee weapon was better than no weapon. Leo had joined us with his shotgun already swung over his shoulder.

"You're coming too?" I asked.

"It's only the immune going, right?" Leo looked around, confused.

"Yes, ignore her. She doesn't know what's goin' on," Rose said.

"Because no one will fully explain anything," I growled.

"Immune people can move among the infected as long as they stay quiet and slow—very slow," Rose said slowly.

"So you keep sayin'," Lucas said.

"It's true," Leo said and we all looked at him. He squirmed under the attention. "I've seen it."

"At the hospital they sure didn't seem to leave us alone," I said.

"That's 'cause you didn't listen, kid," Rose said sharply. She started to tap her foot on the ground, the rubber sole of her shoe slapping against the asphalt. "If you had just held still while those infected were in the room with you, they would have left you alone!"

Rose's ominous words from my first morning at the hospital came back to me. *"Don't move, don't breathe, and the dead won't bother you."*

Was she really right?

"Then how'd you get so injured?" Lucas said, motioning to her ribcage.

Rose's foot tapping stopped and she looked him dead in the eyes. "These weren't from the infected."

I swallowed. Lucas had the good sense to not press her anymore. It was clear what she was saying. They had used her for a live game of operation instead of throwing her to the infected. John looked at me, a question in his eyes. I shook my head. They hadn't done that to me. I hadn't been there long enough to endure that kind of torture. A sliver of pity ran through me for Rose. She may have been bad tempered and all around a pain to be near, but now I couldn't hold it against her. She'd been through some truly terrible things.

I stuffed my Beretta into the back of my pants. "All right then, show us."

Rose didn't say anything as she stormed over to the gate, expecting us to follow, and we did. Two infected had squished themselves up against the gate, their grabbing hands reaching inside. Their rasping noises and motions got more intense as the whole group approached them. John unsheathed his large hunting knife and stabbed them one at a time through the eye sockets. There was a wet suctioning sound as John removed the blade from each skull.

We opened the gate and moved the bodies to the ditch by the road. They would have to be dealt with later as the smell of rot would soon start. John wiped off the knife on the shirt of one of the infected and then handed it to me with the sheath.

"In case you can't afford to shoot off a gun."

I took the knife and looped the sheath on my belt. "Thank you."

"If this works, you'll be able to get into one of these warehouses and scrounge up some food," John said, "but I don't like the idea of you bein' out there with just them."

"I'll be fine," I said, but I wasn't so sure. It wasn't like we had time to do test runs based on Rose's theory.

John ran his fingers along the rim of his hat before taking it off. He raked his hand through his hair and placed the cowboy hat back on his head. "Maybe I should go with you guys."

"You're not immune," I said.

"I might be. Not like I've ever been bit before," John said.

I frowned. "Well, I don't want you to have to find out the hard way. Plus, you need to stay here and hold down the castle while we're gone. I can dub you Sir John before I go if you'd like."

John gave me a tight, brief smile. He wasn't beyond humoring me at the moment. He was worried about letting me go without him.

"Let's just see how this goes with Rose first."

We closed the gate as tight to the wall as we could without locking it in case we needed to make a quick entrance while Rose gave us her demonstration. We followed her across the street to one of the warehouse yards. There were a few infected moseying about, but nothing that we couldn't handle.

Rose motioned for us to stay where we were as she silently crept up to them. They started toward her once they saw her movement. Immune or not, they still picked up on movement. Two infected got within a very uncomfortable distance to her. She stopped moving and held very still, barely breathing. I found I was holding in my own breath as I watched the scene before me.

They slowed down as they approached Rose. One immediately turned and went in the direction opposite of her, while the other sidled up beside her. The infected did some kind of sniffing movement, its arm close enough to Rose that it rubbed up against her. I didn't know how she managed to hold so still. My first instinct was to run every time I got near an infected.

The infected opened its mouth and I pulled out my Beretta. Leo put his hand on my gun, slowly pushing down on it while putting a finger in front of his closed lips. He had more faith in this idea than I did. The clack of teeth reached us as the infected closed its mouth and pushed past Rose, ignoring her completely. He wandered on to the other side of the warehouse lawn.

John and I shared a look. This was promising, but not conclusive. Rose started to move very slowly back to us. The infected were facing away from her, so they didn't come back after her.

"See?" Rose said, looking very much full of herself.

"I told you it would work," Leo said with a smile of his own. It wasn't as big as the one on Rose's face though.

"The dead thing still went after her," Lucas pointed out.

"Can't help that. They're attracted to movement and noise. As long as you stay still when they get near and don't make any loud noises to get them riled up, you'll be fine," Rose said.

"So you're sayin' we have to move as slow as you did and still stop?" Lucas scoffed. "It'll take us a day and a half just to get inside a damn buildin'."

"You got any other bright ideas?" Rose said with her hand on her hip.

"What about a distraction?" I suggested.

"Like what?" John asked.

"I don't know. Something that moves or makes noise—but not too much noise. Just enough to get the attention of the nearest infected," I said.

Too bad we didn't have one of those wacky tube men they used at car dealerships. That would get all the infected's attention.

"We found a little mower in the storage room like an hour ago," Leo said. "Looked pretty old though."

"Show us," I said.

We walked back into the castle motel and they closed up the gate behind us. Chloe met up with us, Amanda close on her heels.

"Is it true you can walk among the infected?" she asked.

"Uh, yes and no," I answered cautiously. One demonstration hardly proved anything. For all I knew, Rose stunk so bad up close that the infected were scared off.

"What's that mean?"

"It means that they still come after you if you're moving, but it looks like they have no interest in us once we stand still," I said.

"That's good, right?"

"I guess."

Leo led us to the maintenance storage room, judging from the worn sign on the front. The door hadn't even been locked. It was a skinny, but long room. At the back there was a red mower that had seen better days. Leo snaked in and around the other equipment and brought the mower out.

"At least it runs on gas; that's somethin'," Rose said.

"We willing to waste that much gas?" I asked.

"It shouldn't take very much. We only need it to last long enough for us to get into a warehouse," Rose said.

"At that snail pace you were goin', a tank won't get us far," Lucas said.

"It doesn't need to keep going. It just needs to get their attention and get them moving toward it," I said.

I don't know if I was trying to convince the others or myself of this crazy plan. I still wasn't sure that I could handle being groped by an infected without screaming and running away.

"How are you goin' to bring back food?" Chloe asked.

Leave it to the kid to point out the flaw in our plan. If we were going on foot to avoid the infected chasing after a noisy vehicle, then we had to bring back the food on foot.

"Round up as many bags as you can find," I instructed.

Within ten minutes, four backpacks and duffle bags had been emptied—one for each of us. The little tank for the mower had also been filled with gas. In one of the courtyard corners away from the front gate, John and Lucas worked on getting the lawnmower working. They had to tinker with it for a bit, but in the end they got the engine to come to life. They quickly shut it down afterwards.

I grabbed one of the empty backpacks and stuffed the flashlight I had found in the motel office inside, then tossed the pack on. Between the four of us—Rose, Leo, Lucas, and I—we could bring back a decent amount of food, but not near enough to feed twenty people for any length of time. While the point of our run was food, it was also a trial run. If this went bad, then we would have to come up with something else. I just wanted to avoid attracting the attention of the infected. This motel was not fortified like Hargrove had been, and it wouldn't stand a chance against a barrage of infected. So we needed our runs to attract as little attention as possible.

If need be, we planned to scout out whatever warehouse we ended up at for a cube van or truck to bring back a larger scale of supplies. It would risk getting attention from the infected though, so it was a 'Plan-B' of sorts. I just prayed that Rose's idea worked and that I didn't get any more digits bitten off in the process.

Chapter 22

"You ready?" Rose asked us.

We were standing at the front gate, waiting to leave. Most survivors had come out to wish us luck on our run. It just made me that much more uneasy. Ethan had wandered out with Crystal dogging him the whole way to the front gate. The mercenary had hit him pretty hard on the skull; Crystal even guessed that they may have cracked it. His balance was still off and he had some pretty bad sensitivity to light. He was speaking clearly, though. Crystal said that was a good sign because if he had internal bleeding it would have created pressure on his lobes and that usually affected speech. Although, nothing was certain without real doctors or exam equipment. All we could do was hope that he didn't have any permanent damage.

Chloe was beside Ethan, keeping a stern eye on him. Not that her ten-year-old frame could do much to stop Ethan's significantly larger stature from hitting the ground should he fall over.

"Be careful out there," Ethan said. "I wish I could help or do somethin'." He scowled as he touched the gauze wrapped around his head.

"You'd be a liability. Injured or not, you ain't immune," Rose said, ever tactfully.

I took a breath through my nose. "Just listen to Crystal, okay? I don't want to come back and find you a drooling mess."

Ethan gave me a small smile. "Bring back some of those strawberry frosted Pop-Tarts, yeah?"

"They grew on you, did they?" I said, thinking back to the time we had raided a Wal-Mart all those months ago. I had squealed I'd been so excited to find those. "I'll see what I can do."

Henry and Sheri opened the gate for us to slip through. John gave me one last hug before they locked the gate up. I turned from the others' pensive faces to the street. Rose was already at the other end of the short side street leading to the castle motel, waving impatiently at us.

We're off to see the wizard...

I must've looked ridiculous trying to hold back my laughter with my bottom lip sucked into my mouth and my top teeth biting down. Leo gave me a strange look as I passed him. I just looked straight ahead, not wanting to bother explaining my hysteria. Lucas paid me no mind as he was already on full alert mode. His head was whipping back and forth, scouting for infected as he pushed the dead lawnmower. He was going to make himself dizzy if he kept that up.

No one talked as we strode down the main street. We were trusting Rose to lead us. The map she had wasn't specifically for this area, but it did focus on the eastern part of New Orleans. If we got cut off and couldn't come back the way we came, Rose should be able to direct us to a different route with the map.

We passed by a bunch of warehouses but nothing stood out specifically as a food company. Some of the buildings were rusting; most were just dirty. An infected wearing a trucker's hat started toward us, stumbling to get from the ditch onto the actual street. Lucas left the lawnmower to run up to the infected and whack it in the head with his crowbar. There was a metallic dinging sound and the infected dropped to the ground, sliding back into the overgrown ditch.

"There," Rose hissed while pointing to a warehouse.

The decrepit sign was missing a few letters but the last word clearly meant to say, "Grocer." We had found our food warehouse. Some of the loading bays even still had big rigs backed into them. A chain-link fence was separating the warehouse yard from the others beside it but it didn't go all the way around, so we were able to just walk right in. Except for the infected standing guard.

"Slow and quiet," Rose said, leading the glacially slow charge.

We basically tiptoed into the yard. It was a bit harder for Lucas since he was pushing our bait. The infected didn't seem to notice us at first, then they eventually caught on that we were moving. They started toward us from all directions. My muscles started to twitch and my mouth went dry as Rose gave us the signal to hold still. We let the infected approach as we stood still like misplaced statues. I tried to control my breathing but it was hard when my heart started to beat rapidly. Lucas went to pull on the engine cord of the mower, but Rose quietly said, "Not yet. Last resort."

They reached Rose first. She didn't even blink. If the infected had any ability to show emotion, it would have been confusion. They circled Rose as their decrepit heads moved from side to side. I heard a crack and one infected's head stayed crooked to the side. It was the most decayed of the group, its nose sunken in, and the left side of its face sagged, drooping the eye off to the side. They did seem like they were continuing to decay once they turned. Maybe they would eventually get to a point where they were so decayed that they just dropped. This was a hopeful thought: extinction of the infected.

I was so lost in thought—a defense mechanism, perhaps—that I barely noticed that the infected had moved on from Rose to the rest of us. They wandered in between our frozen statures, seeming to size us up and down. The one with the crooked head chose me to inspect. *Don't you dare laugh.* I looked straight ahead with my lips tight, keeping the infected in my peripheral vision. It rasped right beside me and I nearly jumped out of my skin as its arm brushed against my side. I was breathing through my nose, but that was quickly aborted as the smell of rot consumed me. This one seemed to have been dead for quite a while. My eyes were threatening to water from the smell.

Stay still. The infected moved from my side to directly in front of me. I desperately wanted to shove it over and stab it with the knife, but any movement would wreck our plan. It got dangerously close to my face. I took a discrete inhalation of air, then held my breath. *One, two, three.* The infected just continued to stare at me as my lungful of air depleted. *Eight, nine, ten.* My face was going to turn purple soon. The breath I had sucked in wasn't as big as it could have been since I was trying to remain quiet. *Fourteen, fifteen, sixteen.*

"Fuck this," Lucas said.

He ran straight for the side of the building, abandoning the mower, not even bothering to turn it on. I sucked in as much air as my body would allow when the crooked infected took off toward Lucas. They all had started going after him, leaving the rest of us alone.

"That dumb shit," Rose muttered. "Well, at least he got 'em off of us. Let's keep movin'."

"What about Lucas?" I asked through a cough. My lungs were burning from the lack of oxygen.

"He made his choice. 'Sides, if he's as tough as he acts, he should be able to take care of 'em."

"What about the lawnmower?" Leo asked, his priorities obviously straight. I could almost hear what he was thinking: *we went to the trouble of bringing it, might as well use it.*

"We might need it when we leave later, so don't turn it on," Rose said.

I bit my lip. Just leaving Lucas to fend for himself felt wrong, even if he was a douchebag. Rose didn't leave me anymore time to contemplate right and wrong as she bolted through the rest of the yard. With no infected, we could afford to move fast. Leo looked at me and jerked his head toward the warehouse, silently telling me to get a move on. With one last look at the side of the building where Lucas had disappeared, I started after the other two.

We tried the front door but it was locked, and there was no way we'd be able to move one of the heavy metal bay doors up. Rose went to the nearest truck first, then to the one after that.

"Come here," she hissed from out of sight.

Leo and I took off after her and found her at the end of a big rig backed into one of the last bays.

"This guy didn't know how to back in here properly."

She pointed to the space between the back and the bay. Sure enough, there was enough room so that we could see into the warehouse. It was dark for the most part.

"Shit, we don't have any flashlights," Rose said.

"I brought one," I said.

I turned around and Rose reached into my backpack. She clicked on the large flashlight and pointed it inside the warehouse.

"I don't see—" Rose flew backwards into us, knocking an unprepared Leo onto the asphalt.

Chapter 23

My ears picked up on the rasping of an infected before I saw it. It sounded like it was trying to clear out a hairball. A handless stump was pushed through the opening, then the head followed. The infected was wearing a crossing-guard style vest which had gotten snagged on the outside of the truck. It was stuck half inside, half outside of the warehouse, continually reaching for us with its ghosted hand.

"Damn thing scared the shit outta me!" Rose growled with a hand over her heart.

I guess she didn't like things jumping out at her. She would have been terrible to go to a Halloween haunted house with. Rose lifted the flashlight to bash the infected's head in but I grabbed her wrist.

"You'll wreck our only light source," I hissed.

I pushed her aside and removed the hunting knife from the sheath on my belt. It couldn't do much with its handless arm, so I easily dodged the stump and brought my knife down on its head. It went limp, still hanging in the spot we needed to go through. Together the three of us tugged at the body. The sound of the vest ripping urged us on until we cleared the infected completely. We dropped it to the ground and Rose pushed the flashlight at me.

"You first."

"How brave of you."

We glared at each other until Leo grabbed the flashlight from Rose. "Fine, I'll do it."

Rose glared at me like it was my fault before turning to watch Leo investigate. He shone the light inside, his shoulders rigid. I think he expected more infected to pop out. When none did, he tested the waters by squeezing through the tight spot and hoisted himself up into the bay. From the outside I could see the beam of the flashlight cross back and forth. After a few seconds, he stuck his head back outside.

"All clear."

"Chickens first," I said motioning to the opening.

Rose flipped me off and easily slunk through the opening. She was pretty tiny in that regard. I went next and Leo helped me up into the dark warehouse. A sliver of light came from the opening we had just come through, but most of what we could see was a result of the lonely flashlight. I looked back to see the door on the back of the truck open. It looked like they had started loading pallets, but gave up halfway through. There was still a dolly inside with a single box left to unload.

"Stay close," Leo instructed.

My lips quirked at the authoritative tone of his voice. It sounded like a kid trying to play grown up. We followed right behind him as we ventured further into the warehouse. The beam showed us the rows and rows of wrapped pallets, and then, in the distance, some metal shelves stacked as high as the ceiling. *Well, I hope nothing good is on the high shelves.* There was no way we could reach that stuff without some sort of jack.

"Shine the light over here," I said.

Using the beam of light to see what I was doing, I cut open the shrink wrap on the pallet with my hunting knife. The plastic squeaked as I sawed. I unwrapped the pallet: a hundred boxes of instant oatmeal stared back at us.

"Nice," Leo said.

"How we going to cook 'em?" Rose asked.

"This is one of those grocery stores that sells everything," Leo said. "We should be able to find a kettle."

"And plug it into what?" I asked.

He made a face. "They probably carry emergency batteries too."

I wasn't familiar with this store, as it wasn't one we had in Canada, so I took Leo's word for it.

"How are we supposed to carry it all back?" Rose asked.

"I'll carry the battery," Leo said.

"If we find one," I added.

"How 'bout we stick to immediately edible foods? We can come back for the rest after," Rose said.

"So basically that leaves us granola bars and salad dressing," I groused. I was so sick and tired of eating granola bars.

"We could try and take one of those trucks outside," Leo suggested.

"I thought the whole point of this trip was to try and make as little noise as possible as we grabbed enough food for the next few days?" I asked. "Isn't that why only we went?" I motioned between the three of us.

"We can turn on the mower when we leave," Leo said.

"I'm pretty sure the noise from a big rig trumps a little mower engine," I said.

"We'll come back after for the truck and supplies," Rose said. "Today is not for the big shoppin' haul, just a small one. Now let's stop debatin' this and get a move on."

We agreed to put a hold on our conversation as we continued through the valley of pallets. I cut a few here and there, most filled with dried goods. We'd found one full of cereal. *Froot Loops for me tonight!* The next one I tried was of course full of granola bars. I made a face as I pictured me eating another one of those dry lumps. I was even growing to hate the ones filled with chocolate chips.

"Shit!" Leo tripped and fell to the ground, the flashlight bouncing off a pallet.

Everything went dark. Rose stumbled to help Leo up as I went in search of the flashlight, praying it wasn't broken. I sheathed my knife, then got down on my hands and knees to feel for our fallen torch. My fingers hit the metal tube, rolling it further away from me. I swore and went after it. As I was feeling around, my hand landed on something far more substantial than the flashlight. It was a leg.

I jerked my hand away, desperately reaching for my knife. By the time I had gotten the knife free, my brain registered that the leg hadn't moved, nor was there any sound of an infected. I swallowed and crawled back over to the leg. Grimacing, I continued to pat the ground. The flashlight had rolled right up against the appendage. I grabbed it and turned the switch on and off. Nothing. I knocked it gently against the palm of my hand and the light flickered, then went off again. I tried it again and the beam finally came back on. I pointed it toward the leg.

It was wearing a beige work boot. I moved the ray of light up the leg to find that there was no body attached to it—it was just a severed leg. I shot to my feet and backed away from the limb. Keeping my eyes on the severed limb, I slowly walked backwards toward Leo and Rose. When I reached then, I turned to shine the light on them.

"You okay?" I asked like I hadn't just, you know, seen a single human leg.

"He tripped over an arm," Rose said pointing to the ground.

Indeed, there was a severed arm on the ground. The bloody stump stuck out the end of the ripped shirt.

"I think I found his leg over there." I hefted my thumb back the way I came. "Careful you don't trip on it." I carefully slid the knife back into its sheath.

"Why the hell are there body parts lying around?" Leo asked angrily as he rubbed the back of his neck. Poor guy must've been embarrassed that he'd tripped over it.

I held the flashlight out for him; he eyed it, then looked at me. With a nod, he took it back and resumed his spot in the lead. Thankfully there were no more random body parts lying

around. We got past all the pallets and hit the shelved goods.
Our heads craned to look up to the top.

Rose let out a low whistle. "No way we can reach those."

"Can you not whistle?" I asked.

So she whistled again with a smirk on her face, which was
actually kind of impressive because that was a hard thing to
manage.

"Get attacked then," I said.

I pushed past them and wandered down the first aisle. Leo
positioned the flashlight on one of the pallets so the beam
illuminated the aisle. It wasn't that bright, but it was enough
that I could squint and read the products on the shelves. Most
of the boxes on the lower shelves were unwrapped; the higher
shelves had the rest of the shrink wrapped pallets. We got to
work looking for any food that required very little prep. My
eyes landed on a box of condensed milk and I smiled. *Milk to go
with my cereal tonight.* I pulled off my backpack and loaded in
half a dozen of the small cans. When I put it back on I realized
how heavy they were. Maybe I could goad Leo into carrying my
bag back.

Leo and Rose were still at the front of the aisle so I opted to
move further down to cover more ground. They were slow.
The boxes at the end were filled with trail mix. Somehow that
was still better than granola bars. I cracked open a box and
pulled out all the bags of mixed nuts that I could. I added them
to my already heavy backpack, hoping that it didn't rip.
Leaving my backpack on the ground, I reached for another box
to open.

I heard slow footsteps come from around the aisle corner. I
yanked myself from the boxes to see an infected wearing the
full warehouse uniform—he even still had a hardhat on. I
fumbled for my sheathed knife, but the infected didn't give me
time. It came at me so I backed up. My foot connected with my
massive backpack and I fell backwards, off balance. My arms

flailed as I hit the ground. The thing wasted no time in diving at me. In the back of my mind, my brain was telling me to stay still. In the lizard part of my brain, it was telling me to fight. The latter won.

As the infected fell upon me, I struggled to reach for my knife. I had only managed to get it halfway out before I fell. Using one hand to hold off the infected, I wiggled the knife free, instantly bringing it down on the infected's head. The knife bounced uselessly off of the hardhat, slipping from my grip as it veered off to the side. I heard it clang to the ground. *Where the hell are the others?* I didn't dare scream for fear of calling the rest of the infected right to us.

The infected *tore* at the stomach area of my shirt. It managed to get a mouthful of fabric, ripping it away like a shark would a fish. I used both arms to try and push it off, but it had me in a terrible position for deadlifting something. I should start doing reps if we ever found a gym.

I pushed again and the thing was flung back. For a brief second, I thought I had obtained superpowers. Then I saw Lucas bashing the infected with his crowbar like a certain super villain. When he was done, Lucas turned back to me and offered a hand. I took it and he helped me to my feet. He winced as he helped me up. *I wasn't that heavy!* I reached back down for my hunting knife, ignoring my wounded ego.

"Thank you," I said.

Lucas just grunted. *Me cave man.*

I looked down at myself to survey the damage. The infected had ripped away most of the bottom of my shirt. Never in my life had I worn a belly shirt before. Now that I had lost weight, it looked rather good.

"It only get your shirt?" Lucas asked, bringing me out of my self-absorbed thoughts.

"Yeah," I said. "I hope they sell shirts here too."

Despite my vain thoughts, I was still not wanting to go around wearing half a shirt. And this was the only shirt I currently owned.

"They sell everythin'," Lucas said.

I finally noticed that there was more light. Lucas had picked up a lantern from the floor and was holding it up. His eyes dropped down to my bare skin and I barely resisted the urge to cross my arms over my torso. It reminded me of the time he'd looked me over in the hospital when I first met him. Like hell I was going to run away with my tail between my legs this time.

"Like what you see?" I asked.

Lucas's eyes popped up to my face with a hint of a smile—or a smirk. It was hard to tell with him. I was starting to sound like Zoe. *Zoe.* At the thought of her name my heart sank with guilt. We were wasting precious time foraging for food, but we needed food to have the strength to do what was coming next.

"There's an aisle of clothin' two down from here," Lucas said. "And a pallet of battery powered lanterns by the door I came through." He held up the one in his hand as if I had no idea what a lantern was. I wasn't that young.

"What happened?" Leo asked, suddenly right beside us. How convenient.

"You didn't hear me getting attacked?" I asked with venom in my voice.

"Didn't hear nothin'," Rose said, then looked at Lucas. "Until you started hittin' the ground with your crowbar."

I picked up my backpack without a word, then stormed away from them, trying to control my anger. "Show me where the clothes are," I commanded Lucas.

He didn't even hesitate as he followed after me with the camping lantern. "You're goin' the wrong way."

I stopped and swiveled on my heel, then stormed in the other direction. *Stupid Rose and Leo. Like hell they hadn't heard anything.* I was pissed. Lucas took the lead and turned two aisles down from where we were. The sign tacked onto the metal shelf said that clothes were indeed down here. Lucas held the lantern in front of him, and it swayed back and forth as we walked through the aisle. It added an extra layer of creepy, like we were in a horror movie walking through a graveyard. I scanned the aisle, my eyes not really reading anything because I was so angry at the other two. I closed my eyes and took a deep breath. I was fine; that was all that mattered. And it was thanks to Lucas. *How did he get in here?*

I turned to Lucas. "How did you get inside?"

"There's an employee side door that was unlocked," he said.

"What about the infected that were chasing you?"

"I took 'em out."

I looked at his clothes. They were stained with brownish blood and skin. His shirt held a rather large pool of blood around the shoulder area.

"Looks like you could use some new clothes as well."

He nodded and placed the lantern down. "Start lookin' at the closest boxes. Don't wander off."

I couldn't tell if that was a jab at me or not. I decided to let it pass—I already had enough to be mad about. Starting with the nearest pallet on the ground, I opened a large box. It was the size of the cardboard boxes grocery stores used for large amounts of produce. Inside was a bunch of plain white shirts. I rifled through, looking for something in my size. I found a tank top that would fit. I looked over my shoulder to see that Lucas was currently engrossed in sorting through a box on the other side of the aisle. Quickly, I set down my backpack and tossed off the ripped shirt, then yanked the clean tank top on. It was a spandex blend, but didn't cling too tight.

"You always undress in front of people you barely know?" Lucas asked.

I could feel a tinge of red spread across my cheeks. Damn, I had thought he was looking the other way.

"Common courtesy dictates that you *look away* when someone changes," I said, proud that my embarrassment didn't leak into my voice.

"I heard the cans clang in your backpack. Thought you hit the ground again." There was definitely a smirk on his face this time.

You're an adult, Bailey. Not a teen anymore. I shrugged indifferently. "Nothing I'm sure you haven't seen before—unless you're not into girls."

Instead of wiping the smirk off of his face, my comment made him grin wider. "If that's what you gotta tell yourself."

I narrowed my eyes; I was pretty sure he'd won this round. With a huff, I returned to my big box of shirts and grabbed a few more in my size. I tended to go through a lot of clothes. As I rolled up the shirts and shoved them into the last remaining space in my backpack, I heard Lucas disrobing and putting on something new. I resisted the urge to turn around and get my revenge, lest he misinterpret my intention.

I skimmed the rest of the boxes. There were tons of generic clothing, enough for everyone back at the motel, but there was no way we would be able to carry it all. Unless we listened to Leo and brought back one of those big trucks with us.

"Come on," Lucas said.

He was wearing a completely clean new outfit. We walked down the rest of the aisle and spotted Leo and Rose sitting on a pallet.

"Ya done?" she asked.

"Are you?" I countered.

"Our bags are full," Leo said. "But I still think we should take back a truck."

"Too much noise," Rose reiterated.

"I spotted a smaller delivery van 'round the side," Lucas said.

"How big?" Leo asked.

"'Bout the size of a small cube van," Lucas said. "I have no idea if it works or not."

We looked at one another as we felt the idea out. The point of this trip had been to stay on foot and grab what we could. But this might also be our only chance to get such a large haul. We wouldn't have to worry about doing another run for a long time if we did bring back a van full.

"Fine," Rose spoke first. "Show us."

Lucas led the way to the side of the warehouse. We passed by two fallen infected with their heads bashed in. Lucas's work, I presumed.

"There are the lanterns." Lucas pointed to a stack of them, then opened the side door a sliver. He opened it further and snuck outside with us quick on his heels.

The daylight assaulted my eyes, forcing me to look down until my eyes adjusted. Damn, that warehouse had been dark. As I was looking at the ground, my eyes moved along the trail of dead infected that led to the front of the yard. How had Lucas taken out that many and been okay? I voiced my question out loud.

Lucas shrugged. "Got a little bite or two. Surprised you didn't see when I changed."

If this were a teen drama, this was the part where the onlookers would be on their phones, immediately posting this on social media and blowing everything out of proportion. Instead, Rose just smirked and Leo looked horrified. He was no fan of Ethan, but he was even less a fan of Lucas.

I shot Lucas a glare for purposely stirring up shit. I was really regretting coming on this run.

"I'm sorry I bothered to ask. Just show us the damn van," I gritted.

We walked to the van in absolute silence. It was unnerving. The van was blocked the rest of the way to the back of the warehouse, like they had parked there in a rush. Lucas tried the door handle and it opened.

"Are the keys in there?" Leo asked.

Lucas hopped into the cab and flashed us a thumbs-up. He turned the keys in the ignition, but the engine didn't start. He tried a few more times and nothing changed.

"Shit, the battery must be dead. The idiot didn't have the ignition turned off all the way," Lucas said as he climbed out of the truck.

He opened the hood and looked at the van's battery.

"If only we were at one of those big box store warehouses ..." Rose muttered.

No one found her funny. We went back inside, each grabbing our very own lantern. Lucas and Leo went off in search of a car battery, while Rose and I waited by the door. There was no point in starting to haul the supplies over until we for sure had the truck running.

"So, what was that Lucas said back there?" Rose said nonchalantly.

I sighed. "He watched me change my shirt like a pervert, that's all."

"And you didn't even peek at him?"

"Nope."

"Right ..."

If someone put a gun to my head and forced me to tell them one good quality Rose had, I'd be dead.

"I think we have more important things to worry about, yeah?" I said.

Rose snorted. "Gotta entertain ourselves where we can. How do you think people came out of that hospital with their minds intact?"

I could kind of see her point—I just didn't like being the "entertainment."

The guys saved me from discussing this further when they returned with a battery under each of their arms.

"Why so many?" I asked.

"They didn't have the exact one in the van on the shelves. One of these are goin' to have to do," Lucas said.

I held the door open for them since their hands were full. Lucas got to work removing the dead battery and tried placing in one of the batteries they had found. The first one wouldn't even get in, but the second one he tried fit. He fiddled with the cables, then climbed in the cab to try the engine. It clunked a few times, then came to life.

"Only got half a tank," Lucas said after he had turned off the van.

"That'll be more than enough," Rose said. "Now let's get to work."

We pulled up the roller door on the back of the van. It was empty. I put my backpack down inside, my back thanking me for the relief. I found a large rock near the back of the warehouse where the cube van was parked and used it to hold open the door while we loaded stuff up.

Once inside, we took off like a university student with an essay due in two hours. I found a dolly to use, which made my trips quicker, and hung my lantern on one of the handles. I started with the cereal pallet, then moved down the aisles. Leo passed by me with an emergency battery in each hand. He eyed my dolly enviously.

I made my way to the back to the clothes aisle. Finding an appropriate sized box was hard; everything was in bulk. I spotted the clothes that Lucas and I had littered on the ground. His heap of clothes was pretty bloody. Just how injured was he?

In the next aisle over I heard a large crash and a string of expletives. I was willing to bet that was Mr. Tough Guy.

Chapter 24

Sure enough, it was Lucas. I had abandoned my dolly to investigate, but brought the lantern with me. Lucas was on the ground surrounded by a bunch of fallen boxes, some leaking fluid onto the floor. I sniffed as I got closer. Beer.

"Really? Alcohol is a necessity?" I said.

He looked at me from the floor. His face was scrunched up in pain and I spotted a fresh stain of blood on his previously new shirt.

"My damn arm gave out," he growled.

He started prodding at the area where the blood was coming from.

"Wait here," I said, running back toward the side entrance.

I had spotted a first aid kit fastened to the wall by the door when Rose and I were waiting around for the guys to return with a battery. It was just a simple metal box on the wall with a red cross on it. I pulled at it but it wouldn't come off. I lifted it upwards and strained. The box came off with a yank, almost throwing me off balance. I ran back to find that Lucas had propped himself up against the shelf, a bottle of beer already at his mouth.

I wanted to run my hands down my face, but the box in my hands was preventing me from it. This had to be the worst group to go on a run with. Pain in the asses, the lot of them.

"I still can't get over the fact that they sell alcohol at grocery stores in America," I said as I approached Lucas.

He stopped sucking down the bottle's contents. "They don't do that in Canada?"

"Not in any province that I've been to."

"Province?"

"Yes, they're on the map and everything," I said sarcastically.

He glared at me, then winced. I kneeled beside him and put down the box, flipping open the lid. I scanned through the contents and pulled out the basics—antiseptic spray, gauze, and large compress pads.

"You need to take off your shirt."

"Thought you'd never ask," he said with a grin.

I rolled my eyes. Worst. Group. Ever. Rose was a pain in the ass. Leo was nice, but a little doe-eyed. And Lucas was a douchebag.

I heard Lucas take in a sharp breath as he pulled of his shirt. I moved the lantern closer so I could get a good look—at his wound. His shoulder was an angry mess of red, fresh blood dripping down his torso.

"How bad is it?"

"Uh ..." I trailed off.

"That bad, huh?"

I leaned in so close that I could feel his breath. There was something in the wound.

"Gross."

"What?" he said, panicked.

I hadn't meant to say that out loud. "I'm not sure."

I went back to the first aid box and dug around for some tweezers. There was a plastic pair in a mini Ziploc bag. I ripped it open and returned to Lucas's nasty shoulder. It looked like the infected had really chomped down hard. The skin was shredded. He was going to have a hell of scar to add to the ones already smattered on his neck and arms. There was even some scar tissue where his lower abdomen met his pant line. The hospital had really done a number on him. *If it was just from the hospital.*

I decided to focus on the nasty task at hand instead of speculating about his many scars. I bit my lip as I prepared to dig into the wound to remove whatever the yellow thing sticking out was. *Please don't be a part of Lucas.* The wound didn't look deep enough to have hit bone or anything like that, so I had no idea what the tiny object was.

"This is probably going to hurt," I warned.

Lucas nodded and took a deep swig of the beer he had started in on. I put my left hand on the unharmed part of his chest to hold him in place and squeezed the object with the tweezers. He hissed in a breath, but to his credit, didn't move. The blood was making it hard to get a good grip. I was starting to push it in deeper. I pushed the ends of the tweezers together and gave up trying to pull the object out. Instead, I would dig. I placed the closed end of the tweezers beside the object and pushed.

Fresh blood started to dribble down, but I kept going. I got in and behind the object, then dug it out with the flick of my wrist. Lucas let out a strangled sound as the object dislodged from his wound and fell into his lap. I had gotten it out. The wound was now bleeding anew, so I grabbed a wad of gauze and pressed it to his mangled shoulder to try and stem the bleeding.

His free hand went to his lap and pulled up the object. We both peered at it.

"It's a fuckin' tooth!" Lucas said flinging it away from him.

Ugh. The infected must have lost it while biting Lucas. I debated making a joke about keeping it for the tooth fairy, but I thought better of it. He looked pretty angry. Lucas finished off his beer while I peeked behind the gauze to see if the bleeding had slowed. There was no point in wrapping the wound up because he would just bleed through the bandages. So, I sat there pressing on his bleeding injury while Lucas stared down the neck of the beer bottle as if willing it to refill.

"Can you pass me another one?" Lucas asked.

"No." I wasn't about to let him get drunk on a run.

"Two beers ain't nothin'."

"Well, your beer here *is* weak compared to Canadian stuff"—he raised a brow at that—"but we need you alert and focused—not buzzed. It's our asses on the line too," I said, choosing my words carefully.

He muttered something along the lines of me being a buzzkill, but in this situation, I was fine with that. He could drink all he wanted when we got back to the motel. I removed the blood-soaked gauze and sprayed some antiseptic on Luca's shoulder, then patched him up with a large bandage. I quickly packed everything back in the first aid kit. This was something we could definitely use.

Lucas got up and put his bloody shirt back on. He picked up a new case of beer off the shelf and while I half expected him to just dig right in, he simply placed it under his arm on the uninjured side and kept moving.

He turned back to me. "You comin' or what?"

I got up with my lantern in hand, hauling the metal kit with me. Lucas went to deposit his *find* in the back of the cube van and I went back to my dolly.

We spent probably a good two hours packing up everything useful we could find. Yes, this trip was supposed to have been more of a quick run, but who knew when we would get a chance to find so many supplies in one spot. Most commercial places had been picked clean, dwindling our choices for supply runs. We hadn't run into anymore infected inside the warehouse, but I could hear some mulling about outside every time I passed near the tiny opening we had snuck in through. That would be fun to deal with later.

I was giving the aisles one last run through for spotting some last-minute items when I heard the sound of a bag rustling the next one over. I pulled out my knife and quietly investigated. With the lantern, I could see pretty well, but I couldn't spot where the noise was coming from. About halfway down the aisle, I heard the noise again and it sounded like it was higher up on the shelf. I jerked the lantern up, almost smacking myself in the forehead with it.

Some tiny rocks fell from the middle part of the shelf, clanging against the rungs as they fell. I walked over and kneeled down, picking up one of the tiny pebbles. It was pet food. I looked up again to see two red eyes reflected back at me. I stumbled back, my heart racing. *What the hell?* I heard a soft meow and placed a hand on my chest, willing my heart to slow back down. It was just a damn cat. The grey fur ball stared at me while it continued to make sounds. I wasn't a pet person so I had no idea if that meant it was mad or happy. At least it wasn't hissing—I knew that one.

"Jesus girl, we're ready to go!" Rose said, yelling at me from the end of the corridor.

I just pointed to the cat. Rose froze when she finally spotted it, and then a grin broke out on her face. She walked at a normal pace toward me and tried to coax the cat from the shelf. At first the cat was wary of her, but then it let Rose pick it up.

"Who's a cute little thing?" Rose said in a baby voice.

The cat was in her arms, letting her scratch it behind the ears as it purred away. I watched her with my mouth hanging open. It was weird seeing her like this. She looked up at me and her smile fell away. "Grab a bag of cat food."

"We're not taking it with us," I said.

"And why the hell not?" She held the cat away from me like she was worried I'd try to grab it from her.

"There's no place for pets in the apocalypse. It's just another mouth to feed." It was cold, but true.

"That's why I said to bring cat food."

"And when that runs out?"

"Then you better bring a couple bags of food," Rose said.

She cooed at the cat and walked away. I jammed my knife back into its holder and started to stomp away, but stopped after a few feet. There was no way Rose was just going to leave the cat there and if I didn't bring the cat food, she'd be using our supplies to feed the damn thing. With a deep, resounding sigh, I headed back to the cat food and grabbed as many bags as I could lift. This would be the last time I went on a run with this group. Rose shot me a haughty look when I reached the truck with the cat food in my arms. I barely resisted the urge to fling them at her.

The back of the van was stuffed. I got a little giddy just looking at it. We would be set for quite a while, and that meant I could leave to find Zoe ASAP. Lucas took the bags from me and squished them into the pile.

"Why the hell did you let her bring the damn cat?" he asked.

I held up my hands. "Hey, I argued against bringing it, but she wouldn't listen." I just wanted to get back to the motel and start planning out our rescue attempt.

"I'm allergic to cats," Lucas grumbled as he pulled down the door to the back of the van.

We all piled into the cab. Lucas was in the driver's seat, me next to him squished in the middle with Leo and Rose—and the cat—sharing the passenger seat. Lucas was about to start the truck when Leo suddenly yelled, "Wait! I'll go start the mower."

The plan was to use the back way out instead of the main road we had come on. There was a tiny alley running behind the warehouse that would lead us back to the motel, with a few twists and turns along the way. Leo hopped out of the cab to start up our distraction. We waited for a few seconds until we heard the roar of the lawnmower and saw Leo sprint back toward us with an infected or two on his trail.

Lucas started the truck. Leo had barely closed the door when Lucas gunned it and we were thrown against the dash. The cat hissed and clawed as Rose was forced to squeeze it tighter. The feral cat caught the edge of her eye when it raked its claws down her face.

She managed to calm it down by the time Lucas had swung the truck around and started going forward down the alley.

"Real nice," she yelled at Lucas.

He didn't say anything but I could see that he was smirking as he stared out the windshield. His face stiffened, and then he let out a sneeze. I looked at Rose, who had a nice raised scratch that started above the left eye and stopped at the apple of her cheek. She was lucky the claw hadn't actually gotten her eyeball.

"You look like a James Bond villain," I said.

The cab was dead silent, then to my utter surprise, everyone—including Rose—started to laugh.

Chapter 25

Lucas started to purposely hit the infected in our way with the cube van.

"Stop that!" I commanded.

We needed our cargo to reach the motel at least.

"This is a pretty big truck, I think it can handle it," Lucas said, veering the truck to the left to take out another.

"You best stop, Mein Fuhrer!" Rose added.

Lucas gripped the wheel so tight I could see his knuckles whiten. I couldn't believe I'd found a person with less tact then myself; Rose truly was terrible.

Arguing and yelling broke out in the cab with everyone trying to get their point across. Lucas yelled about needing to take out as many as we could so that they didn't follow us back. Rose continued to antagonize him with insults, and Leo shouted about all the supplies in the back. And I was in the middle of it. I was suddenly homesick for when I had been on the road with just Chloe. At the time, she'd annoyed me with all her questions, but I'd gladly take that over right now.

"Enough!" I yelled even louder. "Enough!"

They quieted down.

"Just get us to the fucking motel," I said.

The rest of the ride was in silence except for the clipped instructions Rose barked out while reading the map. After a left turn between two warehouses, we reached the main road. I looked out the side mirror. I could see the shadow of a few infected down the road behind us. They had their backs to us, heading in the direction we had come from. It looked as though the mower really had worked.

I let out a sigh of relief when the castle-themed motel came into view and it was still standing. There were a couple new dead infected added to the pile at the end of the driveway. We drove past them, paying them no mind. They must have had a few wander over while we were gone. Henry and the other guy were on the ball and had the gate open for us by the time we pulled up to the fake moat. They locked it up behind us quickly as well.

I had to wait for Lucas to get out before I could shuffle over. Rose and Leo were having a hard time rounding up the spooked cat on the passenger side. John gave me a huge hug as soon as my feet hit the courtyard tarmac.

"You okay?" he asked when he let me go.

I patted his shoulder. "Better than." I led him around to the back of the truck and yanked upward on the roll-up door.

John let out a low whistle. "Well done, you guys."

People started to pop out from wherever they were hiding to see what all the noise was. They started talking excitedly behind us as they spotted all the supplies. Amanda let out a squeal, but not because of the supplies. She launched herself at Rose, who was currently holding the cat. Chloe followed close behind her to investigate.

"You guys found a cat?" John asked.

"Yeah. Rose insisted on bringing the thing back," I said.

Lucas brushed past us and dug through the supplies, producing his case of beer. He left without saying another word. John raised a brow.

"Don't ask," I said.

We got to work unloading some of the supplies. It was easier to leave the bulk of the items in the back in case we needed to get out of there in a hurry. Leo took out an emergency battery to plug a rice cooker and kettle into. Soon plastic bowls of rice and instant oatmeal were being passed around with plastic utensils. Everyone was happy to be eating something other than granola bars. I took a bottle of water from the truck and gulped down the contents. Damn, I was thirsty. I made sure to pour myself a bowl of cereal with the condensed milk. It tasted a little weird at first, but the sugary cereal soon overpowered the grainy milk texture.

Much to Rose's dismay, the cat took a liking to Amanda and was currently allowing the little girl to pet the crap out of it. Chloe didn't find the cat as exciting, but instead came over to badger me about the infected as I took a seat beside John on the sidewalk that ran in front of the rooms.

"Did the infected leave you alone like they did Rose?" she asked.

John looked up from his oatmeal.

"If I didn't move or breathe too loud," I answered.

"So does that mean you're safe from 'em?" Chloe pressed.

I thought about it. "From turning, yes. One bit the crap out of Lucas's shoulder and he's fine, but we can still die of infection and blood loss."

I shoved a spoonful of cereal in my mouth while Chloe digested my words. I had to eat fast or else it would be a bowl of mush by the end of her questions.

"Is that why those people took you?" Chloe asked.

I looked at John. What had they told her?

"Yes."

"How'd they know?" she pressed.

Okay, I was stumped as to what to say to that. I pleaded with my eyes for John to answer that one.

He adjusted his cowboy hat before speaking. "Wyatt found out and sent her to them."

Her eyes narrowed. "Then I'm glad he's dead." She spat on the ground.

"Chloe!" I chastised her.

Me yelling was more of a reaction to the shock of hearing her speak like that than the actual words. Had someone else said them, I wouldn't have had an issue with it. She'd never spoken like that before. Chloe crossed her arms and walked away in huff.

"Don't worry," John said, "I'll get Ethan to talk to her."

That didn't make me feel any better. It was inevitable that people had changed in this new world, but I didn't want that to happen to Chloe. Maybe I was kidding myself. After all that she'd seen, it would be unavoidable. I sure as hell had changed and I didn't particularly like myself—or more appropriately— the things I've done. Chloe shouldn't have to go through that too.

I finished my cereal, not really tasting the rest of it, and hurried over to Rose to ask for the map. She tossed it at me, her attention still focused on the cat in Amanda's arms. A few people had come over to gawk at them like a circus attraction. Having a pet was a luxury of the old world; not one we could afford now.

After I had scooped up the map from where Rose had tossed it, I went to seek out Lucas. He had taken the entire case of beer when we first got back. I wanted to form a plan tonight and leave first thing tomorrow to find the mercenaries compound—to which he needed to be sober for. I checked the hotel room we all had shared last night, but it was empty. I walked by all the open doors, waving to a few people here and there, but still no Lucas. Where could he have gone? *What if he took off?* My heart dropped at the thought. He was my only hope for finding Zoe. There was nothing really keeping him at the motel. Rose and Leo were technically supposed to be keeping an eye on him, but they both had shirked their duties for a cat and handing out food.

I resisted the urge to run. It would only cause panic if I suddenly bolted across the motel. I started to peer inside the windows of the rooms we hadn't opened. Nothing. By the time I was done, I had gotten a few curious stares. I landed back at the end of the rooms, near the office. *The office.* I walked briskly to the office door and pulled it open. The tiny lobby was empty, and the door behind the counter was open.

I let myself in and found Lucas lying on the rundown couch, lengthwise. The beer that was on course for his mouth stopped when he spotted me. He groaned.

"What do you need now?"

I grabbed his boot-clad feet and swung them over to the ground. Lucas let out an annoyed grunt as I plunked myself down on the space I had just created by shoving his feet off the couch. Using the coffee table from the eighties, I spread out the map before us.

"I need you to show me where the compound is," I said.

He continued to lounge on the couch, even with his feet and calves now hanging off the edge.

"I'm busy." He took a big drink of his beer. I looked down to see two empties on the floor.

I stared at him. I really wanted to punch him in the face—my hands were already formed into fists.

"You need to stop drinking."

Lucas snorted. "You my mother now?"

He finished his drink and tossed the bottle next to the other ones. He reached into the case to rummage for a fresh one. Me coming in here demanding things wasn't going to work. I had to appeal to his sympathetic side, which I wasn't sure existed, but it was worth a shot. I took a deep breath and swallowed my pride. This wasn't about me—this was for Zoe.

"Please." I let my fear for Zoe leak into my voice. "You know what they do, and they have my best friend."

Lucas's hand stilled as he was about to twist off the cap of his newest bottle. He pulled himself up to a seated position, then faced the map, placing his unopened bottle on the table next to it.

"You couldn't let me have a moment of peace?" he muttered.

"Once you help me find her, I'll leave you alone," I said. "You can drink yourself into oblivion all you want then."

He looked at me, then shuffled closer to the map. "It's kinda hard to see."

I got up and pulled back the ancient curtains on the only window in the room. It didn't light up the entire space, but it let in enough that Lucas could read the map. I walked back over to the couch as Lucas started running his finger along one of the arteries.

"Prairieville," he said. "That's where the compound I was at is located."

I sat down beside him again. "Where in Prairieville?"

"One of the newer neighborhoods. Filled with mansion-type houses."

"How long will it take to get there?"

"If we can use the interstate, 'bout an hour from here."

"You remember how to get there from the interstate?"

He shot me a droll look. "O' course, but they also left some markers to go by."

"That stupid hand and eye symbol?"

Lucas nodded.

"Why do they use that?" I asked.

"Dunno. I was only with them for a little while before I was shipped off to the hospital. Only met Shawn, their leader, a couple of times before he turned me over."

I had no right to ask, but I did anyways. "What happened?"

Lucas hesitated for a second as he stared at the unopened beer bottle. "One of the guys on my crew saw me get bit on a run so I had no choice but to tell 'im I was immune to stop 'im from puttin' a bullet in my skull right then and there. The shit sack went straight to Shawn." Lucas scowled as he recounted the story. "Shawn had 'em toss me in with a bunch of the dead freaks to prove it. Got torn up pretty bad, but I lived." He let out a humorless laugh. "I was rewarded for my *service* by bein' knocked out cold and shipped off to the place where I had sent others to."

Kind of sounded like he'd gotten what he deserved, but I didn't say that out loud. I wasn't sure why he was telling me this. It sure wouldn't warm me to him. Maybe that was on purpose, so it would be easier for him to leave. I sure as hell wouldn't stop him—after I got Zoe back, that is.

I looked from him to the beer propped on the table. "Are you going to be okay to go tomorrow?" I asked.

Lucas leaned back into the couch. "Only got the one case. Gotta make it last."

I took that as a yes. I folded up the map and got up to leave. Lucas's feet immediately claimed the space I had vacated.

"I had nothin' to do with the girls," Lucas said just before I reached the door. "Just so you know. I wasn't lyin' 'bout that."

I turned to him. "What about killing innocent people to get to the immune ones?"

His eyes didn't meet mine, nor did I get an answer. *Was he one of the mercenaries who had attacked the apartment the first time around?* A chill ran down my spine. I knew he was already in the hospital by the time they had killed everyone and taken Mac, but before that, when they had shot up the place and killed Roy's daughter, then took his wife — had Lucas been there for that?

I couldn't go down that path right now. I needed him to get to Zoe. He'd agreed to help mainly because Rose and Leo had guns leveled at him at the time, but he also said he wanted revenge against Shawn. Maybe he wanted redemption as well. Or maybe I was placing some moral fiber in his being that wasn't there.

Regardless, I was willing to use him until he no longer was of use to me. To ignore his possible crimes until I got what I wanted out of him. If he betrayed us and ran back to this Shawn guy, I wouldn't hesitate to kill him. For his sake, he'd better not try anything.

Chapter 26

"Zoe is my friend too. There's no way I'm not goin'," Ethan said firmly the next morning.

We were standing outside by the cube van. The sun was barely up in the sky and the air was just a little chilly. Back home this would have been considered summer weather, but in Louisiana, this was cold.

"Ethan, you're still injured," I said.

"So are you!" He pointed to my leg.

To be honest, I had completely forgotten about being shot—well, grazed. Between the events at Hargrove, worrying about Zoe and her rescue, and having to find food or risk starving, I had paid no attention to my physical condition. The truth was that I was tired and hurt pretty much everywhere, especially my foot. Once I got Zoe back, I would be locking myself in one of the hotel rooms and sleeping for days. Until then, I couldn't afford to "take it easy." I scowled at Ethan for bringing it up.

"Plus, Crystal said I was fine," he added.

Crystal was with us, her arms crossed. "That's not what I said. *I said* that you are more than likely okay if you're still standing today. That doesn't mean you should run off and go to war." Sheri was nodding in agreement, but it was kind of hypocritical of her. She didn't take it as easy as she should have when she got shot in the kidney.

The thought of Ethan coming with us made me nervous, but I couldn't stop him. If I were in his shoes—hell, I had been—I would have insisted on going as well. My wounds were physical; his extended past that into the brain with his concussion.

I bit at my lip again for the hundredth time this morning. John had already added to my stress when I explained the flimsy plan to him last night by voicing his extreme concern. I had asked him how his plan to rescue me from the hospital had been any different and he gave me that disappointed parent look. But I had been right. Only the two of them had come after me when Wyatt had spilled the beans about where I had been taken. For all they knew, Wyatt was lying—exactly what John had accused Lucas of.

This siege would be different. We would have more people coming along. Me, John, Lucas, Rose, Leo, Sheri, and now Ethan, made seven. I was no idiot. I knew it was going to be dangerous as we were not only dealing with infected; there was an armed militia out there comprised of really bad men. But that was precisely why I couldn't just leave Zoe to them. It would be easy to cut my losses and count her for dead, but that was one thing I couldn't do. John hadn't done that to me and I wouldn't do that to Zoe.

And Zoe was my last link to my old life back home. Without her, there was no physical reminder and I found myself thinking less and less of home as time ticked away. *Would I ever find my way back to Canada? Would I ever see my parents or brother again? Were they even alive?*

Colin interrupted my sad train of thought. "I want to go too. Zoe was hot."

I rolled my eyes. "You sure as hell *aren't* coming."

"I survived by myself all that time. You really think I can't handle this?" He was actually angry.

"You can barely stay awake!" I said, then immediately regretted my words.

"Plus you're a kid." Roses added some dirt to the wound.

"Screw you guys," Colin said through clenched teeth. He stormed off, forcing people to move out of his way.

We already had Ethan to worry about; I sure as hell wasn't taking another person who would be more of a liability than an asset. And it really wouldn't be good for him. I didn't know how much time he had left, and I didn't want to be responsible for cutting it even shorter. Selfish, I know. But a person can only deal with so much at once. One thing at a time.

"You think the kid will listen?" Rose asked.

"I don't know," I said. I starting biting at my lips again. At this rate, they were going to be shredded to bits.

"We should get movin'," Johns said.

Everyone had a weapon. John even hesitantly gave a pistol to Lucas. The look he gave Lucas as he handed over the gun conveyed that should Lucas try anything, John would kill him. It was a chilling look that I wasn't accustomed to seeing on John's face. Lucas quickly placed the pistol in his waistband, still opting for the crowbar at his side. I was given an AR15 and a metal bat in addition to my Beretta. I shuffled from foot to foot. We were practically clearing out the guns and ammo, leaving the others with very little.

Henry and his sidekick had a shotgun and another automatic gun between them, and a few more handguns were given to those old enough and skilled enough to carry. Henry had really wanted to come with us to get revenge for his wife, but John talked him into staying. We were putting them in danger by leaving—and taking most of the weapons, to boot, so we needed to make sure someone stayed behind who was capable of leading the group should something happen while we were away. Henry didn't like it but he understood why. I was still nervous thinking that Chloe and Amanda would be left there, but Henry ensured me that he would look after them with his life.

Chloe was hanging onto Ethan, afraid to let him go. She kept glancing between Ethan and me, like a confused puppy. She was no idiot. She knew something had changed between Ethan and me; she just didn't know what. When she spotted me looking, she unlatched from Ethan, who was currently exchanging some words with John, and came over to me, her face downcast.

When she finally reached me, she looked up. There were tears in her eyes. I kneeled down and placed a hand on her shoulder. "What's up with you?"

She looked over at Ethan before answering. "I don't want him to go. I don't want *you* to go." Her voice was barely loud enough that I could hear.

"Chloe," I said. "We have to get Zoe back." I didn't want to scare her with the details.

"But those men are dangerous!" she said with a few tears crawling down her cheek. "And Ethan is still injured. And so are you."

I couldn't blame her for being worried—I was.

"I promise to look after him. I did last time, didn't I?"

Chloe nodded, remembering my promise to watch out for Ethan when we left the cabin for the first time.

"But you two are fightin'," she muttered.

"Family fights every now and then. It's just how it goes. Doesn't mean I'll let him do anything stupid."

"Family ..." She trailed off. "Is that what we are now?"

"Of course." I ruffled her hair lightly.

She didn't glare at me this time for doing it. Instead, she lunged at me and wrapped me in a big hug. My eyes stung from unshed tears. I didn't want to start the waterworks before we left. We clung to each other until I had to finally push her away gently.

"Ever heard of a comb?" I said, referring to the mess I'd made of her hair.

She gave me her signature glare and patted down her locks.

"You ready to go?" John asked.

He must have wandered over during my exchange with Chloe. Chloe took off back to Ethan.

"Yep."

Our extra supplies were secured into the bed of the truck we were taking while the seven of us worked out the truck cab logistics. John would be driving, but Lucas would also be up front to give the directions. And of course, I would be in the middle of the two. Leo, Rose, Sheri, and Ethan would be sharing the back bench seat. Leo and Ethan chose the ends while Sheri and Rose were stuck in the middle.

Sheri was the wildcard. The only time I had ever been out of Hargrove with her was for the gun training and she had gotten shot, so I didn't know how she would handle herself. She took the gunshot like a champ though, which was reassuring.

Once we all crammed in, Henry opened the gate for us. John lurched the truck forward and we were off. I was already uncomfortable sitting in the middle. Thankfully this was an older truck so it didn't have the center console like the newer ones did. And even better, this one was an automatic with the gearshift on the steering column. No awkward reaching near my legs. Not that there was room to. My AR15 and bat were sitting between my legs and John's automatic rifle was resting against the side of my left leg.

I snuck a peek at Lucas. He had the map out, but didn't seem to be looking at it. I had a feeling he knew his way around and was only using it as a prop. I wondered how his shoulder was doing. As much as I hated to admit it, we needed him in top shape. He was useful. *Until he's not.* I gave my head a shake to dispel my thoughts.

"Take a left after this right," Lucas said when we came to the end of the warehouse district.

"Should I be lookin' for anythin' in particular?" John asked.

"Anythin' that says I-10," Lucas answered.

John was pretty good at avoiding infected. I was glad he had drove rather than Lucas. He would be more cautious. It turned out the east warehouse district we were in was relatively close to the interstate, which made sense. It would be easier for the trucks carrying cargo.

"Take a right here on the 610," Lucas instructed.

We continued down the multi-lane interstate. After a bit, we came up to an area surrounded by green and ancient trees.

"What is this?" I asked.

I could see the tops of huge oak trees. It looked like a nature reserve.

"City park," Lucas said, like it was no big deal.

"In the middle of the city?"

"We're not in the middle of the city, more like north."

There went my confidence in my directional abilities. Everyone stuck their noises to the windows to watch the beautiful green life pass by. It was like I had been transported back to the cabin. We had traded in a cement jungle for a real one. Then as quickly as we had spotted it, the vibrant green was gone, sending us back to our modern landscape—the barren interstate.

"Just keep goin' straight. This road merges onto the I-10," Lucas said when he noticed John scrutinizing the signs.

For a while, we couldn't see anything past the interstate noise barriers. Tops of houses every now and again, but mostly just cement. Anytime there was an overpass the road got more congested. There were multiple lanes, yet we still had to squeeze the truck around the blockage.

John took us through a rather small opening. My teeth clenched as the sound of scraping metal reached my ears. The passenger mirror flew off, but John kept going until we were clear of the traffic jam.

After another ten minutes, I asked, "Are we still in New Orleans?"

"The very west part of it. Should be comin' up to the airport soon," Lucas said.

He was right. First there were signs telling us the airport was near, then we spotted the telltale air-traffic control towers in the distance on our left.

"Ho-ly shit," John said absently. He slowed the truck to a crawl.

I pushed myself up in the seat and craned my neck to see what he was looking at out his window. Planted face-first into the ground were the remnants of a huge passenger plane. It had missed the runway by a wide birth. Debris was everywhere; it even looked like it had reached the interstate. Half-burned seats and suitcases littered the area.

"John!" Sheri screamed.

John slammed on the breaks. We came to a stop a foot away from the back of another vehicle. Everyone sat still for a second. At the speed he had been going, we wouldn't have damaged the truck much, but every little bit counted.

"Sorry 'bout that," John said sheepishly.

We had all been gawking, so no one could blame him.

"Looks like we can't squeeze through this one," Lucas said. "We need to clear a path."

Chapter 27

We cautiously got out of the truck. I left my AR15 inside, but removed my metal bat. Sheri immediately jumped out and stabbed a roaming infected in the head. John was in the process of unsheathing the hunting knife I had returned to him when the dead infected hit the ground.

"Nice one," Ethan said.

Sheri gave him a grim smile at the compliment. Perhaps she wouldn't be a wildcard after all. We hesitantly approached the traffic jam. It was about three vehicles deep, but none looked to have crashed into anything other than the back of the vehicle in front of it. The first cars were empty, with their doors wide open. The next set of cars were worse for wear. Windshields were shattered and bloodied.

Sheri gasped when we peered into an old Jeep. The driver's head was sticking out of the windshield, glass embedded deep in the skin and completely shredded to the bone around the jawline. Grime and blood stained the rest of the glass. Then we found the reason for the crash.

The foremost vehicles had crashed straight into a section of the plane wing. The metal wing must have flown off and was currently imbedded in the interstate sticking straight up. As I looked up, I could see that the debris piece was about a foot taller than me.

"It cut the damn car in half!" Rose said, her finger pointing toward the back half of an old Toyota pressed up against the wing—the front half of the car nowhere to be seen.

"How are we going to get past this?" I asked.

The wing had hit the interstate and sliced it all the way to the other side. There was a deep path leading to where the wing had finally stopped. As I tested it with my foot, the cement started to crumble and fall into the void.

Lucas reached into the truck and pulled out the map. Everyone hurried over to take a look except for me. I continued to test out the broken path. Cement and asphalt chunks crunched under my feet every time I tried to move closer. Something yellow caught my eye and I looked to the left of my foot. It was the cup part of the oxygen mask found in planes. A shiver ran up my spine. I'd never had a problem with flying before, but now I knew I forever would. Not that planes would be up and running anytime soon—or possibly ever.

The familiar rasping of infected dragged my attention from the cut in the road to looking past it. It didn't sound like just one or two. I went on my tiptoes and tried to look around the wing, but only spotted the tops of abandoned vehicles. A hand was shoved at me, then disappeared as the infected fell through the wide path the plane wing had created. I watched it drop with my mouth open.

There was no way we were getting past something wide enough to swallow a body, not to mention the rasping hadn't stopped. I was willing to bet there were a lot more infected where that one had come from waiting for us on the other side. This was a dead end.

"Bailey, come one," John said.

They were already loaded back in the truck. I ran over and scrambled back into the middle, John following in behind me. He reversed until he could swing the truck around to face the way we had just come from. I looked at him.

"Detour," he said.

We had to backtrack a bit until we came to a turnoff that led us down a non-interstate road. It eventually connected to a highway that Lucas reassured us would lead back to the I-10—eventually.

It felt like we had just taken a giant ride around the airport. That stupid blockage had cost us gas and time. Once we got back to the I-10 via a major overpass, we were back on the trail again. It was almost immediate, the scene change. No longer were we in the city. Wetlands surrounded us. I could see a huge body of water off to my right reflecting the sunlight back at us. Then there were the swamps.

I crinkled my nose as we passed by. The smell reminded me of a wet dog, damp and stinky. Aside from the smell, it was a cool sight to see. Thick, dense trees seemed to float on the water. Green sludge drifted along the top of the water with the occasional tree root sticking out. Something moved under the water, causing the green muck to shift and sway. I swallowed.

"Lots of wildlife in there," Lucas said, more than likely having seen the same thing I had just witnessed.

"Alligators?" I asked.

Lucas grinned at my hesitant tone. "Could be, or wild hogs. They like to roll around in the muck."

I would be staying clear of swamps. Since we had stuck to mostly the city and the surrounding towns, I hadn't actually seen a genuine Louisiana swamp until now. Even at Ethan's cabin there hadn't been any nearby.

We continued mostly north along the interstate. For a while there was nothing but land, but then we could see smaller towns clustered off of the road.

"Prairieville should be comin' up soon," Lucas said.

He peered out the passenger's window, his nose practically pressed to the glass.

"There!" Leo said.

He was looking out the same side as Lucas, but spotted the interstate sign first. As we got closer to the exit, the inside of the cab got even more quiet. There was a giant, red hand with an eye in the middle spray-painted over the Prairieville turnoff sign. They should have just used a hand giving us the middle finger—it would've had the same effect.

John brought the truck down the turnoff onto another road. We didn't immediately arrive in the town, we had to keep driving to get to it. We came to another non-interstate highway before we saw the 'Welcome to Prairieville' sign, also graffitied with the ominous symbol. A warning.

"Okay, now which way do I go?" John asked Lucas.

"Keep goin' straight," Lucas answered.

We could have started to play I-Spy with all the symbols plastered around town. It felt like a dog marking their territory.

"I don't see any scouts or anythin'," John said.

"They don't waste manpower on that. They think the markin's are good enough to keep people away," Lucas said. "But just in case, take a left here."

John obliged and we turned off of the main road we were on to a one-way street. Lucas led us down some more deserted streets. The further we went, the more residential everything became.

"You telling us their hideout is in the 'burbs?" I asked incredulously.

Lucas nodded. "In the newer area, to boot."

There seemed to be an overkill of schools. I had noticed them when we first entered the town limits. Surely they didn't used to have a population that big that they could support that many schools, did they? Maybe this town took education very seriously, which wasn't a bad thing; it just seemed unnecessary. In the town I grew up in, there'd been only three elementary schools to choose from—the third one having been built long after my K-9 days.

We passed by older, but well-maintained houses. The few vehicles parked outside weren't old beaters, but they weren't expensive either. This seemed to be a middle-class neighborhood. My dad always said you couldn't judge a person by their car because for all you knew, that person driving around in a fancy BMW could be taking fifteen years to pay it off while flipping burgers at a fast-food restaurant. I always thought he'd just said that to make himself feel better about driving a Subaru. For all I knew, this was the rich part of town.

That thought was turned on its head when Lucas directed us down another road. Instantly the word *estates* popped into my head. Like most towns in North America, there was clearly a line divide of wealth. Okay, *this* was the rich part of town. The houses were huge. Most were sporting three car garages, white columns, and immaculate stone fronts with castle-like peaks. They really liked the bricked-front look here.

"Stop here," Lucas instructed. "The house they use is just around the next block. We don't want 'em to know we're here."

John slowed and parked the truck off to the side of the road. We got out of the vehicle quietly. I shouldered my AR15 and gripped the handle of my bat tight as it fell to my side. Everyone else was saddling up as well. It looked like we were preparing to go to war, which in a way, we were. They destroyed Hargrove, killed innocents and took one—possibly more—of us prisoner. In my book, they had declared war and if it was a war they wanted, then a war they would get.

Chapter 28

Lucas led our silent group across the lawns of the massive houses. No doubt they were once manicured; now they were full of uneven grass and rotting foliage. Lucas held up his hand as we approached the side of the house on the corner. The next street was where the mercenaries would be. The blood in my veins started to pump faster and faster. I couldn't tell if I was anxious or excited. My nervous system was fried by this point.

Lucas peeked around the corner. I heard him suck in a breath. He turned back to us, his brows furrowed, and then he took another look.

"...the hell?" he muttered.

"What?" I asked.

"I don't see anyone," Lucas said.

He turned back to us again and crouched down, motioning for us to do the same.

"I'm goin' to go scout it out by myself. If it's clear, I'll wave you over," he said.

"No way!" Rose hissed. "How do we know you won't just go runnin' back to 'em?"

Lucas scowled. "I want 'em dead as much as you do."

"You could be leadin' us into a trap. We ain't lettin' you go up there yourself," Rose said.

She had a point.

John held up his hands. "We'll split up. Lucas, Bailey, and I will go check it out. The rest of you stay here. If somethin' is up, I'll pop off a round and you'll know to come runnin'."

"We need to stay out of sight; that's why less is better," Lucas said, his arm jerking down with his harsh exclamation.

"Son, I ain't stupid. You're not goin' in there alone," John said.

John and Lucas stared each other down and I swallowed at the tension. They better not start fighting. Sheri hitched in a breath and extended her arm, grabbing our attention. She was pointing at an infected shambling toward us. It bumped into the curb, barely catching itself. No one moved. We let the thing get closer to us, to the point where it was on the same lawn as us, and then Rose and I shot out. I tripped the thing, swiping out with my foot. It collapsed to the ground and I stuck my boot-clad foot on its chest. Rose then brought her knife down on the infected's head while it struggled to free itself from under my hold.

We returned to the group huddle, leaving the dead infected where it had fallen. Lucas frowned.

"There's no way they would have let a dead one get that close to the compound. Usually they had one or two guys patrollin' the immediate grounds at all times," Lucas said, then added, "plus it's too damn quiet."

"What do you mean?" John asked.

"There was always loud music goin' or shots goin' off. Somethin' ain't right." Lucas tugged at his collar.

"You think they abandoned it?" I mused out loud.

"Only one way to find out," John said.

He motioned for Lucas to lead the way. Lucas no longer looked mad; instead he looked concerned. That made my pulse raise—this time I knew it was my nerves. Something had spooked Lucas.

"If you hear anythin', you come runnin', all right?" John said to the others.

They nodded. Ethan looked a little angry that he hadn't been selected, but he didn't dare argue with John.

Crouched low, we crossed the front of the lawn into the next one. I kept my head low, the ground becoming a blur of green. Lucas stilled so we stopped behind him, and then he pointed to the largest house yet. It made the other mansions look tiny. No wonder they had chosen that one. It looked like it could house fifty people. There was a tall privacy fence surrounding the property and a wide-open iron gate at the front.

Inside, there were fallen bodies and a couple roaming infected. One still had an automatic weapon attached that was dragging behind it via a strap. Every time the weapon hit a stone or something to make a sound, the infected would stop and whirl around to look for the source of the noise.

"Those bodies belong to your *friends*?" John asked.

Lucas swallowed, but didn't answer. He entered the gate and we were forced to follow. The infected came straight for us. I raised my bat and John took out his hunting knife. There would be no gunfire until absolutely necessary. I met the infected that was dragging the automatic weapon halfway. My metal bat whistled in the air as I swung—hard. It connected with the infected's skull and it crumpled to the ground. I brought the bat down again and it stopped moving.

John reached down and yanked off the rifle it was dragging. The outside looked scratched up, but John was able to eject the magazine. He flashed me the top. There were still bullets inside. John pocketed the magazine and gently placed the rifle back on the ground.

We killed off the rest of the infected as we made our way up the sprawling driveway. There was even a damn fountain in the middle. It wasn't spraying any water, but it still looked impressive—except for the dead body floating face-first in the murky water.

Lucas stopped to turn over the body. As he did, some pinkish water splashed onto the cement driveway.

"Knew 'im?" John asked.

"He wasn't a mercenary," Lucas said.

"What?" I asked, confused.

"The mercenaries aren't the only group out there," Lucas said, which answered nothing.

"Meaning?" I prompted.

"They were kind of in a gang war."

John and I looked at each other. "What the hell does that mean?" John asked.

"I'm willin' to bet the other crew got to 'em; that's why it's so quiet in here. They're all dead like the ones out here," Lucas said.

"How big is the other gang?" John asked.

"Not near as big ..." Lucas trailed off, then spoke to himself. "How'd they do it?"

John didn't look pleased with the news. As if the mercenaries weren't enough of a menacing presence, now we had to worry about another gang? Why the hell did people care about being the fucking head honcho? There were so many more important things to worry about! At least the other gang had done our work for us.

My shoulders slumped. If they were all dead, how were we going to find the other compounds? I started to panic as a more frightening thought streaked across my mind.

"Do you think Zoe is in there?" I asked, my voice thick.

"I highly doubt it," Lucas said. "Like I said, this wasn't the location for that side of their *operation*."

"We'll check inside just to be sure," John said, placing a hand on my shoulder.

Lucas pushed open the ornate front door. No creaking or anything. Right off the bat, we spotted dead bodies strewn around the entrance. The air was heavy with the scent of rot and copper. Blood coated the white tiles, leaking in between the grout, forming a series of red lines. Bullet holes and arterial spray marred the paint job. Broken decorative pieces lay mixed among the bodies. I almost slipped on a broken vase as we walked among the bodies.

We canvassed the carnage-filled first floor. No one had been left alive. I noticed that there wasn't one woman among the mix. I highly doubted any females had stuck with the mercenaries willingly. Lucas pointed to a couple of the bodies, saying they weren't part of the mercenary crew. It looked like they had invaded the place. Guns were still next to their fallen owners, leading me to believe that they hadn't attacked for resources. They just wanted to eliminate. We moved onto the upper floor when we finished our loop. The only sounds we could hear were our own breathing and footsteps. This place was a tomb.

The upstairs was filled with dead as well. Lucas pushed open one of the doors to reveal a large office. A huge wooden desk sat in the middle with papers and maps scattered on and around it. There was a large map nailed to the wall in a crude manner. We walked up to it to see a bunch of red circles and pins.

"Are these all the compounds?" I asked, scanning the map.

"Compounds and drop-off zones," Lucas said.

"Drop-off zones?" John asked.

"They're certain areas they secured for tradin'," Lucas hesitantly answered.

"You mean where they traded people like goods?" I didn't disguise the anger in my voice.

Lucas didn't answer.

"Where do they keep the girls they take?" John asked. His eyes were narrowed and lasered in on Lucas.

Lucas took a deep breath. "They didn't tell us grunts much, but the guy in charge here once got so drunk he told us that compound was in Baton Rouge, but I don't know *where* in Baton Rouge."

The map we were looking at was a large area chart. Prairieville was circled, along with the outskirts of New Orleans and Gretna, and Baton Rouge. But there was nothing specific enough to tell us where the places were located within the cities.

"Let's look through the rest of these papers," John said.

We put down our weapons and started going through the papers and maps. I found a small notebook that looked like it was a ledger. There were tables of weighted items for trading values. I stopped at the page labeled 'Immune.' One immune was worth a crate of food and six cartons of ammo. Or a few drums of gasoline. Or a rifle and a handgun.

My heart stopped as I read that the drop-off zone was listed as the East Louisiana State Hospital. They fucking delivered straight to the front door. I started to giggle. *Thirty minutes or less, or it's free!* Lucas and John stopped their rummaging to peer at me. I ignored them as I counted the tally on the next page, feeling every indent of the pen marks. Twenty-seven people had been caught and transferred. Which mark was mine? There was nothing personal about the ledger. We were simply something to be bartered and traded, like a crate of oranges.

It made me remember when Tim had traded me for a sack to the mercenaries at the apartment. Whatever was in the bag, Tim had deemed me worth. Is this what they did for the girls they captured? Were they weighed and valued like the immune people? I suddenly felt nauseous. Was Zoe already in one of these ledgers? I threw the book down in disgust.

I turned from the mess and looked out the big bay window. The dead bodies were still there. *Good.* The mercenaries deserved everything they had brought on themselves. Hell, I'd shake the hands of the gang who did this except chances were they were just as bad.

"Found somethin'," Lucas said, and I tore myself away from the window.

We crowded around him to see what he was talking about. It was a hand-drawn map by someone who had the shakes or was drawing it while moving. The top said South Baton Rouge and the X-marked destination was a hotel. The bottom of the paper said *Girls, Girls, Girls!* My vision clouded over as I clenched my teeth. When I found these men, whether John tried to stop me or not, I was going to kill them all.

"Think this is it?" John asked.

"Your idea of what's goin' on is as good as mine at this point." Lucas shrugged.

"It's all we have, so we're going," I said. "We have to at least try. Even if it isn't the place we need, don't they mark up the area with their symbols? We can track them that way. How far into the actual city do you think they will be?"

"This says South Baton Rouge, so I'm guessin' we won't have to go downtown, but whoever drew this clearly drank too much." Lucas frowned at the paper as he turned it sideways. "The mercenaries don't like to hunker down in populated areas. There's a good chance we won't have to go too far in."

John took off his cowboy hat and ran a hand over his hair. "All right. Let's go back and round up the others."

We descended back down the stairs and out the front door of the mansion. The frosted crystal glass surrounding the door twinkled like Christmas lights as the sun broke through. This place would have been beautiful in its heyday. When we reached the others, I spotted two more fallen infected. At least they were capable of taking care of them.

"Anyone in there?" Rose asked.

John shook his head. "All dead."

None of us mentioned the other gang and the war that was erupting. There was no point in scaring them anymore. We loaded into the truck and circled back around the way we had come. The I-10 would also take us to Baton Rouge if we kept heading north.

Once back on the interstate, Lucas and I took turns memorizing the "map." The shaky drawing wasn't anything concrete, but with everyone being dead at the last compound, we were starting from scratch again. The mercenaries were everywhere it seemed, so all we had to do was keep looking and we'd find someone. *Hold on Zoe, we're coming.*

Chapter 29

We had already spotted the mercenaries hand and eye symbol as we approached the edge of the city limits.

"Take the forty-two exit," Lucas said.

"That's not what it says here." I pointed to the hand-drawn map.

"If we take the 3246 exit, they'll be lyin' in wait. The hotel looks like it's just off of it. We need to sneak up unnoticed," Lucas said.

I narrowed my eyes at him. "How do you know that?" I noticed the others out of the corner of my eye shuffle in the back seat.

"I'm gettin' real tired of tryin' to convince you. Believe me or don't, I don't give a shit," Lucas growled. "I just don't wanna be shot as soon as we pull up."

John listened to Lucas's advice and turned off on forty-two. We took an immediate right down another road until we connected with 3246. Everyone tensed as we drove through the south part of the city. Infected had started to come out from the woodworks. John was going fast enough that they couldn't catch up to us, but it was still an alarming amount. Hopefully we wouldn't be forced to come back this way.

We got to a large paved area with a bunch of retail stores.

"Stop," Lucas ordered.

"How do we know which hotel from here?" I could barely see the rest of the retail stores to our right, let alone the area just off the interstate where the hotel was supposed to be.

"We don't until we get closer, but we need to be on foot, otherwise they'll hear the engine," Lucas said.

John parked the truck behind Joe's Crab Shack, which left us a fair distance away from the hotels. We loaded up again with weapons, this time leaving the melee ones behind. This would be a firefight. John threw on a backpack and filled it with all the ammo we had taken. He attached a suppressor to the end of his handgun.

"Got any more of those?" I asked.

John shook his head. "Just the one."

I went back to ensuring I had enough ammo. I had one extra magazine for my AR15, but didn't have one for the Beretta so I had to pocket a bunch of loose 9mm rounds. The cool metal bullets felt weird in my jean pockets—the tight material had pushed the ammunition right against my leg.

For a brief moment, I felt the urge to pray, but I was conflicted as to what I would pray for. Did I hope they were dead like in the last compound, or did I hope they were there and that we could kill them all? *If they were all dead and Zoe was in there...* I shook my head. No point in clouding my mind with these types of thoughts beforehand.

We watered up and ate a light meal before we crossed the set of one-way roads. Even though I knew no one was driving along the road, I still looked both ways before crossing the street. It was too ingrained in me. I had to keep adjusting the AR15 on my shoulder as the strap kept slipping. I peeked over at John to see he wasn't struggling with his automatic rifle, but it was mainly because of the backpack strap was helping hold it in place. He had the silenced handgun at the ready in case we ran into anyone or anything. We didn't want them to know we were here until we had the upper hand.

We passed by another restaurant before we reached the hotel. I would have asked which hotel it was except the sound of loud music drifted obviously from the one on the left. A bunch of discarded, dead infected surrounded the area. I cringed at the smell. *How did that not bother them?*

"Keep down," Lucas hissed.

We practically crawled over the mound of dead infected to get to the backyard terrace wall. The bass was cranked up enough that I could feel the vibrations. Were these guys stupid? The music would bring in the infected for miles; except we hadn't spotted any live ones nearby yet. Maybe the rotting smell was keeping them away. After all, the infected didn't go after the dead. Plus, they were wasting all that power. They must have rigged up some sort of generator as the lights inside were also on.

"Give me a boost," Lucas said to John.

John and Leo kneeled down and lifted Lucas up so he could look over the wall. We all heard a scream—a female one—the surprise causing them to lose their hold on Lucas. He came tumbling down on them with a muffled curse.

"What was that?" Sheri asked. Her eyes were ablaze with anger.

I knew exactly what she was thinking because I was thinking it too. The girls were indeed in here and being subjected to the mercenaries.

"I couldn't tell before you *dropped* me," Lucas said as he rubbed his head.

"Well, what *did* you see?" I asked.

"There's a patio and doors leadin' inside, but I didn't spot anyone outside."

"See a spot where we can climb over?" John asked.

Lucas nodded and pointed to the corner of the terrace wall. "There's some thick bushes over there that would cover us."

John and Leo boosted Lucas up again to double-check the area. He gave us a silent thumbs-up and scrambled over. We listened intently to hear if he had been spotted. After a beat of no yelling or gunfire, the rest of us helped each other over. John lifted Leo up; then from his perch on the wall, Leo assisted

John by pulling him up until John could latch onto the wall himself.

My eyes kept darting from the two on the wall to the sliding doors that led inside. *Please no one come through right now.* The patio was empty of people, like Lucas had said it was. Finally, John and Leo plopped down on the ground next to us. We sat crouched for a few seconds to make sure we hadn't been spotted. Lucas motioned forward with his hand and we followed him in a single line along the building. He peeked in through the large glass doors. When he turned around, he didn't look pleased.

"There's at least ten guys that I can see, but part of the sittin' area is out of my view."

"Do you see any of the girls?" I asked. I didn't want them to accidently get caught in the firefight.

"No," Lucas said. "But that doesn't mean they aren't down here. No spray and pray, got it?" He looked at everyone accusingly.

"Son, I've been handlin' a gun since before you were born," John said, sounding insulted.

Lucas smirked at that, then his smile fell away as he realized what we were about to do. I had to take a few breaths to calm my nerves. I looked back at the others behind me. Their faces were a reflection of my own anxiety, each pinched with a mix of worry and determination. I had been so focused on getting to Zoe that I hadn't even thought about the others. What if I had just led them to their deaths? Would *I* survive this? Our own mortality was something we faced every day, yet never *really* thought about. I purposely put it from my mind, but I couldn't shake it this time. We weren't about to face a horde of undead; we were about to *slaughter* a bunch of living, breathing men. *Bad men*, my mind corrected me. *Think of your best friend.* I had to do this.

Leo did a silent Hail Mary while Rose muttered something quickly under her breath. It sounded like a prayer. I swallowed to try to dispel the dryness in my mouth. Ethan gave my hand a squeeze and I crushed it back in response. His betrayal seemed so insignificant in comparison to what we were about to do. If we survived this, I would tell him that I forgive him. I didn't want to do it now because it might undercut whatever confidence we had, as if the seriousness of the situation would suddenly come crashing down on us. Nothing like last-minute confessions and forgiveness to instill confidence.

"Weapons ready. We only get the benefit of catchin' 'em off guard once," John said.

His eyes locked with mine and he gave me a grim smile. Lucas grabbed onto the patio door handle and pulled the sliding pane open. We burst through the opening with Lucas leading the charge. Time really did seem to slow down; even my heart beat lulled. I caught the looks of utter surprise on the mercenaries faces as they spotted our team.

The first guy to recover reached for his own weapon, but Lucas spilled first blood by shooting him right in the chest. He flew back over the couch he had jumped up from. Then time resumed to normal speed.

Gunfire flew. Pieces of the walls and decor exploded. The mercenaries started to dive for cover. The loud bass thumped in my ears.

We spread out to make ourselves less of a target. We pushed on and around the furniture the mercenaries were hiding behind. One guy jumped up and made a run for the other room. I brought my AR15 up and shot, hitting the guy in the and back propelling him forward onto the floor. John grabbed me by the back of my shirt and we crouched behind a thick wooden table as gunfire was starting to get returned.

John held up his finger until there was a break in the spray of bullets, then sat up and shot his automatic rifle. Bullet casings hit the ground around us as I joined in. We shot through the couches where we knew they were hiding. Leo shot off his shotgun and the music suddenly cut out, leaving us with just the defining sound of the weapons being discharged. Lucas and Ethan were the furthest in the room, shooting at the men who were trying to get away, then took off after them, disappearing from my view line. Sheri was pressed up against a pillar looking terrified, and I had lost sight of Rose. I could hear her hunting rifle going off, but couldn't actually see her.

"Move!" John yelled and we got up, but stayed low.

We pushed further into the hotel to the bar area. Unlike the mercenaries in the seating area, the guys in the bar part had one of the girls with them. She looked terrified: whether it was because of us or the mercenaries holding her captive, I couldn't tell.

I took out as many men as I could. Beside me, Leo lifted his shotgun and pulled the trigger. I saw the guy he was aiming at grab the barely-clothed girl and throw her in front of him like a coward. The girl's chest exploded in a spray of red and she let out a harrowing scream. The guy dropped her dead body, then tried to flee behind the bar. Leo's face fell as he stared at the dead girl, realizing what the guy had done. He was frozen, but I wasn't. I took off after the guy, jumping over a fallen bar stool and the dead mercenary that had been perched on it. I let loose on the coward with my rifle.

The bottles of booze behind the counter exploded as I shot up the bar. When my magazine clicked empty, I swung the rifle onto my shoulder and pulled out the Beretta from my waistband, making my way behind the bar. The mercenary looked like a sponge. His dead eyes were looking at nothing while the various holes in his chest leaked and pooled in a puddle of red underneath him. I may have gone overboard on that one.

Gunfire being aimed my way had me dive around the corner of the bar. I heard a masculine grunt of pain and dared a peek. Leo had been kneeling over the dead girl when he had been shot in the back. He slumped forward and I let out a scream. The mercenary shooting our way started toward me but was cut off as Rose blasted him straight in the face. His feet actually lifted off the ground from the impact, and half of his head exploded like a firecracker.

Rose didn't waste any time looking at her handiwork as she ran to Leo's fallen form. Another mercenary appeared from the hallway to our left and I bolted from my hidey-hole, taking two shots from my Beretta. I hit his shoulder with one and he spun backwards, letting off a shot of his own. It ricocheted just a foot from me, pounding a hole in one of the stool legs.

I ran at him as he started to fire aimlessly. My mind didn't even register that I was in danger; it just kept pushing me forward until I was upon the injured mercenary. I unloaded two rounds into his chest, hearing an odd whistling sound as his lungs deflated. More gunfire from all around me went off as the rest of the mercenaries gathered on the first floor to fend off our team.

"Bailey, get down!" I hit the ground, not even questioning the order.

I felt the whiz of bullets pass over me, then heard a body hit the floor only a few feet from me. I looked up to see a fallen mercenary in front of me and John standing behind me with his gun.

John yelled, "Come on!"

I got up and grabbed at the back of Rose's shirt. She let out a sob, but let me guide her over to John, then we followed him down the corridor. I couldn't bring myself to look at Leo's dead body. *Don't think about Leo, don't think about Leo.* Grieving was for later; anger was for now. I put my Beretta back in my waistband, then ejected the empty AR15 magazine, jamming the spare one back in.

We had used up a lot of our ammo in the initial shooting spree when we had entered the hotel; now we would have to be more conservative as we picked off the rest of the mercenaries. Ethan, Lucas and Sheri were out of my sight, but they had to still be on the first floor as more gunfire erupted from the rooms surrounding us. The lights flickered and went out overhead as bullets hit all around us. Mercenaries were coming down the hallway after us. Just how many of them were there? We had already killed so many...

John shot out the glass pool doors and we ducked for cover from the spray of gunfire. My nose was instantly assailed with the smell of stale water and chlorine. I slipped on the wet tiles, only to have John steady me. He held a finger to his lips and we pressed ourselves against the wall, waiting for the mercenaries.

The nasty looking pool water lapped against the edges, spilling over onto the tile. It was like something was in there, but no *human* would willingly swim in the disgusting water. The sound of glass crunching drew my attention back to the shattered pool entryway. John held up three fingers, silently counting down. When his last finger fell, he spun around and began shooting into the hallway. I did the same, shooting my AR15 before I could even aim. Bodies were flung across the hallway and into the opposite wall. We stepped out of the pool area and shot up the rest of them.

John let out a yelp and hit the floor. My heart threatened to stop, but I kept shooting until all the attacking mercenaries had been eliminated. Dead bodies lined the hall, some slumped against the walls with bloody tracks running down the busted drywall. I shouldered my gun and leaned down to John. He was still moving.

"Just got my leg," he grunted.

Blood was seeping through his jeans about an inch above the knee. Rose ripped off her windbreaker and used it to tie off John's leg just above the bullet wound.

"Didn't hit nothin' major," he said, "but hurts like hell. Help me up."

Chapter 30

We both took one of John's arms and wrapped them around our shoulders. This position made it difficult to hold up my weapon, but not impossible. John was still able to use his other leg and limped along with us pretty good despite the fact that we were both shorter than him. It was a slow go getting over all the men we had gunned down. I couldn't even bring myself to feel bad about it, even if I had wanted to.

The hotel had taken on an eerie silence. My ears were still ringing from all the gunfire and adrenaline pumping my blood throughout my body at warp speed. We nearly dropped John as Lucas came around the corner.

"Don't shoot!" he barked as he retreated back around the corner.

I lowered my weapon and shuffled John's arm back in place. He had almost slipped off when I'd jumped at the sight of Lucas. Rose and I helped John over and onto one of the shredded couches. I winced in sympathy as he let out a grunt when his leg hit the cushion. The sitting area and bar were a mess. The expensive furniture had been destroyed in the firefight. Bodies were lying all over the place. Blood was everywhere. I didn't imagine there would be so much blood ...

Rose hurried over to Leo's fallen body after we dumped John. Everyone else had survived. I gave Lucas, Ethan and Sheri a weak smile. Lucas kneeled down and began to examine John's leg wound.

"Looks like the bullet went right through. Tore up your muscle pretty good though," Lucas said. "We just gotta get the bleedin' to stop and you'll be fine—eventually."

John shrugged off the backpack he still had on and handed it to Lucas. "There's a small bit of first aid supplies. I figured we might need 'em."

Lucas pulled out a small jar of peroxide and other first aid fixings. He untied the windbreaker around John's leg and ripped his jeans all the way around until the entire rest of the material came off. It was like John was wearing a pair of jeans on one leg and jean shorts on the other. Lucas dumped some of the peroxide on the wound and John let out a hiss. Blood and liquid poured onto the floor, streaking the white linoleum pinkish.

"You pack a needle and thread?" Lucas looked up at John.

John nodded grimly. Lucas kept digging in the backpack until he pulled out a spool of medical thread and a needle encased in plastic. He ripped the plastic off the needle with his teeth, then threaded the needle with surprisingly steady hands. My own were still shaking slightly. When Lucas sank the needle into John's leg I turned away and went over to Rose. Sheri was talking to her lightly, trying to coax her from hovering over Leo's body.

I closed my eyes for a brief second and took a breath, then looked down. Rose had maneuvered Leo so that he was no longer hunched over the dead girl but was lying beside her, his eyes closed. I was about to place a hand on her shoulder when a loud bang on the floor above us had me jerking my head toward the ceiling. My eyes flashed to Ethan, who was at the ready with his own semi-automatic rifle.

Lucas hurried to finish tying off John's wound. He made a loop and cut the rest of the thread with his teeth. *Ick.* He pushed himself up and got his own gun ready.

"We did a sweep down here. The rest must be upstairs," he said, ejecting his magazine and stuffing it full again.

I sprinted over to them and did the same, filling up my first AR15 magazine.

"Did you see any of the girls?" Sheri asked.

She had managed to get Rose up and back over to us. Rose looked lost, her cocky and rude demeanor completely washed away. *Don't think about Leo, there's still work to do.*

"Just the one in the bar area. They gotta be on the next floor," Lucas answered.

Another bang above us had everyone spurring into action.

Lucas pointed a finger at John. "You stay." John froze in the middle of getting up.

"Like hell I'm stayin' here!" John said with venom.

"You'll just slow us down and we're gonna need to take the stairs, which you can't do with that injured leg," Lucas said. There was no hint of superiority, just cold hard truth.

John let out a very unlike John curse. He knew Lucas was right. We couldn't afford to look after him if we had to have another shoot-out. John held his gun close as his eyes swept over the floor.

"I don't like it, but fine."

"All right, let's go."

Lucas led the remainder of us down the hallway. I gave John one last look just before he disappeared from sight. He gave me a clipped nod, letting me know he would be fine. He wasn't one to let ego get in the way. Together, the rest of us ran down the hallway heading for the stairs, just past the dead elevator. Whatever power they were using to keep the lights on didn't extend to the lift. Lucas opened the door to the stairs and we ascended upwards in grim silence.

We still needed to find the girls and Zoe. There was no way they would be up there by themselves, so I prepared myself for more carnage. The door to the second floor flew open as we were still climbing. A burly man without a shirt burst through and began shooting. We all returned fire and the guy was hit many times. He stumbled back into the hallway as we took the rest of the stairs two at a time.

Lucas reached the door as it was about to close and held it open. He lifted up his hand, stalling us right behind him. The mercenary we had gunned down was lying on his back in the hallway, one of his feet stuck in the doorway. Lucas shuffled the guy's foot out of the way and stuck his head out the door. A bullet nearly hit him, implanting itself in the frame beside his head. Lucas returned fire with just his gun sticking out of the doorway, his body still in the stairwell. They took turns shooting at each other until the other person stopped. Either they were out of bullets or Lucas had hit him with his random shooting.

We burst into the hallway. Indeed, another man lay dead about midway down the corridor with bullet holes decorating the wall space around him. Sheri let off a couple of nervous rounds even though there wasn't anyone actually shooting at us anymore. Lucas yelled at her to stop and she did. She looked deathly pale from fright. Slowly, we inched our way down the second floor hall. Door after closed door passed us. I heard knocking and screams from the inside.

"Help us!" a distinctly female voice sounded from the other side of room 215.

"Get back from the door!" I yelled.

I pulled out my Beretta and shot at the card reader door handle. It blew apart and the door creaked open. Three terrified girls looked back at us as they scuttled away, having spotted our weapons.

"We're here to help," I said, holding up my arms.

"All that shooting downstairs, was that you?" one girl asked.

She couldn't have been more than fifteen. Her dirty and tattered clothes hung off her small frame still skinny with adolescence. *Those mercenaries deserved worse than a bullet to the head.*

"Yes. Do you know where the rest of the men are?" It was a long shot, but I had to ask.

The young girl shook her head, but the oldest of the three spoke up.

"T-they use the meetin' room at the end of the hall. It overlooks the pool." She pointed due north toward the end of the hallway.

I looked at Lucas. "Why aren't they out here shooting at us?"

"Don't know." He narrowed his eyes, squinting the rest of the way down the hallway. "Probably hidin' away like cowards."

I turned back to the girls. "Do you know another girl by the name of Zoe?"

All three shook their heads. My heart sank. "T-they keep us in here until they"—the oldest swallowed—"until they need us. We don't get to see much of the other girls." My heart picked itself back up. Zoe might still be in here.

I could see bruises lining her naked arms and her lip was busted. *If they hurt Zoe...*

"Stay here until we come back," I said.

The youngest jolted forward and grabbed my arm, her eyes desperate. "Please don't leave us!"

"I'll stay here with them," Sheri said, taking the girl's hand from my arm. "You go free the rest of the girls and send them to this room."

The girl seemed to relax at Sheri's words. She led them back inside the room so they were out of the line of fire should someone start shooting. The inside window had been boarded up so the girls only way out was the room door. Somehow they had managed to lock the doors from the outside. That was a scary thought. I didn't know hotels had that ability.

We continued down the hallway, knocks and yells coming from behind the doors we passed. Each room that we cleared had more girls, but none of them contained Zoe. We were running out of rooms to check. Some of the girls thanked us profusely, while others visibly slunk away from Lucas and

Ethan. I could only imagine the horrors they'd gone through at the hands of the mercenaries. It made me what to kill them all over again.

I stood in front of the last hotel room door on that floor, my hands scared to open it. *What would I do if Zoe wasn't in there? Where did I go from here?* Lucas noticed my hesitancy and pushed me aside, opening the door with his own gun. His was way louder, causing a fit of screams on the other side of the door. *Please be Zoe, please be Zoe.* The door swung open, but the girls were out of view. Probably hiding from the loud shot.

I cleared my throat. "Zoe?"

No answer.

"Zoe?"

Light footsteps approached me. I hadn't realized I had been looking at the ground, unwilling to face the possibility of my failure of not finding Zoe. Two girls stood in front of me, neither of them my best friend. Tears threatened as my brain worked through what this meant. Zoe wasn't there. She was more than likely dead. I wiped away the rogue tears and instructed the girls to head to 215 and wait for us to finish clearing the second floor. All that was left was the boardroom the first girl had told us about.

I don't know how I was still clinging to hope that Zoe was in there, but I was. One group of girls had told us that the mercenaries didn't use any of the floors higher than two. Too much energy to upkeep the entire building. So, this was my last hope for finding Zoe. I dragged my heavy feet over to the set of closed double doors to stand beside the others who were waiting for me.

I listened closely, picking up on movement inside. I nodded back to Lucas, Ethan and Rose. We got into formation around the doors with our guns pointed and ready. Lucas and I kicked in the doors at the same time, the meager lock not standing a chance against both of our strength. Gunfire immediately started from behind the boardroom table.

I aimed for the guy at the end of the table who was partially exposed. One of my bullets landed in the middle of his forehead, sending him to the floor with a spray of blood that coated the blank whiteboard. The others were able to take out the rest of the men.

"Stop! Lucas!" one of the men cried out.

Lucas's head knocked back and he motioned for us to stop firing. The room was still. No one dared to move, as if one little sound would send us back to war.

The guy hesitantly popped his head out from behind the table. "Lucas, my man, you know I didn't—" The man didn't get a chance to finish his sentence as Lucas shot him in the face.

I looked at Lucas for an explanation.

"He was the traitor who turned me over to Shawn," Lucas said. "Don't know what he was doin' here. Bastard should've been at the first compound we checked."

His voice was cold as he regarded the guy he just shot. I walked around the table, surveying the damage and searching for a female. No Zoe. She really wasn't there. I had failed her. All this had been for nothing. *Not nothing. You saved those girls.* It was a small consolation prize to my grief-filled mind. *I didn't even get to say goodbye...*

A noise came from the closet, pulling me from my aguish. Lucas approached the closet and turned the knob. A guy came tumbling out—he was already sniveling.

"Please don't kill me!" he pleaded.

His head was downcast and he was practically bowing in submission to us. His whole form was shaking. I didn't care how pathetic he looked; he was one of the sick bastards in this place. He wouldn't be shown any mercy. Lucas walked over to him calmly.

"You got one chance and one chance only. Where else are the men in the buildin'?" Lucas said.

"I don't know! Please don't—" he was cut off as Lucas shot him in the calf.

The man let out a cry and fell to his side, clutching his injured leg. He cried into the floor, a string of drool leaking from his mouth.

"Where are the rest?" Lucas asked again.

Ethan gave me a pleading look. He wanted me to stop Lucas from torturing the guy, but I had no intentions of stopping him. This was the last chance we would get. Snot bubbles joined in as the man became even more of a drooling mess. "Just the first floor and s-second." Just as the girl had said.

Lucas turned to me. "You and Rose stay with him, while Ethan and I verify."

"Sure."

After Lucas and Ethan thumped away, the man looked up at me with his eyebrows drawn and his face scrunched in pain. "Please just let me go. I'm not like those men!"

I gave him the most apathetic look I could muster, which was hard because I wanted nothing more than to bash his face in for Zoe. "Then why are you here?"

He started to snivel again. "It was either that or they killed me!" He turned his pleading look onto Rose, which was a bad idea.

She wound up her leg and kicked him square in the gut. "Your *friends* killed mine!"

Another kick. "Your *friends* kidnapped me and sent me off to that damn hospital!"

An even harder kick. The man let out an unholy squeal. "Your *friends* killed Leo! He was like a son!"

She didn't kick him again because she was too busy falling to the ground in tears. Sobs shook her entire body. I placed a hand on her shoulder and she let me. She didn't swat me off like a wild animal—which I half expected her to do. Everyone had their breaking point, and Rose had just found hers. I was pretty sure I was nearing mine. The goal of finding Zoe had kept me going, but now what did I have? Nothing. Just a missing toe, haunted memories and dead friends.

Lucas and Ethan came back into the room a short while later. Rose had composed herself and was no longer crying. Her eyes were swollen and red, giving away the cold demeanor she had tried to put back into place.

"There's no one on the other floors," Lucas said, not taking his eyes off of the man.

The mercenary was curled into the fetal positon, staring at the corner of the room.

"Where's Shawn?" Lucas asked.

This got the man's attention. He went to speak and then started to cough. Maybe Rose had kicked in his lungs as well.

"Well?" Lucas prompted.

"J-just kill me," the man whimpered.

It was a good thing John was downstairs. I didn't think he would approve of our interrogation. Ethan was already squirming, clearly uncomfortable with what was happening. He kept trying to catch my eye with his own, but I ignored him. This would be for Zoe. If I couldn't find her, I would kill every mercenary I could find until they were no more.

"Not until you tell us where Shawn is!" Lucas raised the butt of his rifle and brought it down on the man's leg where he had shot him earlier.

The man struggled against Lucas, so Lucas brought down his knee onto the guy's throat, trapping him in place. The mercenary clawed at Lucas's leg, but he didn't budge. Lucas shouldered his rifle and pulled out a switchblade, flicking the blade up. The mercenary's eyes bulged even more. He looked at us like *we* were the bad guys, and I suppose for just this moment, we were.

"I'm goin' to ask you again. Where. Is. Shawn?"

Ethan took a step forward, but I grabbed onto his arm. "Don't."

"Are you seein' this? You can't be okay with this?!" Ethan said, his voiced strained.

"He's one of them," I said simply.

Ethan's jaw dropped as he peered at me, taking a step back. "You can't be serious. I know you Bailey, this ain't you."

Rose and Lucas had turned to watch our interaction. Lucas let out an annoyed grunt, and turned back to the mercenary trapped under his knee. He raised the knife and the man screamed, "He's at the river drop-off zone with a couple of girls. He's tradin' 'em to stop the gang we've been havin' trouble with. A peace offerin'!"

The air disappeared from my lungs. *Zoe could still be alive!* I stepped forward, interrupting Lucas.

"When did he leave?" I asked.

"This mornin'."

Damn. It was at least noon now.

"When was the meet?"

"All I know is that they aren't expected to be back until late."

That bode well for us. Maybe they would still be there by the time we reached them.

"Do you remember the girls' names?"

The man shook his head. Of course the sicko didn't; the mercenaries wouldn't care about that.

"Do you remember what they looked like?"

The man started to shake.

"Answer her!" Lucas raised the knife again.

The mercenary raised his hands to stop the blow. "Blonde! One was blonde!"

Natural blondes are rare these days. The words of the mercenary who killed Roy echoed in my head, making my hands twitch.

"And the others?"

The guy took in a deep breath. "The only other one I saw was sort of Asian."

My body went still. *Could be Zoe.* I needed to calm down. Zoe wasn't the only half-Asian girl in the world, but hope reared its head again. I had to check.

"Where's the river drop-off zone?" I finally asked.

"They don't tell me those things," he squeaked out.

Lucas gave him a warning look.

"B-but Keenan would know. He looks after this place," the man answered in a rush.

"Who's Keenan?" I asked.

"Big guy. His was up here just before you came."

The big guy from the stairwell? Shit, he was dead.

"You're the only one left alive in here," Lucas said.

The man let out a low wail. "Keenan wou—*will* have a log of all the areas. He was Shawn's pet dog."

"Where?"

"He had his own room on the main floor. It'll be there."

Lucas removed his knee and the man relaxed, only to be pulled up by the scruff of his neck. Lucas was still strong enough to lift the man up despite the bite on his shoulder he'd sustained yesterday.

"You're goin' to show us," Lucas said, shoving the guy toward the door.

We walked out with the hobbled man. He stumbled a few times, but Lucas just yanked him back to an upright position. I could hear all the girls' voices in 215 as we approached the room on our way back to the stairs. They stopped as they saw us pass by. One of the girls started to cry when she spotted the mercenary. Another girl comforted her while shooting daggers at the man. Any sliver of sympathy I may have felt for the man stopped right there.

"Should we come too?" Sheri asked.

There had to be at least thirteen females we had rescued; this was going to be tricky logistic-wise.

"Yes. You guys can stay with John in the seating area while we check something out," I said.

They followed us down the stairs, and then Sheri led them over to where John was nervously waiting for us. He relaxed when he spotted all the girls. His eyes fixed on mine and I shook my head. *No Zoe.* The girls were clearly uncomfortable. They wanted to leave, but they would be sitting ducks if they ran out there unarmed.

Ethan stayed back with John and Sheri, more than likely unwilling to be partner to what would eventually happen. This guy was as good as dead once we found what we needed—if he was telling the truth. Lucas shoved the guy forward and we continued on.

Chapter 31

I blew open the lock on the door to Keenan's room and Lucas forced the injured mercenary in first just in case it was a trap. No people were lying in wait inside the room, just an unmade bed and messy desk. We did a quick sweep just to make sure, then Lucas threw the man onto the bed. He bounced on the mattress, letting out a cry when his leg with the bullet hole in it got caught underneath him. Lucas threatened that if the guy so much as got up, he would be killed slowly. The way Lucas said it even sent chills down *my* spine.

We went through the scribblers and papers on the desk. It mirrored what we had found at the first compound—I even found the ledger. I was too disgusted to even open it. There were a couple sets of car keys hanging on small hooks above the desk. I pocketed them. We would need another vehicle to get all the girls out of there.

Rose held up her own find—a map of south and west Baton Rouge where it touched the Mississippi River. Lucas took the map from Rose and held it in front of the man's face. He pointed to the red circle. Was it a dock or a port?

"This it?"

The mercenary swallowed. "I don't know! They never told me anythin'. If it's in here, then it's your best bet."

Lucas dragged his tongue along his teeth as he regarded the man. Now came the tough part. What did we do with the man?

"Maybe we should make you come along. We can get you back to Shawn. I'm sure he'll be happy to see you," Lucas taunted.

I bit my lip. I didn't like that Lucas was toying with the guy. If he was going to kill him, Lucas should just get it over with. The unmasked fear on the guy's face told me that being turned over to Shawn would be a terrible fate.

"Let me go or kill me! Just don't that," the guy cried. "Please."

"Just how bad is this Shawn guy?" I asked more to Lucas, but the mercenary answered instead.

I mean the mercenaries were bad in their own right, but if this Shawn guy's own men feared him that much, he must be really awful.

"He's the worst of us," the guy explained in a rush. "There's a rumor that he was awaitin' sentencin' for a huge homicide when the dead bastards took over. Killed an entire family, kids and all."

He did not sound like a pleasant guy. In a room full of starving wolves, he was the bloated lion. I looked at Lucas for confirmation.

"I heard the same thing too. Guy is scary as hell. Only had the *pleasure* of meetin' 'im once or twice, the last time I saw 'im was when he forced the dead ones on me when I was discovered. Calm and collected type, not some ragin' lunatic who goes off at the drop of a hat," Lucas said.

And now he possibly had Zoe with him.

"Then what do we do with 'im?" Rose said, pointing an accusing finger at the mercenary.

Lucas looked at the man, who had started to cry again as his fate was called into question. I motioned for Lucas and Rose to meet me back out in the hallway. It seemed really ... cold to discuss a man's fate in front of him. We were only far enough to be out of earshot, not eyesight. I could still see the mercenary sniveling away on the bed.

"There's no way we're actually takin' 'im with us, right?" Rose asked Lucas. "He'd be a liability."

"No," Lucas said.

He confidence faltered a bit as he stared at his rifle.

"How about we just leave him here?" I suggested.

After everything that had happened since we invaded the compound, the last thing I—or anyone else—wanted was to play executioner in cold blood. I was sure the guy deserved it, but I didn't have it in me to shoot a guy who was utterly helpless. Maybe if he was coming at me with a machete I could do it.

"What if he comes after us?" Lucas challenged, but it was only half-hearted. He needed to save face.

"With his injured leg? He'd be caught by an infected before he even got to us," I said.

"What if he gets to a weapon and shoots us as we leave?" Rose asked.

"We lock him in a closet then. Seems only right since that's where we found him," I said.

He'd eventually get out and by then, we would be gone. Lucas nodded and charged back into the room. He ripped open the accordion closet doors, then grabbed the mercenary and tossed him in. The guy was barely able to get out a "what" as it all happened so fast. I passed Lucas an extension cord that had been plugged into an emergency battery. He wrapped it around the gold doorknobs and tied it off.

There was no yelling or kicking on the other side so we left him, closing the room door behind us. The girls were crowded near the patio doors while Sheri, Ethan and John looked to be having an intense conversation. They stopped when they saw us. Ethan looked us up and down, more than likely looking for signs of the mercenary's blood. When he found none, his shoulders relaxed and he gave me a relieved smile.

"Where's the guy?" Sheri asked.

"Don't worry 'bout 'im," Lucas said. "Worry 'bout how we're goin' to leave here with thirteen extra bodies. They can't all fit in the back of the truck."

"We were just talkin' 'bout that," John said. "Ethan took a look out the front and there's a couple of big SUVs we could take, if we can find the keys."

I pulled out the two pairs of car keys I had lifted from Keenan's room. "Think one of these will do?"

John gave me a smile. "Perhaps. You and Ethan see if either of those are a match and we'll gather up the girls."

I passed a set to Ethan, and he led the way to the front of the hotel through the immaculate lobby. The automatic doors didn't open for us, so we had to part them a smidge to get through. An infected immediately jumped out from my left and I instinctively kicked at it. It flew down to the cement and rolled over into the dead flowerbeds. It looked like a dog rolling around in mud. I didn't have my bat so I had to use my Beretta to shoot it dead.

The shot rang out and then the infected lay dead among the decaying shrubbery. Ethan gave me a concerned look. We were going to be gone soon, so one bullet couldn't have mattered. I looked down at the keys to see that the fob had the Chevy symbol on it so I tried the Tahoe first, leaving the other SUV to Ethan. The engine roared to life, the gas needle landing just above the halfway mark. Ethan didn't have any luck with the other SUV, so I turned off the engine and joined him out front.

"You think this one will hold them all?" I asked.

"Them bein' squished in the back seat is the least of our concerns," Ethan said as we ran back inside.

I informed the others that we had found the keys to the Tahoe. As I went to help John up, Rose said, "Wait. We can't just leave Leo here."

It shamed me to admit, but I had forgotten about Leo in the midst of everything.

"How are we supposed to carry him?" Lucas asked.

Rose glared at him. "We're in a hotel. There's sheets everywhere. I'm sure we can find some to carry him in."

Lucas took a breath through his nose. "Fine. Come on."

Rose and Lucas took off down the hall where Keenan's room had been. The rest of us were forced to wait for them to return. It only took them about five minutes before they came back with two large white sheets. They must have found a housekeeping cart. They laid the sheet flat beside Leo and then Rose took his feet while Lucas lifted his shoulders. Together they placed Leo's dead body on the sheet, bunched up a handful at each end and lifted him as if they were a pair of medics.

"So what's the plan?" Lucas asked when he and Rose had shuffled back over to us.

"I'm going to that drop-off location," I said.

I knew we were tired, injured and broken, plus saddled with thirteen extra bodies that had no way of defending themselves, but I was going to try dammit. The longer we took, the further Zoe would get away.

John let out a harsh breath. "Bailey ..."

"Don't Bailey me. It's Zoe we're talking about!"

"I'll go with her," Lucas said, surprising me. He must really want to get to that Shawn person

"Me too," Rose added.

"And like I'd let you go with just them," Ethan said.

"What about the girls?" Sheri said. "They have no way of protecting themselves."

"You and John can take them back with the Tahoe. The rest of us will take the truck," I said.

"I don't like the idea of splittin' up," John said.

"It's the only choice we have."

John and I stared each other down. Usually we were on the same page, but not about this. From the torn look on his face he knew that once we let go of this opportunity to find Zoe, there would be no more leads or chances to find her. If only it had been as easy as finding me at the hospital had been for him and Ethan. Then Zoe would more than likely be here with us right now. I knew I was putting them and the girls in danger by spreading our group thin, but we were in a tight spot.

"I feel like I'm makin' nothin' but concessions," John muttered. "I know I will just slow you down with my leg, so I'll stay with Sheri, but we're not headin' back without you."

"What do you mean?" I asked.

"We'll stay here until you get back," John said. "Then we'll leave together."

Some of the girls vocalized their displeasure with John's plan. I couldn't blame them. I wouldn't have wanted to spend any more time than necessary at the hospital after being released.

"I'm *not* staying here," one of the older ladies said.

"There's the door," Lucas said, rather unkindly. I gave him a look telling him to shut his mouth, which he ignored of course. "We ain't holdin' you here."

The older lady nodded stiffly and picked up a gun from one of the fallen mercenaries. She ejected the magazine with practiced efficiency and seemed placated by what she saw. A handful of other girls joined in and scrounged up a few more guns.

"Don't you dare shoot those off near here," Lucas said.

God, he was a douche. The older lady flipped him the bird and he scowled. Can't say he didn't deserve that. She gathered up the others who had armed themselves and headed for the front door.

"Let's go," I said. The daylight wouldn't wait for us.

John and I traded sets of keys. I stuffed the truck keys down in my pocket, making sure they wouldn't have a chance of slipping out.

"Be careful," John said.

"You too." I gave him a tight smile. He tipped his cowboy hat at me. "Oh, and be careful of the guy we locked in the closet. He might get out."

"Huh?" At John's confused look, I explained what we had done with the mercenary we found hiding upstairs.

"You could've mentioned that before," he muttered. "Yeah, I'll keep an eye out."

Lucas and Rose set Leo down, then the four of us followed behind the girls who had decided to leave. New infected had crawled through the opening. They were staring at the infected, no one willing to take a shot thanks to Lucas's warning. I pulled out my Beretta and shot the two infected loitering in the lobby. The girls' heads whipped toward me.

I felt bad just leaving them there with their mouths hanging open, but we had to get to that truck. The outside air was fresh in comparison to the smell inside the hotel. By the time we got back, the smell of the dead bodies may have forced the others outside. Not that there wasn't a smell out here. Still had no idea why the mercenaries had left the dead infected right outside the hotel.

We started a jog toward the restaurant where the truck was currently parked. From the time we had entered the hotel, more infected had gathered. They were sprinkled all over the cement wasteland like chicken pox dots.

Gunfire erupted behind us as the girls had left the hotel and started shooting at the infected in the distance. I had sympathy for them and what they had been through, but they really should have listened. I chanced a brief glance back to see them retreating back into the hotel. Good, maybe they saw that our plan was indeed best. Unfortunately, their brief bout of shots had the infected coming right for us.

"Stupid," I heard Lucas mutter under his breath. I'm pretty sure there was a rude noun that followed his harsh declaration.

I was forced to start shooting my Beretta as infected got closer to our crew. Then everyone else started to shoot. One by one the infected were going down, but more appeared to take their place. I had a strange feeling that we had been led into a trap, like the infected had made themselves purposely scarce when we had found the hotel, only to converge on us as one later. I knew the infected weren't capable of such thought and planning, but it was still eerie.

"We can't waste all our ammo here," Lucas said. "Run for it."

His plan made me nervous because while Lucas, Rose and I were immune, Ethan was not. We couldn't just hold still as the horde inspected us. Lucas and the others didn't give me a chance to voice my concerns as they bolted away from me.

"Fuck!" I yelled, then started to run, already trailing behind them.

A group of infected cut the others off from my sight. I tried to dodge around them but one snaked around my leg and I tumbled down to the pavement, my gun sliding a few feet from me. They started to converge on me and I lashed out with everything I had. I hit one in the knee with my foot, knocking the joint back in an unnatural angle. I heard bone crack and the infected toppled over as its leg gave in. Another one fell on top of me, its snapping teeth dangerously close to my neck. With an unholy yell, I shoved it off of me and rolled on top of it, yanking my AR15 from my back. I used the butt of the gun to bash the thing's head in.

I could feel the other infected groping at my back so I swung the gun around, knocking them backward. A new infected dive-bombed me, taking us both back down to the pavement. There were too many of them. The rational part of my brain was telling me to hold still, but I was beyond listening to it now. I fought and scratched again until a break in the infected appeared. Slowly, my mind registered the sound of gunfire as I started to get smothered in dead infected weight. A hand was thrust into the pile and yanked me out from underneath.

It was Ethan. I looked up at him with thanks in my eyes until one of the non-dead infected burst from the pile, sinking its teeth deep into Ethan's side.

Chapter 32

I let out a scream that eclipsed whatever noise Ethan had made. *He's a dead man. He got bit saving me.* Ethan knocked the thing off of him and put a bullet in its brain. For a brief second our eyes met. Ethan saw the terror in my face and smiled. He fucking *smiled,* a sad smile, but a smile nonetheless. I got to my feet, the world having fallen silent around me. Ethan and I looked at each other, both knowing what came next.

"What the fuck are you guys doin'?" Lucas hissed.

His foot hit my Beretta so he picked it up and handed it back to me. I took it from him with a limp hand. Lucas looked from me to Ethan, his eyes landing on the blood soaking Ethan's torn shirt.

"We gotta keep movin'," Lucas said, his eyes still glued on Ethan's bite.

Ethan nodded and grabbed my arm, starting me up again. I was in a daze; my brain couldn't handle anymore. Why was Ethan not freaking out like I was? We ran toward the restaurant where our truck was parked as more infected planked us on all sides. The truck would have a hard time getting through this many infected.

"We gotta get inside!" Rose said, jerking her finger at the restaurant.

Lucas raised his gun and shot out one of the glass doors. I barely registered the infected I shot. All I knew was that they went down. We piled through the opening and Lucas immediately turned over a table and shoved it toward the front door as a blockade.

"Grab every table you can!" he yelled at us.

I put my Beretta into my waistband and we began piling up all the tables, even throwing in a few chairs for good measure. Soon the entrance was clogged with furniture, the infected unable to get through for the moment. Ethan let out a pained gasp and hunched over, his hand pressed to his bleeding wound. I led him over to one of the booths and had him sit down. I lifted up his shirt to reveal the angry bite mark the infected had left. His bite location mirrored my own scar from the scratches I'd gotten months and months ago. The difference being that his wound was already festering, where mine acted like any old injury. His bite had taken on a purplish hue with the engorged veins running from it pumping the poison throughout his system.

Ethan looked me deep in the eyes, seeing the hopelessness behind them, before reaching for his gun. He pointed it at his head, but I managed to whack it away before he could pull the trigger.

"Let me do it! I don't want to be one of those things!" he boomed, reaching for his weapon again. I threw it out of range, and the rifle clattered to the floor, skidding away from us.

"You might be immune too! Just wait!" I said desperately, trying to hold him in place.

We both knew it was a long shot, especially considering the state of his wound, but Ethan listened, eventually slumping against the booth seat. In the end, no one really wanted to die. Fighters would keep fighting until the bitter and bloody end.

Both Rose and Lucas cast me a sympathetic look. *Why were they looking at me like that?* Ethan was the one who was dying! Then they both took off to ensure the infected couldn't breach the restaurant for the moment, giving Ethan and I some privacy. Infected banged and clamored against the windows but we paid them no mind.

I didn't think it was possible to physically see the moment someone's heart broke, but when Ethan whispered Chloe's name, there was no denying it. Ethan grabbed me by the arms, a wild look in his eyes.

"Please take care of Chloe!"

I laid a hand on his. "I'll protect her with my life."

He slumped back down, tears streaming down his face. "I won't even get to say goodbye."

"I'll tell her whatever you want me to," I whispered.

"Tell her I love her and to not be sad," he said with a faraway look, like he was imagining telling her himself. "Tell her to be strong for the both of us—and to listen to you."

My eyes teared up. This wasn't how it was supposed to go. I had gotten Chloe back to her brother only to have him die. It wasn't fair. Ethan just had to play hero. He would have been okay if it wasn't for me. Chloe would still have a brother if it wasn't for me. Guilt weighed my heart down. *This is all my fault.* I should have never let him come out here in the first place while he was still recovering from his concussion. Chloe would hate me for this. I'd broken my promise to keep her brother safe.

Ethan snapped out of his trance. He looked at me, then pulled me in for a hug, sliding out of the booth. We sat there on the ground, holding each other, trying to hold back the hysterics.

"I'm so sorry, Bailey. I know you said you didn't want to hear it but please listen."

I nodded into the crook of his neck. He was right. The last thing I wanted from him on his deathbed was an apology—I should be the one apologizing—but if it made him feel any better, then I would listen.

"You have no idea how much I regret tellin' Wyatt about you. And when we found out they had sold you off..." He paused to swallow. "I don't think I've ever felt so low."

"It's okay. I forgive you, Ethan," I said, trying to contain my sobs. "Do you forgive me?"

He pulled back and held me at arm's length. "For what?"

"For this. You wouldn't have been bitten if it wasn't for me." My voice broke at the end. *I'm to blame. He got bit saving me. And* I'm *the immune one.*

"This isn't your fault, Bailey. *I* wanted to help you. That was my choice."

I didn't say anything. Ethan wrapped me in a big hug again as if willing me to listen to his words. My mind drifted toward us. I wondered that if the world hadn't gone to shit and if I'd met Ethan during my time in Louisiana, if we would have even said a word to one another. I was no fool. Our relationship was more of a result of circumstance than of true love. I didn't believe in that nonsense. But that didn't mean that he meant nothing to me. My eyes clouded with tears again and I let out a sob so he hugged me tighter.

His body was a furnace. Our grip started to slip as Ethan slumped to the ground. His breathing was ragged and harsh. I helped him down to a lying position and took his hand in mine. I briefly heard footsteps behind me, but they quickly disappeared.

"Promise me you won't let me end up like *them*." He refused to say the word "infected" but I knew what he meant.

"I won't." He squeezed my hand as he let out a wet sounding cough.

"Promise me you'll take care of yourself."

More tears fell from my eyes. "I will."

"Promise you'll love Chloe like your own sister."

"I already do."

He closed his eyes, his face pinched. "It feels like I'm burnin' from the inside out."

"Do you want me to find you some water?" We were in a restaurant. There had to be bottled water around here somewhere.

"No! Just stay with me."

I wiped away the hair matted to his sweaty forehead. He didn't look like he would last much longer. He was suffering. As if reading my thoughts, he let out a loud cough, blood starting to dribble down his chin. Shivers traveled up his body, shaking my hand along with his. But he never let go. He took a couple of deep, grasping breaths, then let out a long whistle of air. His chest never rose again, and the grip on my hand finally loosened until his hand fell away completely.

I stared at his dead body. *No, no, no.* He couldn't be dead. I started to shake his torso.

"Ethan, please wake up," I cried.

He will wake up, my unsympathetic brain reminded me. He just wouldn't be Ethan anymore. A hand touch my shoulder—I shook it off.

"He's gone," Rose said lightly. She was standing behind me.

"No," I mumbled, my eyes still glued to Ethan.

"We gotta take care of him before he turns," Lucas said.

I heard a smack. "Fuck you. Give her a minute," Rose hissed.

Had Rose not just gone through this with Leo, I'm not sure she'd be so understanding. As it were, I did need a minute for my brain to come to terms with Ethan actually being gone. He was lying right in front of me and I couldn't wrap my head around it being real. *Maybe it was a prank. A terrible one. Don't be stupid. He's dead.*

I wiped at the new tears streaking down my face. My fingers curled around the butt of my Beretta and I pulled it from my waistband, flicking off the safety. Another hand touched my shoulder.

"You don't have to be the one to do it," Rose said.

"Yes I do." This was my punishment to bear.

I pointed the gun at Ethan's head and whispered, "I'm so sorry, Ethan. I hope wherever you are, that you're at peace." I wiped at my running nose with my free arm. "And thank you— for everything."

I pulled the trigger.

Chapter 33

To say I was numb was an understatement. We were barreling through the streets of South Baton Rouge with Ethan's dead body tied up in tablecloths in the bed of the truck. I was simply dead inside. I had refused to leave him in the restaurant to be eaten by the infected. This was the only way. I must have looked crazy because neither Rose nor Lucas argued with me. Instead, they helped me scrounge up some table clothes to tie together and wrap Ethan in.

We had a hell of a time clearing the infected, but we eventually got them to rally to the side of the restaurant while we made a run for the truck with Ethan's body. I shot the infected without feeling. I couldn't even register fear as all the infected surrounded the truck. Lucas managed to get us out of there without too many dents, but the whole time I just stared blankly out the window.

Find Zoe. Don't think about Ethan. Find Zoe. Don't think about Ethan. This was my new mantra. If I expected to make it through what we were going to face soon, I needed to keep repeating it to myself.

Lucas had given the map to Rose to read and she was currently telling him where to go. She was good at that. We were heading west toward the river. Street signs passed us by, but I wasn't paying attention. Soon Lucas was slowing down the truck; I could see the reflection of dark water in the far distance. We were on the edge of a massive parking lot that was close to one-thirds full, all cars nestled in their painted parking stalls. If anyone dared a glance, we looked like just another vehicle parked among the others. It was good camouflage.

"You goin' to be okay to do this?" Lucas asked.

The way he said it sounded like he was accusing me of something. We were there because I insisted on going after Zoe so I needed to nut up. I took a shaky breath, Rose and Lucas eying me warily. I hadn't said a word to them since I had them help me wrap up Ethan. Now wasn't the time to check out. I could do that after, even if all my body wanted to do was lie down at the moment. It seemed all I was doing lately was pushing my mental breakdowns to the side.

"Yes," I answered.

They didn't look convinced.

"Shawn ain't goin' to be as pleasant as the guys at the hotel."

That was his version of pleasant?

"I said I'll be fine," I snapped. He didn't say anything more.

I filled up the magazines to both my guns using what little ammo I had left over—it wasn't enough to fill them. Lucas and Rose did the same. We had used a fair number of bullets killing all the infected after leaving the hotel. I looked around the area Lucas had parked us in. There was an enormous casino and hotel in the middle of a roundabout road, and a parking lot fit for a stadium.

"You think this is it?" I asked. There didn't appear to be any people near the casino.

Lucas extended his arm, his index finger pointing into the distance. "See that giant black SUV?"

I squinted until I spotted the vehicle. It was just a small speck on the asphalt horizon, off to the side of the casino. I had no idea how Lucas had spotted it. It looked like it was in the middle of the road blocking the throughway.

"That's one of the lookouts. They usually have one when deals like this go down. Most guys don't play fair. Chances are, they're in the buildin' closer to the river."

I could barely spot the building Lucas was referring to.

"Think he can see us?" Rose asked.

"He would've taken off by now or warned 'em if he did. Probably sleepin' on the job," Lucas said. "We're goin' to have to sneak up on 'im. No firearms."

I gripped the hilt of my metal bat more than willing to go Babe Ruth on their asses. We filed out of the truck, closing the doors softly behind us. I didn't dare a look at Ethan's covered corpse in the back, in fact, I specifically avoided looking past the cab of the truck.

In a single line formation, we followed Lucas as we made our way to the large SUV, using the random cars in the parking lot for cover. The numbness slowly trickled away, replaced with the familiar rush of adrenaline. It took forever as we zig-zagged through the casino's surprisingly full parking lot. All the vehicles were empty. Just how many people had decided to come to the casino instead of an emergency shelter? Some addicts were just hopeless.

We got to the last car in the parking lot, bringing an end to our cover. The SUV was still parked in the middle of the road. Behind it was the Mississippi River, glinting in the late afternoon sun, and a waterfront bar and grill. There were more cars parked outside the bar, but they weren't inside the designated stalls, instead haphazardly parked at all angles. Had to be the mercenaries.

A couple of infected were sniffing around the large, blacked-out SUV. Whoever was inside didn't seemed too concerned with a couple.

"I'm gonna try and sneak up on 'im. You two wait here till I'm done," Lucas said.

Before we could argue, he took off in an awkward crouching/running position across the rest of the distance—he looked like a monkey. I just hoped the infected were enough of a distraction. I dared a glance through the windows of the car we were hiding beside to see Lucas pull open the driver's door. The two infected that had been sniffing around previously were now lying dead on the ground. He stuck his head in, then shut the door and came crouching/running back to us.

"He was already dead. Someone slit his throat," Lucas said when he returned.

"What the hell?" Rose asked.

Lucas shrugged his shoulders. "No clue, but I could definitely hear noise comin' from the bar and grill. Sounds like they're havin' themselves a party."

Find Zoe. Don't think about Ethan. This was one party I would be happy to crash.

"We're gonna approach from the side." Lucas motioned to the left of the bar and grill. "And scope out the perimeter before we make a move."

Lucas led the way again. We crossed the roundabout road before we came to the side of the building. There were two men talking and laughing outside the front door. I crinkled my nose; I smelled the cigarettes even though I couldn't see them. One would think that the apocalypse would be the ultimate time to quit, seeing as you had to risk your life to find a pack of smokes. I guess smoking was risking your life too, so whatever, wouldn't ever be my problem.

The men had been too engrossed in discussing whatever they had been to notice us sneak up to the building. I gave Lucas a 'what now' look. He leaned in close and waited until Rose did the same before whispering, "We need to secure the perimeter. Rose, you stay here and keep an eye on this side. Bailey and I will continue to the other sides."

Rose nodded and squished herself against the side of the building, slowly daring to glance into the giant windows. Lucas and I kept going until we reached the back side of the building. My eyes were immediately drawn to the river. It had been a while since I'd seen such a big body of water. It was a relaxing sight with the water sparkling in the sunlight and the gentle movement making the sparkles look like they were winking.

Lucas didn't wait for me to finish my admiring as he disappeared around the next corner to check out the north side of the building. I tore my eyes from the river to the back side of the building. I had to stand on my tiptoes to even reach the windows. They were giant to allow the patrons inside to view the river. Footsteps crunched behind me. I whirled around expecting to see Lucas or Rose, but instead I found a strange man. We both froze as we regarded one another. He must've come from the direction of the river because we hadn't spotted him two seconds ago.

He didn't sound an alarm or start yelling—he held a finger up to his lips. His eyes were wide with fright. I had a distinct feeling that he *wasn't* a mercenary. He cautiously approached me with his arms slightly in the air to indicate he didn't mean any harm. I still didn't lower my bat. He had a pleasant face. It reminded me of Ethan. My heart clenched at the comparison.

"What are you doin' here?!" he asked accusingly.

"Me? What are *you* doing here? Are you a mercenary?" My hand itched to pull out my Beretta, but I didn't want to make any sudden movements.

"I'm not one of those animals," he scowled. "We're here to shut 'em down."

I was now completely confused. That's what we were here for. "What?" was all I could get out.

"My team and I are here to take those *men* out," he said.

I spotted more movement along the river, this time from walking bodies, not the water.

"You trying to take out the other gang as well?" I asked.

The man smiled. "We are the *gang*." He used finger quotes for the word gang.

At my confused look, he continued. "We pretended to be a gang to get in with the mercenaries. We needed to gain their trust so they'd tell us where they were takin' the kidnapped

THIS WOULD BE PARADISE

girls and the immune. Our leader is in there right now pretendin' to be tradin' a couple of girls for peace."

"You were the guys who took out their other compound," I said.

The guy nodded. "We went to the hospital where they were shippin' off the immune they grabbed, but it was lost to the infected."

"I may have had a hand in that," I said.

The guy regarded me completely different now. "Why are you here?" he asked again. He was growing impatient with having to explain all this to me.

"They took my friend and we came to get her back."

"She one of the girl's inside?"

"Possibly. I haven't gotten a chance to check. Been here chatting with you."

The guy gave me a droll look. "She'll be fine. Once that scumbag Shawn hands her over, we'll get her outta harm's way."

I had zero reason to trust this guy, but for some reason I did. He seemed so sincere. It only seemed logical that if there were bad people, there were a couple good ones out there as well.

"I'm Bailey, by the way." I lowered my bat and held out a hand.

He took it and shook. "Mercer."

"So why are you out here, Mercer. Not in there?" I hefted a thumb at the bar.

"We're the cavalry in case somethin' goes south. One guy on the inside has a walkie. If we get one distress call, we storm the place."

"You the ones who killed their lookout?" I asked.

"Had no choice. Can't afford for our cover to get—"

He was cut off by someone inside yelling, "Ambush!" then gunfire erupted.

Oh God, Lucas and Rose.

"Shit!" Mercer yelled.

He waved his arm toward the river and more bodies emerged. I tensed until I spotted a few women mixed among the armed men. Clearly, they wouldn't be with the mercenaries. They stormed up to the building. Mercer grabbed my elbow and steered me further away from the building. One of his men pulled out a rather scary looking gun and pulled the trigger, the bullet shattering the giant glass windows. The shards rained down on the spot Mercer had just pulled me from. These guys were a lot more organized than we were.

I turned to Mercer. "I'm here with two other people. A big guy with scars on his neck and a small Mexican woman. If you see them, don't shoot!" I hated using stereotypical descriptions, but it was the fastest way to get it across.

"They inside?" Mercer asked.

"No."

"Then they'll be fine."

Gunfire came from inside, directed right at us. We returned fire as we snaked around the side for cover. Rose came running up to me, her eyes wide.

"What the hell's goin' on? One of the mercenaries yelled ambush on the other side of the bar and then they started shootin'," Rose said. "Who are these guys?"

Had they spotted Lucas?

"I'll explain later. They're on our side," I said.

I ran past her toward the front of the building. I had to get in there. Rose followed behind me as well as Mercer and a couple of his crew. Rose was giving them curious glances, but didn't say anything. Mercenaries were spilling from the building, trying to run from the firefight. I tossed down my bat and swung my AR15 from my shoulder and started firing. One leather-clad guy was thrown against the car he was trying to open as my bullets impaled him.

Mercer's crew opened up fire as well, helping me kill the cowards who were running away. Once they were taken care of, we ran to the front doors to head inside. I was pushed aside as Mercer maneuvered his crew in first. They looked like a professionally trained SWAT team. Maybe one of them had been a police officer beforehand. Rose and I followed in behind them, the smell of booze and stale smoke permeating the air. The floor was sticky under my feet. *So gross.*

Most of the firing had stopped. Dead men lined the entryway. The dining room had been turned into a battlefield. Tables were toppled over for cover, and they were periodically shooting at each other from opposite sides of the room.

"Give it up, Shawn. We have more men than you, especially since we just decimated half of your guys," an authoritative voice echoed throughout the room.

"Fuck you!" Bullets sprayed, some in our direction.

I ducked away behind one of the dining room walls with Mercer. He was whispering something to another one of his cohorts, them nodding intently. They took off through the swinging kitchen door, leaving Rose and I at the edge of the dining room behind the wall separating it from the entryway. We were not part of their crew, so I wasn't sure if we should follow them. I dared a look around the wall again. I couldn't spot Zoe or any females, just overturned furniture and the occasional knee from the men hiding behind the tables.

They were at a standstill, neither side daring to make the first move. Rose leveled her rifle, aiming for something inside the dining room. She let off a round and we heard the sucking sound of a bullet hitting flesh, then a crash to the floor. I yanked her behind the cover of the wall just as fire was returned.

"You just gonna get your men to pick us off one by one then?" an angry voice yelled.

"Eh," the first voice I had heard when we entered said. "Looks like there's more than just my guys here."

Our presence must've thrown the guy off. Oops. We were technically on their side. A hand touched my shoulder and I practically jumped out of my skin. It was Lucas.

"What the hell is goin' on? I saw you enter with a bunch of other people."

"Apparently, they're on our side," Rose said with a shrug.

"They're the ones pretending to be the gang, and somehow the operation didn't go according to plan," I whispered.

"Yeah, one of the mercenaries spotted me," Lucas said, his hand rubbing the back of his neck.

So, it had been him.

"Shh," I said, returning my attention to the stand-off.

The two leaders—I assumed—were arguing back and forth. The one guy was trying to negotiate a surrender for the other side, while the other was just refuting every effort.

"Fuck you," snarled the angry voice. "I always knew somethin' was up with you, man. Shoulda listened to my gut."

More bullets.

"Just surrender, Shawn, and you will walk away from this," said the authoritative voice. "And the rest of your men."

Someone spat, and then there was the sound of a gun being cocked.

"This what you want?"

A tall and lanky man stood up and began firing at random. A few men on his side started to shoot as well. The other side returned fire from their cover and a hailstorm of bullets took over the bar. Stray shots started to get closer to us until a new barrage of weapons joined in. Mercer and his people, who'd snuck into the kitchen, appeared through another door behind the mercenary's side and began shooting them up from behind.

They were completely taken off guard. A bunch of errant bullets pounded into the wall we were hiding behind. We dove for cover, Lucas covering my body with his. I couldn't tell if that was on purpose or just the way we had landed. His body was tense and rigid above me as the bullets ricocheted off of nearby surfaces. I let out a yelp when a round landed not even a foot from our heads. When all the noise stopped, we slowly got up from the floor.

My ears were ringing and I had to wipe off drywall plaster from my clothes. The bullets had shredded the wall we had been using for cover. Not a smart choice in hindsight. Tables scraped across the floor and I tensed. Who had won? There was no way the mercenaries walked away from that play.

"Bailey, you and your people can come out," Mercer's voice said.

Lucas and Rose both raised a brow at me.

"We introduced ourselves outside," I explained. "That's how he knows my name."

Cautiously, we rounded the corner to see Mercer and his team still standing. Couldn't say that for the mercenaries, though. They were bloodied and slumped over dead on their side of the dining room. A rather short man from the other side walked over and peered down at the fallen mercenaries with a scrunched look on his face.

"You kind of ruined our operation," the leader said. It was the authoritative voice from before. "Now we'll never find the compound where they keep the girls."

He was talking to us.

"We just came from there," I said.

The man looked up from the carnage to me. His gaze was intense.

"Where is it?" He calmly sauntered over to me as if this was just another day on the job.

"It's a hotel off of the I-10. We took it out and freed the girls. We're heading back there; you can follow us if you'd like," I said. "But first, have you seen the girls they brought here?"

The man looked at one of his team members and nodded. The other guy scampered off to another portion of the bar and grill.

"Once Shawn handed them over, we had our people bring them to another room to make it look like we were *sampling the merchandise.*" The disgust in his voice was obvious. "Needed to keep up appearances."

I held my breath as footsteps from the hallway to our right got closer. *Please be Zoe.* The first girl that came through was the blonde one. She looked terrified and refused to let go of the man escorting her out. Behind them a head of black hair came into view.

"Zoe!" I yelled.

She looked surprised at first, then ran past the men to us. I couldn't move—I was in shock. Relief and a dozen other emotions ran through my body. I wanted to cry, I wanted to smile, I wanted to yell. I had finally found my best friend. She hugged me tight as she shook and cried. We pulled back and I noticed the busted lip and shiner she was sporting. Huge black circles hung under her eyes.

"How did you find me?" She sounded incredulous.

It was like a miracle at the end of a hard road.

"Good detective work?" I said.

I didn't really want to tell her that we shot up a compound at the moment.

"I take it she was the friend you were looking for?" Mercer asked.

"Yes, thank you."

Zoe turned from me to the leader of the crew. "Thank you for getting me away from those monsters." Her voice broke a little at the end.

The man gave her a smile. "Just doing my job, miss."

"Job?" Lucas asked.

The others regarded him like they had forgotten he was there.

"Well, not a job in the sense that I get paid," the man explained. "I just like to do what's right. These mercenaries have been plaguing this area worse than the infected."

The man held out his hand for me. "Name's Wesley."

I took his hand. It was a firm grip. "Bailey."

"Well, Bailey, mind taking us to that compound now?" Wesley asked.

Chapter 34

I sat in the back seat with Zoe while Lucas took us back to the hotel compound and tried to engage her in conversation. Other than at our initial reunion, Zoe had pretty much resorted to one word answers. I tried to draw her out, but she wasn't ready to talk about what had happened to her. She asked what was in the back of the truck and when I told her, she barely reacted. She just turned from me and peered out the window.

She was acting like a husk of the Zoe I knew. *What had those men done to her?* Maybe she would come around when she saw that we had killed all of them back at the hotel.

"So those people were pretendin' to be gang members?" Rose asked.

"Yes," I said for the second time. She didn't seem to be grasping the concept of them being double agents.

"They comin' back to the motel with us?"

"I ... don't know," I answered honestly.

I had no idea what really came next. Once we got back to the compound, we could leave for the motel. Wesley's people never mentioned that they had a place, but if they were looking for the girls, chances were they had a place to bring them back to. Were the girls even going to come back with us? It was selfish, but I was kind of hoping that Wesley's people took them. We didn't need more bodies to take care of. *We were coming back with less mouths to feed, though.* I shook my head violently, refusing to think about Ethan's death and what I would have to say to Chloe. I was the queen of procrastinating.

The hotel was within sight, infected still roaming around. A woman in Wesley's crew was standing in the back of one of their trucks, picking them off with deadly precision as we drove up to the compound. How she was keeping her aim straight was a mystery. Lucas brought the truck to a stop and we got out, shooting the nearest infected, no longer concerned with making noise. Once they were dead, we re-entered the building, our people meeting us in the lobby.

John limped over to me and gave me a one-armed hug. It was all he could do without toppling over thanks to his injured leg.

"Glad to see you," he said. He looked from me to Zoe with a smile. "And you too, Zoe."

They had their own awkward embrace, Zoe slinking off to the side when they were done.

"Who are they?" John jerked his chin at Wesley's crew.

They were all on red alert with their guns at the ready as they entered the lobby.

"That would be the gang the mercenaries were dealing with," I said.

When John's eyes bulged, I continued. "They aren't really a gang; they were just acting so they could gain access to this compound and free the girls."

"Wesley?!" one of the girls cried out and ran to him straight across the lobby, leering eyes be damned.

He scooped her up and swung her around, placing a wet sounding kiss on her head. "Mary." He was practically in tears. They pulled apart and started kissing until it became awkward.

Mercer cleared his throat until they toned it down, but he had a small smile on his face as he did it. John pulled me away from the scene by placing a hand on my shoulder. "I don't see Ethan."

I dropped my eyes. "He got bit."

"Oh God, Bailey, I'm so sorry."

Why was he telling me he was sorry? He should be feeling sorry for Ethan—he was the one who was gone. But I guess the dead were just that—dead. They weren't the ones left to pick up and carry on. That was for the living.

"Where ...?" John asked.

"Just outside here. He saved me from a pile of infected," I said, struggling to relive it. I'd rather pretend it didn't happen. "His body is in the back of the truck. I couldn't just leave him there."

"We'll give him a proper burial when we get back, along with Leo," John said. "That way everyone can say goodbye."

By everyone he meant Chloe; he just didn't say it. Wesley walked over to us with Mary tucked under his arm. He looked like he wouldn't be letting her out of his sight for a while.

"Thank you," he said sincerely. "They took my love here." Mary smiled at his words. "And I wouldn't rest until I found her." Wesley looked back at his crew before adding, "Would your people want to come with us? We built a little community on a small plot of farm land. Nothing fancy, but there's some walls and a roof to sleep under," Wesley offered.

"Thank you, but we have some people waiting for us," I said.

"Well, our doors will always be open for you should you change your mind," Wesley said. He crooked his finger. "Mercer, come here."

Mercer walked over as he pulled out some paper from his jacket pocket. He scribbled some stuff down and handed it to me. It was directions.

"When you get back to your people, this is how you'll find us," Wesley said. "Now, let's get these girls outta here."

Most of the girls had decided to go with Wesley, thanks to Mary's coaxing. Only a handful decided to come with us, which was the best-case scenario at this point. We couldn't take on the burden of thirteen more mouths. Sheri was wary of their crew at first, but Mary explained how she loved and trusted

Wesley. After all, he had become like an undercover cop to find her.

John informed me that they had neither seen nor heard from the mercenary we had locked in the closet, so we just let him be. Chances are he wouldn't make it very far being injured and by himself, to boot. He'd get what was coming to him one day.

I helped Rose get Leo's body into the back of our truck alongside Ethan's. I took a moment to say something while Rose rejoined the others standing by the front of the truck.

I'm so sorry, Ethan. You gave your life to save me and to find my best friend; to help rid this world of some truly bad men. I wish that you were still here and that I could still see you run your hand through your hair or laugh with Chloe. I promise you that I will take care of her. I will treat her like my own sister. We all will. Goodbye, Ethan.

I dabbed at the small tear hanging from the corner of my eye. I meant every word.

Epilogue

1 Month Later

"Make one more comment about me bein' Mexican and I'll skewer you," Rose growled at Lucas.

They were at it again. I would have thought after everything we had been through that we could all get along, but alas, that wasn't the case. Rose was trying to heat up a can of refried beans with some camping gear and Lucas was giving her a hard time.

I found myself still surprised that Lucas had stuck around. Out of all the people we had met, I figured him for the runaway. Too bad that damn cat had stuck around too. It had scratched up my leg more than once while trapped in the truck with it for hours on end. Colin threatened to eat it once and whatever Rose had said to the teen had him staying miles away from her afterwards. I had eventually gotten the chance to have my talk with Colin about his sickness. He told me that he just wanted to live what was left of his life without being treated like he was dying.

"Do I look like Augustus to you?" he joked, then on a more serious note, he continued, "I don't want to be known as the sick kid who people pity. I want to be the funny kid with the blue hair. I want to go out like that."

It was a hard thing to hear from anyone, let alone a fifteen-year-old boy who was supposed to have a full life ahead of him. I struggled with what to do, but in the end I went against my better judgement and let the subject drop—not that there was anything I could even do for Colin. I would honor his request. That much I could do.

We were currently hunkered down for the night in an abandoned field with our vehicles surrounding us, protecting us from the blustery night and any wandering infected. Of course we still had people on look out, but with our smaller numbers it was impractical.

Once we had returned to the castle-themed motel with less, yet more faces, we had a decision to make. Did we stay or did we go? After Ethan and Leo were put to rest properly, with a side service for Roy, Mac, and all the others we'd lost at Hargrove, we decided to seek out our new life. A new start.

The directions to Wesley's little paradise burned a hole in my pocket. They didn't aggressively sell us on the place like the welcome committee at Hargrove had done. This was the real deal. I could feel it.

I looked over the fire to see Chloe and Amanda sharing a plate of food. I was just glad Chloe was eating again. After we came back with Ethan's body, she had gone into shock. She wouldn't eat or talk much. She wasn't sleeping at night. She just stayed away from everyone. Slowly, she had come around, turning back into the kid I remembered, the one who was too big for her shoes. Kids are resilient.

Zoe too was mostly back to normal, but she never talked about what happened while the mercenaries had her. I didn't push her on it. She didn't force me to talk about Ethan or what happened at the hospital either. It was an uneasy truce. Not a very healthy one either. I knew you weren't supposed to keep things bottled up, but I just wasn't ready. My time at the hospital, Ethan's death—they were still fresh wounds.

I took out the folded piece of paper and re-read the directions for the hundredth time. I had long since memorized the words, but it was more like a ritual at this point. John noticed me reading and leaned over from his spot beside me, his finger pointed at the creased paper.

"That paper ain't long for this world."

Maybe I *had* taken it out one too many times.

"Don't worry, I got it all up here." I tapped a finger to my temple.

"That don't make me feel any better." John grinned at his joke.

I sighed. "Sure, I forget to pick up *one* magazine and suddenly I'm senile."

John had asked me two weeks ago during a quick run to pick up an Old Farmers Almanac and I had completely forgotten. He would have come but his leg was still recovering, the muscles having been torn up pretty bad. He'd more than likely have a small limp for the rest of his life.

"A very important magazine," he said with no real anger.

I shook my head and returned to staring at my paper.

"You think this place will be okay?" he asked conversationally.

I shrugged. "Who knows? They could've already moved on for all we know. Or maybe they're actually a commune that worships lizard gods."

John rolled his eyes at that.

I smiled into the fire, the flames dancing before my eyes and whispered, "Or, this would be paradise."

THE END

Author's Note

Yes, this is the end, my friends. Well, the end of this series, anyways. I am so happy that you decided to give my little slice of fiction a try (at least I assume you have if you're reading this). *This Would Be Paradise* was my very first book and my first series. There will always be a special spot in my heart for it, but that's the thing with hearts—they have lots of room. I will be moving on to another series that will fall under the Urban Fantasy genre. If you are interested in hearing more, please check out my website: http://ndiverson.weebly.com/

I will be giving away *free* advanced reader copies of the first UF book (when I actually write it) in exchange for *honest reviews*. If this is something you would be interested in, please contact me here and I will put you on the list: http://ndiverson.weebly.com/about-the-author.html (disclaimer: you must have a valid Amazon account where you can post the review from)

And, if you enjoyed this series, please consider leaving a review. Reviews and word of mouth help support indie authors and keep them typing away. Know that you would have my eternal and undying gratitude (too cheesy?) and somewhere out there, you would be putting a smile on my face!

Thank you once again for reading!

Want the latest news about new releases and sales (not spam, never spam!) sent right to your email? Sign up for my mailing list here: http://ndiverson.weebly.com/sign-up.html

19973330R00162

Printed in Great Britain
by Amazon